AMAZING GRACE

KIM NASH

Boldwood

First published in 2019. This edition first published in Great Britain in 2024 by Boldwood Books Ltd.

Cover Design by Head Design Ltd

Cover illustration: Shutterstock

A CIP catalogue record for this book is available from the British Library.

Paperback ISBN 978-1-83603-592-3

Large Print ISBN 978-1-83603-591-6

Harback ISBN 978-1-83603-590-9

Ebook ISBN 978-1-83603-593-0

Kindle ISBN 978-1-83603-594-7

Audio CD ISBN 978-1-83603-585-5

MP3 CD ISBN 978-1-83603-586-2

Digital audio download ISBN 978-1-83603-587-9

Boldwood Books Ltd
23 Bowerdean Street
London SW6 3TN
www.boldwoodbooks.com

1

Grace was woken from her slumber by the rattle of the letterbox and the thud of post hitting the door-mat, followed by a grizzling, subdued woof. When she realised this was an Archie-free day, she sighed and then remembered that she'd offered to work to-day, just for something to occupy her. She looked at the clock: 7.30 a.m. Much as she'd love to roll over and have a few more minutes, she'd better get a shimmy on. Grabbing her fleecy dressing gown from the hook on the back of her bedroom door, she trun-dled downstairs, still a bit bleary-eyed, to make her first coffee of the day. There at the bottom of the stairs, lying on the front doormat with a pile of post on his head, was Becks, her most handsome and faithful furry friend. Every single morning without fail, he greeted her with the biggest wiggle of his bum and a face that scrunched up in a lopsided doggy smile. What a perfect start to the day.

She sat on the bottom stair and he climbed onto her lap. Ecstatic with his early morning fussing session, he couldn't get any closer if he tried. As a labradoodle (or a 'mongrel', as her dad would say) he was quite a big dog and way too big for sitting on laps, but he was also the second love of her life, so she let him. After minutes of him trying to suffocate her with affection, Grace shooed him off and grabbed the pile of post, flinging it on the breakfast bar on her way through to the kitchen.

While the kettle boiled, she stretched and rolled her neck to relieve her aches and pains. Crikey, if she felt like this at thirty-seven, how would fifty feel? And then seventy... Didn't bear thinking about.

Putting the milk back in the fridge, she sat on one of the bar stools and noticed that a gold envelope peeked out from the normal brown ones that she always tried to ignore.

'Oooh. Becks, what have we here?' she asked him, wondering who she used to talk to before she had a dog. 'Fancy-schmancy.' Whatever was in the envelope felt stiff, like a card. She ripped it open carefully and then her heart hit the floor when she read the words imprinted on it.

Grace Carnegie and Guest
are cordially invited to the
Lord Mayor's Chambers to celebrate
The Stafford and District Business Awards Ceremony
At 7 p.m. on 8 May 2018
Dress Code: Black Tie

So many things ran through Grace's mind as she re-read the invitation. What would she wear? Who would she take? Who would be there? Would she know anyone? Who else would be on her table? What did 'Black Tie' even mean? *Did she even want to go?*

This was her worst nightmare. She hated public events and she stressed so much about what to wear, she usually made herself ill. She hated making small talk with people she didn't know, feeling awkward and totally out of her comfort zone. Normally, she avoided occasions like this at all costs.

She was also feeling more sensitive than usual at the moment, after a very traumatic incident on the school playground the day before.

Grace loved the fact that her job allowed her to

pick up her son Archie from school two days a week, and she usually really enjoyed seeing him come out of school. Yesterday, however, just as the kids were lining up with the teacher, a lady who was around sixty wandered over to Grace and said, 'Isn't it fabulous that we're able to pick our grandchildren up from school? Don't you just love this part of being a granny? I wonder if our grandchildren are in the same class? Which one is yours?'

Grace was well aware that on that particular day she hadn't had time to put her face on, and that yes, she wasn't the youngest mum in the world, but she was way too embarrassed to tell this lady that Archie was her son, not her grandson, so she nervously smiled, mumbled, grabbed Archie's hand as quickly as she could and walked away holding her head high, even though she felt totally gut-punched.

Now she was looking forward to next term, when she wouldn't have to do the school run any more. Archie was ten, and in the last year of primary school, when they encouraged the kids to walk to and from school on their own, getting them ready for high school. At least then she wouldn't have to face that woman again.

It had played on her mind all evening, and when

her friend Monica happened to call her that night, she burst into tears and confided that she already felt like a fat old frump without someone thinking she was a good few years older than she actually was. Monica was really supportive and said she had an idea to make her feel better. Grace had no clue what she had in mind, but they had arranged to get together in a fortnight, the next time that Archie was at his dad's.

And now, as if it wasn't bad enough that she had been mistaken for Archie's granny, Grace had been invited to this formal event. She knew she'd be expected to go, as she'd been told this week that she'd been nominated for an award for her cutting edge work at the family run estate agency that she worked at, and she'd been dreading the invitation arriving, but now, on top of her usual nerves, she was worried that tons of other people would obviously think she was way older than she was.

Grabbing her phone, Grace searched 'black tie'.

'Shit the bed, Becks! I have to wear a cocktail dress! What even *is* a cocktail dress?' Her anxiety levels rose even higher.

Grace was a practical soul at heart, a list-maker, so she did what she did best to get rid of stress. She grabbed an empty notepad from her stationery stash and started making a list of pros and cons of going to this event.

PROS

It would be good for business.

I might win.

CONS

I need to lose three stone – FAST!

I don't have a guest to take.

I've never owned a cocktail dress in my life.

I'd have to find a cocktail dress.

Where do you buy a cocktail dress?

Do they sell cocktail dresses in Asda?

I won't know anyone there.

I might have to sit next to a stranger and eat dinner.

I'd have to make small talk.

If I did win an award, which I won't, what if I fall over when I have to go up to collect it?

What if I throw up with nerves?

I'd have to have my hair coloured, get rid of those grey roots.

Oh crap! I'd have to shave my legs!

So the cons outweighed the pros. It was obvious

what she had to do. She'd just have to find an excuse not to go.

* * *

When she went into work that morning, the awards event was the talk of the office. The three young girls who worked there were discussing what they were going to wear and talking about having spray tans and booking in nails appointments with the local beautician. Grace's worst nightmare was their big dream.

'How exciting!' said Melanie, who was the office manager as well as the boss's wife. 'Our Grace, nominated for "Business Superstar" and the agency nominated for "Estate Agency of the Year". We are so proud of you all.'

Grace smiled but underneath she was already dreading the event and trying to think of every excuse she could to get out of it. She went over to the desk she used when she was in the office and picked up a pile of particulars that needed putting into some semblance of order, starting to pair photographs with their relevant descriptions. Before Grace had started at the agency, houses had been detailed in the usual way, paper copies being given out to prospective buyers. Grace had had the idea of filming the rooms and sharing the videos on the agency's Facebook page, which was also new, so that people got a real feel for the house they were looking at. It had been quite revolutionary for this small family firm and had increased business by 200 per cent.

Nicki, Jo and Julie, all twenty-something single girls, fawned over her.

'Oh, Grace,' said Nicki. 'We were just saying before you came in that you've inspired us all to think of new innovative ways to do things to make us better than our competition. And if you can do it at your age, then we absolutely can.'

Grace laughed at the backhanded compliment, and she and Melanie grinned at each other.

'Seriously, Grace,' said Melanie, 'we are so delighted. Since you joined us, it's like a breath of fresh air has wafted through the business. We were very stuck in a rut, too busy to even think about changing things. We really did hit the jackpot when you applied for this job.'

It was amazing, really, that Grace had been so desperate to get this job, so that she could fit work around Archie, and that they were so pleased to get her. It had been a super match, and it had worked wonders. However, her bosses telling her she'd done a good job was enough for her. She didn't need to go through all the stress of the awards ceremony for affirmation. They could buy her a bottle of gin and a thank-you card and she'd be made up.

She had a busy few weeks ahead of her. Perhaps if she didn't think about the awards ceremony it might go away. Or she'd come up with the best excuse ever for why she couldn't go. It wasn't like she was going to win, anyway...

2

'BIN!'

'But I feel comfortable in black. And it hides everything!' Grace whined as Monica put yet another black top on the pile.

'How many black tops can one person have, for goodness' sake?' Monica muttered. 'You'll feel comfortable in colours too by the time I've finished with you, lady! No longer will you hide behind baggy, colourless, *miserable* clothes! It's no wonder you feel like crap sometimes. You have to face facts, Grace. You are curvy, so you are going to show off your curves, not hide them away. Blooming heck, I wish my boobs were as big as yours! Loads of people I know would be *so* jealous of your cleavage. With my help, you, my darling, are going to flourish and bloom and feel fabulous in everything you wear!' Monica stood behind Grace, bringing her arms around her front and giving her boobs a grope. 'And be proud of these mammas!'

'Get your hands off me, you bloody perv!' Grace couldn't help laughing at her friend, even though she was quite devastated that most of her favourite clothes were being packed into bin liners. She was concocting a plan for how she could retrieve them later when Monica walked around and stood in front of her, hands on her hips, apparently reading her mind.

'And you needn't think you are getting these back either, madam. I'm taking them straight to the charity shop! Although I'm not sure even they'd take some of this stuff, it's so bloody awful!'

'God you're tough!' Grace growled at her. 'Brutal!'

'And that's why you love me so much.' Monica grinned. She flung another black bag down the stairs towards the front door and blew her a kiss. 'And *that* is a very special bag that we're taking somewhere else.'

* * *

It was Saturday, a beautiful crisp spring morning, and Archie, the love of Grace's life, was at his dad's for the weekend. Since she and Mark had split up over a year ago, she usually moped around the house on the weekends that Archie wasn't there, just trying to fill time. If truth be told, she missed them both dreadfully. She missed being part of a family, but Mark had changed so drastically since becoming a head teacher, it was almost as if the power had gone to his head.

The excitement of organising and finally moving in to their forever house gave her something else to think about, and the other main thing that had brightened up her days and dragged her out of the house every morning was the second love of her life; Becks, named after her hero, David Beckham. They had rescued Becks from a dog's home in Birmingham. Although she now wondered who had rescued whom.

Getting a dog was her idea to cheer up Archie, as he was struggling a little bit since the split, and she hoped that it would help him to heal, but in truth it was *her* that the dog had healed more. He was her shadow. Although she wondered whether between Becks and Archie she'd ever go to the loo in peace again.

She loved it when she, Archie and Becks were all curled up on the sofa, Becks resting his head on her or Archie's lap. And now that Archie was getting to an age when he didn't really want to hold his mum's hand any more, and snuggles were becoming few and far between – a development that Grace found, frankly, quite devastating – her cuddles with Becks were the most physical contact she had these days. He really was the most adorable dog and she hadn't realised when he came into their lives just how quickly she would love him. She wouldn't be without him now. It also meant that she didn't have to keep talking to herself, which was a really bad habit she'd fallen into.

So she wasn't really alone any more, even when Archie was at his dad's, and today the effervescent Monica had turned up on her doorstep wearing a raincoat and pink stilettos, looking like a flasher. She also had a glint in her eye, which could only mean that she was up to no good. While Grace put the kettle on to make them both a cuppa, Monica whipped off her coat and flaunted a cerise pink t-shirt which, in diamanté letters right across the front, read 'Changing Grace'. Grace sighed inwardly. She was obviously going to be Monica's latest project.

'Don't worry, darling, I've got one for you too,' she

said, grinning as she flung a plastic bag at Grace. She also appeared to be brandishing a roll of bin bags, which made Grace raise an eyebrow. The kettle boiled and as Grace turned to make them both a drink, Monica disappeared up to Grace's bedroom quicker than greased lightning, and by the time Grace had taken the drinks upstairs, Monica had pulled everything from the wardrobe rails onto the bed.

Three hours and seven bin liners later, Grace's wardrobe was looking rather sparse. There was one pair of black trousers, a pair of skinny denim jeans that had been bought in a moment of madness and never been worn, and a couple of tops that had been given to her by her sister before she emigrated.

Forced by Monica to clear out her underwear drawer, she had been shocked to find seventy-seven pairs of manky old pants and five ghastly old bras that didn't even fit her – all now consigned to the bin bags.

'You seriously need some new undies! What colour do you fancy and what size do you need?'

Grace just looked at her in stunned silence. 'Well, obviously one black and one nude or neutral. What else would I need?'

'Are you kidding me?' Monica stood and stared at

her with her hands on her hips.

'What's so wrong about that? You wear black with your dark stuff and the nude one with everything else. Surely that's what everyone else has?' Grace shrugged.

'For God's sake – you *so* need help!' Monica told her sternly, but with a smile on her face. 'Come on then, grab your handbag. We're going undie shopping once we've dropped these bags off at the charity shop.'

Grace had forgotten what a force of nature Monica could be. They'd been best friends at school but at the age of sixteen, in their final year of high school, Monica's parents had moved miles away. Even though they'd tried to stay in touch, their lives had taken them in different directions. Grace had enrolled on an intensive interior design course at college and Monica embarked on an exciting new adventure as an 18–30s rep in various places in Europe, and they'd sadly lost touch over the years. So it was such a delight when one day Grace was scrolling through Facebook and a friend request popped up from Monica. They re-connected, first online, and then they moved to phoning one another; the years slipped away as they very quickly fell back into their easy friendship and became firm friends once more.

Monica had settled in Greece where she lived for ten years with her husband Alessandro until he was killed in a motorbike accident, when she returned to England to be with her parents so they could take care of her at that traumatic time in her life. Sadly Grace didn't know that this had happened and now felt some guilt that she hadn't made more of an effort to stay in touch over the years and be by her friend's side.

She admired Monica for starting a new life, knowing that Alessandro wouldn't have wanted her to grieve forever. Little Ollington was an affluent village and Monica saw an opportunity, deciding to follow her natural path, retraining to be an image consultant, personal stylist and shopper. Which was why she had apparently taken it upon herself to make Grace her latest client. After a hair-raising drive in Bertha, Monica's flame-red VW Beetle, they arrived outside the closest thing to a department store in the Staffordshire sticks. Little Ollington was a fabulous place to live if you fancied a cream tea or an afternoon's romp in the countryside, but the nearest shopping centre was miles away and visiting major stores meant a forty-five-minute train journey into Birmingham.

They headed straight for the underwear section

and Monica danced around, holding up a few bras, and asked, 'OK, what size bra do you need?'

'Well, before Archie was born I was a 36DD,' Grace replied.

'And now?'

'Erm, not entirely sure,' she said in a voice that she projected towards the floor, sounding like a naughty schoolchild being scolded by her head teacher.

'Not sure! *Not sure!* Are you for real?' Monica spluttered. 'Your son is now ten!'

People in the shop started to look around to where the noise was coming from and Grace wanted to crawl up her own backside. Monica lowered her voice. 'Grace, are you really telling me that you have no idea what bra size you are?'

'Erm, yes,' Grace whispered, and she hid her head in shame.

Monica tutted loudly in pure disgust and amazement and disappeared in a huff. A few minutes later she returned with a pretty, young bra-fitting assistant who introduced herself as Amy-Louise. She quickly offered to measure Grace and dragged her off to the changing rooms for the most embarrassing encounter of her life. Amy-Louise recommended a completely different size and style bra to the ones

Grace had been wearing for the last God knows how long and suggested that it might be worth browsing online to see what styles and colours she might like in the future.

Grace looked at Amy-fricking-Louise and sighed. *I won't be needing to worry about droopy boobs for a good few years yet*, she thought as the young assistant showed her how to scoop her boobs into her hands and hoist them into her bra, ensuring all the breast tissue was supported. It had been a while since anyone had been anywhere near her boobs and she'd never thought that 'getting back into the swing of it' would be quite like this. Grace was mortified by the whole incident and couldn't get out of the shop quickly enough, although she did come away with four new bras – the white, black and nude that she needed, plus a pink lacy number that Monica had bullied her into buying.

'Come on, sweetheart.' Monica tucked her arm into Grace's. 'I think you and I need to have a chat on the way to swishing.'

'Swishing?' questioned Grace. 'What the hell is "swishing" when it's at home?'

'You'll see!' Monica was grinning like a Cheshire cat. 'And you're going to *love* it!'

3

Bertha the Beetle screeched to a halt outside Rita's Rags to Riches. As they walked through the door, a voice shouted out from behind a curtain at the back of the shop: 'Won't be a tick, ladies!'

Within seconds, one of the most glamorous people that Grace had ever met appeared, dripping with jewellery and oozing natural style and charm. 'Now, you must be Grace. Hello, sweetie, I'm Rita.' She took Grace's hand in both of hers. 'Thanks so much for coming along to my little swishing shop today.' She air-kissed Monica on both cheeks. 'Dahling, it's so fabulous to see you again. It was so lovely to get your call to say you were coming in with another of your ladies. So, Grace, this is how it works.

First, you check in the clothes you brought along.'
Rita started rummaging through the 'special' bin bag
of Grace's clothes that Monica had handed over. 'You
have brought fifteen items so you get to choose fifteen items from the rails. These clothes have been
brought in by other people who have cleared out
their wardrobes. You can choose more, but for every
additional item after fifteen, you have to pay two
pounds fifty per item. But then as Monica is a regular
customer, she knows the rules, don't you, darling?'

'Sure do, Rita.' She turned to Grace. 'This is one
of my favourite upmarket charity shops in the area.
I've brought so many of my ladies along to give them
a wardrobe make-over that I feel like part of the furniture. Come on, Grace, let's start! This is going to be
sooo much fun!'

Grace doubted it very much. Since she'd put on
weight over the last few years, shopping for clothes
had become one of her least favourite activities –
next to having her bikini line waxed. Which was, in-
cidentally, something that she hadn't had done
since... she couldn't even remember when. It wasn't
like she had anyone who would even notice!

She browsed through the racks while Rita and
Monica were nattering away, grabbing things off the
rails and putting them in the changing room.

A black dress caught her eye but as she picked it out to look at it in more detail, Monica's booming voice cried, 'No, no, no, no, NO! *Absolutely not!* From now on anything black is banned!'

Oh God, Mum, what am I letting myself in for? Grace silently entreated, looking towards heaven. She talked to her mum all the time. She knew some people thought she was a bit on the crazy side, including her ex, but it was the only way she'd been able to cope since her mum lost her battle with cancer twelve years previously. It was the routine daily tasks that she found difficult to get through. Sometimes she still went to pick up the phone to share something with her mum, momentarily forgetting that she was no longer there. The shock and sadness of remembering that she could no longer speak with her took Grace's breath away and she would stand, holding the phone, stunned by her loss all over again.

This time though, she heard a voice very clearly saying, *Darling girl, it's about time someone took you in hand and showed you what you are capable of. I'm sorry if it seems harsh, but if I were there right now, I'd be doing it myself. Love you!*

She often heard her mother's words and had got used to it now, even though she originally thought she was going a bit bonkers. She dreamt about her mum a lot too, dreaming that they were shopping together, or out having dinner; routine, normal activities for a mother and a daughter, but when she woke, the realisation that it wasn't real was always heartbreaking.

Rita's excited voice jolted her back to the present.

'So, Grace!' Rita said, clapping her hands. 'Why don't you tell me what your style is and I'll see what I can come up with?'

Grace tried to think how to answer the question. Since she'd had Archie, she didn't think she even had a style. She spent most of her working time in suits and that was what she felt most herself in. While some of her friends were comfortable at the weekend in jeans, a hoody and a pair of trainers, Grace knew that she was a bit stiff with her clothing. Smart jeans were probably the trendiest things she wore but she always wore them with a nice jumper and a pair of boots because that was her personal style – such as it was. Unless she was walking the dog of course, when she usually donned a pair of old joggers and a sweatshirt. People would never notice her for her dress sense, that was for sure; the only style she had was anything that covered her fat arse.

'OK, Grace, get in there and get your kit off!'

Monica manhandled her into the changing room and pulled the curtain shut. 'The first thing you are trying on is the blue jumpsuit.'

'You have to be kidding me! Surely jumpsuits went out years ago? And besides, what if I needed a wee while I had it on?' she exclaimed.

'Neither of those facts bothered you enough to stop you having three of them in your wardrobe though, did it?' Monica laughed. '*Having* been the operative word! They must have been in there since 1985!'

'I loved those, thank you very much!' Grace responded. 'Can't believe you chucked them out – and now you're making me try on another one?'

'I chucked out three jumpsuits with shoulder pads that Krystle Carrington would have been proud of – very different to what you're about to try on!' She cackled with laughter.

Grace stomped out of the changing room in the jumpsuit. Her shoulders were slumped, her posture was poor and her face was really miserable.

'I hate it!' Grace said, pulling a face and sounding like a truculent teenager.

'Look at the state of you! Push your tits out and hold your stomach in!' Monica scolded. 'And stop slouching! That's better. Ooh, you're like a naughty child!'

'I still hate it!'

'Shut up and turn round!' Monica snapped as she handed her a wide silver belt and a long sparkly silver and blue necklace, which Grace noticed was actually rather nice.

'But I really don't like it!' Grace said, turning to head back to the changing room.

'Did I not just tell you to shut it?' Her friend flicked her on the shoulder. 'Trust your Aunty Monica.'

'I'm sure Gok Wan wasn't this rude to the ladies on his show,' Grace said, rubbing her crystal necklace between her fingers.

'Oh, stop moaning, you! Now hoist your bangers up and let's see that amazing cleavage which, by the way, most women would die for, put these heels on and get out here!' Monica handed her a pair of sparkly silver wedges, and Grace took them from her and slipped them on her feet.

She looked in the mirror. Actually, it looked OK. In fact, the more she looked at herself, the more she realised it wasn't bad at all. Perhaps Monica did know what she was doing, although Grace wasn't going to admit that in a hurry. She perked up a bit and turned this way and that. Her backside didn't look quite as huge as she thought it would. Perhaps all that worrying about the house move, and how much it was going to cost to do it all up, along with all the other worries of a single parent, had resulted in a bit of weight loss after all? Silver lining and all that. Something sharp was digging into her thigh. She found the culprit – it was the label.

'Bugger me, it's still got the label in! It's never been worn! And it cost a hundred and fifty pounds new.'

'And that's the beauty of swishing,' chorused Monica and Rita in perfect harmony.

Perhaps this is going to be fun after all, Grace thought as she tried on more outfits that Rita and Monica had chosen for her. She particularly loved a turquoise silk cocktail dress that Rita had brought into the changing room and said would be perfect for her even though Grace had laughed at first at the thought of needing a glamorous dress in her wardrobe – she couldn't see herself wearing that while walking Becks, or watching Archie play football on a freezing Saturday morning. But then she remembered that she *did* need something swanky for that event she was trying so hard to forget. The empire-line cut of the dress fitted her perfectly on her top half, making her look curvy instead of busty, and the longer-length chiffon skirt skimmed her legs gracefully and ended just above her ankles (or her 'cankles', as she frequently referred to them). It felt comfortable yet fashionable at the same time. Rita really knew her stuff.

Shopping with a girlfriend was actually far more fun than shopping alone. Years ago she wouldn't have dreamt of wearing an outfit unless it was labelled Dolce & Gabbana – but these days the closest she got was Florence & Fred. Rita handed her a glass of Prosecco at one point and as she very rarely drank these days, she was feeling particularly tiddly.

Grace eventually chose some smart-casual items she could wear for work, some stuff for relaxing and wearing around the house and some swanky things she could wear if she ever went on a night out, including the cocktail dress. And there wasn't a black item in sight!

Rita packed up the outfits they'd chosen and handed Grace five bags that were bursting at the seams. 'It's lovely to see ladies who come in feeling miserable go out with smiles on their faces. That's what makes it all worthwhile. That'll be twenty-five pounds then, please, my darling.'

'Twenty-five pounds! Is that all? Are you sure?'

'Yes, lovely, you had fifteen items for free as you brought fifteen items in, then another ten items at two pounds fifty each which makes twenty-five pounds.'

'Wow, that's an absolute bargain!' Grace exclaimed as Monica and Rita sang in unison, 'And that's the beauty of swishing!'

Back home, Grace flung herself on her settee, exhausted from her morning of being prodded, poked and cajoled.

'God, I'm knackered!' she said to Monica who was standing over her. 'I'm so looking forward to getting my jimmies on, ordering a Chinese and having a relaxing night in watching *The X Factor* tonight!'

Monica grinned. 'Ha! No bloody chance, sweetie! I'm so glad you like the blue jumpsuit the best, because you're wearing it when we go out tonight. Come on, shift your butt! Get in the shower right now! You'd better be quick, though. You've got an appointment at the hairdresser's in fifteen minutes.'

4

Carlos, Monica's brother, who just happened to be a hairdresser, was a magician in the salon. He worked wonders. He was a dead ringer for Idris Elba and the ladies loved him. As he chatted to Grace, he blended three different shades of deep brown, copper and rich red into her hair and then snipped away.

As he swung the chair round to finally face the mirror, he grinned and said, 'Ta-dah!'

The mousy, lacklustre, shoulder-length nothing style she'd had for years had been transformed into a funky, flicky bob that Kate Silverton would have been proud of. It knocked years off her and she felt light and carefree for the first time in a very long time.

'OMG! I love it!' Grace exclaimed.

'Darling, you look like spring!' Monica squealed.

'Spring?' Grace enquired.

'Yes, darling, you looked like winter before. Dull, dreary and miserable. But now you look like spring – exciting and full of promise for the future.'

'I think there's a backhanded compliment in there somewhere,' said Carlos, winking at her. 'What she's trying to say is, you look hot, girl!'

'Right, come on, stop flirting with Carlos, babe, it won't get you anywhere, I can assure you. He's so in love and happy with Fernando that they make me want to throw up!'

Carlos stuck out his tongue at his sister and handed Grace over to Fiona, a young and stunning beautician who did stage make-up at the local theatre.

Oh please, Mum! I know I ask loads of favours of you, and it's normally to find me a fabulous parking space, but please don't let me leave looking like Widow Twanky! Grace mouthed silently to somewhere up above. She felt soothed, as if someone was reassuringly resting their hand on her shoulder.

After around twenty minutes titivating, Fiona said, 'It's time. Close your eyes... and now you can look in the mirror!' She swung Grace's chair around.

Grace held her breath, and slowly opened one eye and then the other. She blinked and blinked again. Was that really her? She could not believe it.

'Is that me?'

'Sure is! Do you like it?' Fiona asked nervously.

'*Oh! My! God!* What have you done to me? That's not me, surely?' She stared straight at the mirror, sideways on and back to straight on. 'Like it? I bloody *love* it!'

Fiona laughed. 'I know I do the stage looks but I've been learning how to do subtle make-overs too and how to enhance a person's natural features. Are you sure you're happy? You didn't think you were going to end up looking like a pantomime dame, did you?' She laughed.

'God! Of course not!' Grace said, mentally crossing her fingers at the lie. 'I'm bloody delighted, Fiona. I'm going to tell everyone about you and how amazing you are! Between you, Carlos and Monica, you've transformed me on the outside. Thank you sooo very much.'

'Well, let me know if you fancy a pizza-and-Prosecco night and I could teach you how to do it for yourself, if you fancy it?'

'Now you're talking. Thank you so much, Fiona.'

Monica sniggered. 'Yes, that's the outside done,

Grace, and you look amazing. We're ready for our night out and then we just have the inside to work on!'

* * *

My darling girl. I wish you could see yourself through my eyes. I wish I could reach out and touch you and take you in my arms once more. If I could wish for anything in the world, I would wish that you would learn to love yourself. You need to realise just how beautiful you are, inside and out. But you're not ever going to be able to let love into your life until you love yourself.

I'm so glad that Monica has taken you in hand. I know you are sad and still really struggling with losing me, and I only wish I could help you more. I wish you could feel it when I touch your face and wipe away your tears. I wish you could feel my hand in yours when you sleep at night. I wish you knew how much I still love you even though I can't be with you in body. I'm just a breath away, my darling. So close but yet so far.

Mum xxx

5

Grace turned the key in the lock. Monica had given her two and a half hours until she was being picked back up for a night out on the town. As she closed the door, she realised how painfully quiet it was without her son in the house and, as always, it made her heart twang.

She was so glad that her life had changed for the better now, even if that meant being alone and being a single mum. When she and Mark first split, Grace had worried most about how Archie was going to handle it. She'd waited forever to meet the love of her life, and on the day her son was born, she did. He was her pride and joy. Her life. Her everything. She had a pang of sadness every time she thought about just how much her mum would have loved him, and that she'd never had the opportunity to share Archie and his wonderful self with her.

Grace tottered down her long hallway, the new high heels that she'd promised Monica she'd get used to click-clacking on the Victorian tiled floor, and plonked down her shopping, handbag and keys on the large wooden bureau at the far end of the hall. She'd always longed to walk through the front door and be welcomed by someone who simply couldn't live without her. And she knew that in just a few seconds, she would be getting such a hug and a heart full of love coming her way.

The thud of a tail thumping on the floor could be heard as she opened the kitchen door, and there he was.

'Hewo, my gorgeous boyyyyyy.' She tickled Becks behind his ears and squatted down to his level where he leant into her, sat straight on her lap and knocked her off balance. 'Hewo, my bootiful baby. Mamma's home now! Do you need to go do a wee-wee?' She laughed at herself and wondered why people talked to animals and babies in a stupid voice.

Since Becks came into their lives, she understood why dogs were used in therapy. Just stroking this gorgeous bundle of fluffiness always restored her spirits.

He just seemed to sense that she needed to laugh and be loved. She was so glad that he was part of her life.

She opened the French doors, which led onto the patio, to let Becks out. Seeing how much of a state the garden was in, Grace remembered that she wasn't the only thing in her life that desperately needed some love and attention. She glanced at her watch as she flicked on the kettle and grabbed her favourite Cath Kidston mug from the cupboard. She had a bit of time before her big evening out.

Off came the high heels, and she sighed in relief as her feet hit the cold stone tiles. She grabbed the slipper boots that had been warming on the radiator, slid her feet inside and soon started to warm up. It was early spring and even though it had been a day of bright sunshine, the afternoons were still a little chilly, especially when you had a tiled floor.

She went over to the huge chrome American-style fridge freezer and as she grabbed the milk from the fridge door, she spotted a bottle of Pinot Grigio. *Mmm!* She thought. That might just hit the spot and give her some much-needed Dutch courage. She dreaded to think what Monica had planned for their big night out.

She grabbed a large wine goblet from the cupboard next to the fridge, filled it halfway and took a big swig. As the cool liquid hit the back of her throat, she sighed and took another large gulp. Rolling her shoulders in a circular motion like her Pilates teacher had taught her to, Grace closed the French doors after Becks wandered back in. He followed her through to the lounge, a homely room with two huge brown leather sofas opposite each other separated by a wooden coffee table. She switched on the two table lamps, which cast a low cosy glow into the room. Lighting her Jo Malone Pomegranate Noir candle, her decadent present to herself, she slumped down into her big comfy reading chair, in the large bay window, Becks curled up with his head resting on her feet.

Grace remembered the first time Mark had taken Archie away for a week's holiday. All her friends had tried to comfort her, saying that they'd love a week off from their kids, but it broke Grace's heart to hear people say that. She hated being away from Archie. He was the person she was closest to in the world. He was her best friend. She loved spending time with him, whether it was going to theme parks – which they could rarely afford these days – visiting friends or just chilling out at home.

When he was away from her it felt like she'd lost

a limb, and she had a constant dull ache in her heart. She thought she'd get used to it in time, but she never really had. The fact of it was that even before Archie was born, Grace realised why she'd been put on earth. Her job was to be a mum. Archie's mum. It was the best job she'd ever had.

At first, she'd made sure that she planned to do something or go somewhere on the nights when Archie went to Mark's flat. Then the nights that he was with her would be their special time. She hated sharing her son, even if it was only every other weekend and one night in the week. She certainly had never thought that she'd be in the position where she'd have to do that. She even wished sometimes in her really dark moments that Mark had died so that she didn't have to share Archie, but then she pulled herself back in check, realising that it was best for their son to have both his parents in his life, even if one of those was an arsehole sometimes.

When she and Mark were together, she'd been the main carer for Archie. Mark was always at work and when he did have some free time, he spent it on going to the gym, or out with his friends, or playing squash. At least that's what he *said* he'd been doing. Grace found out later that it was just a ruse for going out for drinks with other women. He denied it of course, every time she asked him where he was. In fact, he used to tell her that it was nothing to do with her – where he was – and that he didn't have to tell her anything. She had always found that suspicious – if he didn't have anything to hide, surely he would just say where he was going? Mark's rejoinder was that they were two people in a relationship, not fused at the hip; they didn't have to do everything together. But they actually didn't do *anything* together, so Grace spent her time lonely and worrying what Mark was up to on the nights he wasn't at home. She just wanted someone who loved spending time with her.

She spent her life making excuses for Mark, not telling her friends the truth about him. Whenever they came round, he always made out that he was the perfect husband, offering to make cups of tea and charming them with his sparkling conversation, but behind closed doors Mark treated her like she was his skivvy.

He certainly blamed Grace for their lack of sex life. His idea of foreplay most of the time was not speaking to her for a week, then getting into bed and asking abruptly if she fancied a shag. Strangely enough, that didn't really do it for her, and nor did his mood swings, spinning between the roles of attentive husband and mardy bastard, so that she never knew which Mark she was going to come home to. The worst part about it was that because he was so manipulative, she always ended up questioning herself and starting to wonder if she was in the wrong.

On those occasions when she did agree to have sex with him, it was because she felt like she should keep the peace and because if she did it with him, it might shut him up for a week or two. His sexual technique left a lot to be desired too. He seemed to think that grabbing her boobs and twiddling her nipples like he was trying to tune into a radio station would be a big turn-on. Most of the time, she was glad the lights were off so he couldn't see her grimacing, wishing it would be over as quickly as possible.

But on his great days, he was the most attentive person ever, running her a bath, pouring her a G&T; she'd wished she had that Mark all the time. That was the Mark she had fallen in love with; the Mark that had made her want to have his child. It wasn't until afterwards she found out the times he'd been nicest to her were when he'd been up to no good.

Deep down, Grace had known for a long time that things weren't quite right between them, but she also knew that families stuck together through thick and thin, and marriages were forever.

Finding out about Lorraine was a blessing in disguise in a way, Grace thought now as she wondered whether she'd have been brave enough to do anything about ending the marriage without a catalyst kicking it all off.

Grace's train of thought was interrupted when the doorbell rang. She wasn't expecting anyone, let alone the dashingly handsome bearded man standing at her door. He had tousled dark brown hair, which he casually ran his fingers through as he spoke.

He introduced himself as Vinnie. He leant forward and his strong hand, slightly rough perhaps from hard work, shook hers as he stared deep into her eyes.

'I'm so sorry to bother you on a Saturday. I'm from the landscaping company you left a message for earlier in the week. I didn't have the chance to call you back so I just popped round on the off chance that you might be in as I was in the area,' he said. 'I wondered if I could take a look at those overgrown trees that you mentioned. Would that be OK?'

It would be more than OK, Grace thought. It was not every day that a hot sexy beefcake with a warm, seductive, yet soothing voice turned up on your doorstep and made your heart flutter. All her Christmases had come at once!

'Yep, sure. Shall I take you round the back?' *Why did she say that?* They both blushed.

'Well, that's the best offer I've had for a long time.' Vinnie laughed and his whole face lit up, eyes sparkling. They were the most amazing, piercing, intense blue that seemed to look right through her to her innermost secrets. *Crikey*, Grace thought to herself. She hoped he *didn't* know what she was thinking...

Becks came to investigate who was at the door and Vinnie bent down to stroke him. 'Hey there, fella, you're a beauty, aren't you?'

Becks looked as if he was glowing with his compliment and stuck by Vinnie's side, following him down the side path into the back garden as if he'd known him forever.

As she walked him into the garden, Grace took the opportunity to check out Vinnie. He was around six foot two and broad, with lean long legs that ended in a rather muscly yet perfectly shaped bum. His hair was dark with a few grey streaks around the ears. He was wearing a royal-blue polo shirt with the company logo, jeans and boots. As they reached the bottom of the garden, he leant over the fence and his t-shirt rode up his back, giving her a glimpse of an Armani waistband. She was just pondering over whether he wore boxers or briefs when he turned round and caught her staring at his backside. She quickly averted her eyes.

Blushing again, she pointed out one of the trees that really needed cutting back, and as he reached up to grab an overhanging branch, the front of his t-shirt rode up, displaying the most ripped six-pack she'd ever seen on a man that wasn't in an advert. Her breath caught in her throat as their eyes met.

'Yoo-hoo!' Belinda from next door stuck her head over the fence, breaking the moment. 'Hello, favourite neighbour,' she beamed.

Grace let out a breath that she hadn't realised she'd been holding in. 'Hey, lovely, how are you?'

'I'm good, darling, thank you, are you? And *who* is this gorgeous young man you're hiding away at the bottom of your garden?'

'Vinnie, this is Belinda. Belinda, this is Vinnie. He's come to have a look at my bush.' Grace blushed as red as a beetroot. She'd done it again.

'Mmm, interesting.' Belinda's eyebrows rose. She was clearly trying not to laugh, but Grace could see her shoulders were shaking and her eyes twinkling more than normal. Grace breathed in a few times and tried very hard to control herself, not wanting to make Vinnie feel uncomfortable. But an uncontrollable laughing fit took over and she found herself giggling helplessly.

Once Belinda and Grace had pulled themselves together, she explained to Vinnie, who had turned away to take some photographs, that the trees were shutting a lot of light out of the garden and that she had to chase round the last bit of sunshine towards the end of the day through the summer.

Belinda nodded. 'It's a shame for poor Archie when he's out playing, isn't it, love?'

'Archie is my ten-year-old son,' Grace explained.

Vinnie slipped his phone back into his pocket. 'Ah, I did wonder, what with the football goal and three hundred footballs by the patio doors. Although I suppose you might have been trying out for the England ladies' team.' He chuckled. 'Well, we can't have Archie playing football in the dark now, can we? We'll try to get a bit more light sorted out for him then.'

They chatted about the landscaping for five minutes or so and Vinnie took more photos on his phone of the trees that needed attention. Then he turned round and snapped one of her too. 'Just so that when

I pass on the photos, the guys who come out know who to ask to make them a cuppa.' He grinned.

Belinda's eyebrows rose and she winked at Grace behind Vinnie's back. Grace smiled. She had been truly blessed the day she moved into the house next door to Belinda and Bill. All she ever heard from their home was laughter. After many years of marriage, this wonderful couple were still the best of friends and madly in love with each other. It was a delight to see and gave her hope in love and marriage. They looked out for Grace and Archie, and Grace looked out for them. In fact, they were more like family than neighbours. They loved helping out with Archie, seeing him as a surrogate grandson who they could make a real fuss over. They looked after him sometimes when Grace had to work in the evening, and Belinda sometimes picked him up from school in an emergency. And Bill even gave in to Archie's demands to play football with him from time to time until he needed to have a sit down and get his breath back. It was good for Grace to have someone to support her, without her mum around. Her dad was not really well enough to look after Archie. She didn't know what she'd do without her fabulous neighbours.

Vinnie rubbed his hands together. 'Right then,

I'd better be off. I have the pleasure of going out on a
stag night with my mates tonight, for my sins. God
help me! I'd better go and make myself look respectable.'

He looked more than respectable to Grace. Since
she'd split up with Mark, she didn't think she'd actually come across anyone that she even marginally
fancied, yet here was a man that she couldn't take
her eyes off. It was a shame that he'd now walk out of
her life and she'd probably never see him again.
Vinnie said his goodbyes to Belinda and walked up
the side path to the front of Grace's house. A ping
from his phone signalled a text message, and a frown
crossed his brow when he looked down at the screen.
However, it quickly disappeared as he turned to say
goodbye.

'It's been really lovely to meet you, Grace.
Thanks so much for letting me pop in on the spur of
the moment. Perhaps I'd better arrange to come
back and make sure my team are doing a good job.
You never know, I might get a cup of tea and a
Hobnob next time?' They grinned at each other and
their eyes held just a second longer than they
needed to. 'You'd better give me your number
again... erm, if that's OK, of course, and I'll plan a
date in the diary when the boys can come and get

the work done and we'll get you some sunshine back into your life.'

Grace smiled, as she realised that he'd already done that. 'Thanks, Vinnie, that would be great.'

She waved as he drove off in his four-wheel-drive truck. Turning towards the house with a stupid goofy grin on her face, like a teenager with her first crush, she literally bumped into Bill. Laughing, she said 'Hello' and gave him a quick hug before heading into the house.

Bill always made Grace laugh, particularly his ongoing feud with the local wildlife. Their side paths ran parallel and she often heard Bill yelling, followed by the sight of the top end of a broom above the fence. She took no notice now, but the first time she'd seen it, she'd wondered what the hell was going on. All she could see was Bill yelling and running up and down the path trying to shoo something up high with the broom. 'Bloody shitting bastards!' were the only words she could make out. She had gone over to speak with him and as they'd started to chat, he had suddenly broken off to yell into the sky: 'Look at 'em, up there. They wait for me to jet wash the path then they shit all over it! Beady-eyed sneaky little bastards!'

Looking up, Grace had seen three pigeons sitting

on the aerial of her neighbour's house. As they stared, there was a swooshing noise followed swiftly by a sound similar to that of an egg splatting, and she realised that one had pooped, missing Bill by mere millimetres. She had tried very hard to keep a straight face and muttered how naughty it was of them. Making a swift exit, Grace had closed her back door and couldn't help but giggle. It was at times like that she wished she had someone to share a right good laugh with.

As she closed the door, her phone pinged to say she had a text from Belinda.

> Phwoar, he was a bit of all right! Get in there! I'm going to christen him 'fit bloke'.

Grace laughed out loud and texted back:

> Not every day you get a hotty like that turn up on your doorstep. Must have been my lucky day!

Normally on a Saturday afternoon, she'd be in her dog-walking clothes with not a bit of make-up on and her hair in a ponytail. Thank God for Monica right now, as on this particular Saturday she had been dolled up and looking really rather fabulous when the hot gardener arrived. Perhaps Lady Luck was on her side for a change!

She looked at her watch and saw that she had time for a quick cuppa before the big night out that Monica had planned. While the kettle boiled, she looked out of the kitchen window at the garden and realised that there was an awful lot of work to do, not just getting the trees cut back. She dismissed the thought that more work in the garden might mean more chances to meet the hot gardener, and laughed at herself.

Grace opened up the French doors and took her tea out to the garden, sitting on the cast-iron bench on a patio that had seen better days. Daffodils and snowdrops were starting to appear through the borders. Spring was her favourite time of year; crisp but bright mornings signified the start of a promising new season, and the days getting longer made her feel so much brighter. She thanked her lucky stars for this beautiful house that she now lived in.

* * *

Grace fell in love with her home in Little Ollington the moment she saw the details at the agency, sitting on a pile for her to type up. It was a house that she drove past every day on the way to the office and she'd always loved it but never thought it would be within her price range. She immediately asked if she could go and see it before the For Sale board went up. She hoped and prayed that it was as lovely as it looked from the outside.

It exuded charm and character from the moment Mrs Robinson opened its duck-egg blue front door and introduced herself and welcomed Grace and Archie inside. Grace's heels click-clacked down the stone-tiled hallway, and she walked through the kitchen door and gasped.

'Oh, Mrs Robinson, what a fabulous room.'

The kitchen was everything she'd ever wished for: cream gloss units and black marble worktops, with a central island breakfast bar to die for. If this was the first room, she couldn't wait to see the rest of the house.

'Call me Gladys, dear,' she said. 'Mrs Robinson makes me feel so old. Please do join me for a cup of tea. It's nice to have some company for a change.'

Grace gazed out of the kitchen window looking at the huge garden as Gladys pottered around, laying a tea tray with what looked like the best china.

'Why don't you go and look round the rest of the house while I wait for the kettle to boil? And take your time. I'm in no rush today.'

Grace meandered around the house. Sadly, the kitchen was the only room which had been renovated; the other rooms needed a great deal of love and attention. But with her eye for interior design, Grace was able to visualise how each room could look under different circumstances. There would be a lot to do; there were no two ways about that. But it had the bones of a stunning house. The cast-iron fireplaces with tiled surrounds in the lounge and dining room were simply beautiful. She'd always dreamed of having a real fire, the smell always bringing back such happy memories of her childhood. The high ceilings with ornate cornicing gave a wonderful feeling of space, and the huge sash windows throughout reflected light into every room. She just loved it. She knew it would take a lot of hard work and money, but with her design skills and knowledge of using colour, light and shade, and co-ordinating the soft furnishings, this house could be totally exquisite – the perfect home for her and Archie.

'What do you think, Arch?'

'It's a bit old and gloomy, Mum. I'd prefer to live somewhere newer, like Dad and Lorraine's flat.'

Grace's heart sank, but then his face lit up as he walked into one of the bedrooms that overlooked the back garden. Staring out of the window at the lawn, he said that there was room for a full-sized football goal. Grace agreed that it was definitely a possibility. And when Archie saw the huge TV screen on the wall of the bedroom, he claimed the room as his immediately. 'We could get a TV like that for my Xbox, Mum! Can I have this room? Please, please! I love this house now. I've changed my mind.' He did a strange dance move, and Grace did a funny move back at him.

'Really, Mum! No one dabs any more. It's all about the floss. Get with it!'

Grace grinned and heard the kettle whistling downstairs. A memory flooded back to her of her nanna's house, where there was always a whistling kettle and tea leaves with a tea pot, china cups and saucers, and a tea strainer. She'd spent many hours as a young girl there, as her own mum worked so hard to keep the bills paid and a roof over their heads. Grace's dad wasn't good with money; he was old-fashioned in his ways and as quick as her mum could earn it, he could booze it away with his mates down the pub. Nanna was always there for her and her sister, Hannah, when Mum was working. There was a huge Nanna-shaped hole in all of their lives when she passed away not long after Grace turned sixteen. But right now, thinking about Nanna didn't make her sad, it made her think about how much Nanna would love this house, and that warmed the cockles of her heart.

She returned downstairs, aware that her heart was beating a little faster. Since Mark had left there hadn't been much to smile about, but looking around this house, Grace felt the first stirrings of antic-ipation.

'Let me.' She took the tray from Gladys and fol-lowed her through to the lounge where original leaded French doors overlooked the garden. It was strange but she felt a sense of peace in this house, as if she'd come home. It felt familiar and warm to her and a delicious shiver of excitement ran down her spine. Grace realised that it was enthusiasm, mixed with trepidation. She already knew she wanted this house for herself.

'Do excuse the garden, my dear, I haven't been able to keep on top of it. The house too. I've tried my best, but the time really has come for me to move to a smaller, more manageable, place. This house is way too big for me now and it's time for someone new to come in and make wonderful memories like Charles and I made here with our family. I hold ours right here in my heart.'

A lump formed in Grace's throat, and she hoped she and Archie would make amazing memories here, too. Memories that would make Gladys proud.

As Gladys reminisced about bringing up her family in the house and asked her questions about her life, Grace found herself opening up about Mark and her divorce. She told Gladys how they'd moved to Little Ollington when Mark had been offered a job out at a smaller school, after being sick and tired of schools in inner-city Birmingham. She confided that when they'd moved out to the countryside, they had known nobody, and about the fact that the split with Mark meant that they were living in a rented property but that they were now ready to find their forever home. She smiled at Gladys, hoping fervently that this would be the one.

She glanced over at Archie, who was sitting cross-legged on the floor playing Fortnite on Grace's iPhone. Grace was going to have to start limiting screen time, as he had been a little obsessed lately, and it was becoming a real issue with him getting way too stroppy when she asked him to do something. Setting the boundaries was increasingly difficult when his dad let him play on the computer as much as he liked, which Grace knew he only did as it was easier than interacting with his son. But while she was chatting to Gladys that day and he was quiet and happy, she let him play.

Over tea, Grace told Gladys all about her family. It felt really natural to share so much with her; she was such a sincere, interesting and open character, and Grace had warmed to her immediately, thinking how much her mum would have liked her.

So Grace told Gladys about how her dad had recently moved out of his house and into a local retirement village. He had gone to pieces when her mum died – they had been together for fifty years – and Grace was so happy that he was finally starting to enjoy life again. He had his own private flat, but it was in a community where lots of people were in the same boat and he could have company if he wanted, but he could also choose to be alone. There was a small supermarket onsite, and carers and cleaners popping in and out for those who weren't quite so mobile. And he had made new friends who were constantly visiting him. It was perfect and it had given him a new lease of life.

When her dad still lived at home, Grace had made sure to keep popping in to keep him company even though he was quite demanding and often grumpy. Mark was charming in front of his father-in-law but behind closed doors he didn't like that Grace spent lots of time with her dad and didn't understand his neediness. But Grace knew her dad was lonely and craving attention. He'd been with her mum so long that he didn't know how to exist on his own. Sometimes she'd be driving home from his house when she'd get a call on her mobile from her dad's neighbour to say that he was feeling unwell. Grace knew it was attention-seeking, because he'd been perfectly fine when she'd left him not that long ago, but he constantly needed the reassurance of people around him.

The retirement village was therefore the perfect answer and doing her a favour too, as it meant that she got some time out from her dad giving her ear-ache about her son coming from a 'broken home'. Her father's mindset was old school; he thought that people should stick together through thick and thin for the sake of their children and not be selfish and divide their family. Grace was aware that her father totally disapproved when she kicked out Mark and felt that they should have worked through their differences – which was rich, really, coming from him, who had been a bit of a lad in his day. But Grace knew that now she had Archie, she couldn't put up with what her mum had lived with, although times were different then.

She remembered a conversation she once had over a cup of tea one afternoon when her mum was having a moan about the lack of respect that she was shown in her marriage. Her mum's view was that you either put up with the person you'd chosen to be with and got on with it or you worked hard to sort it out and fix it. You made your bed and all that. But Grace knew that if she stayed with Mark, not only was she not being true to herself, but she was also showing Archie that it was OK to act that way too. She was determined that she'd make sure Archie would grow up to know how to treat people properly. Grace wanted to show him that relationships were meant to be happy, not tolerated.

Gladys took the details of the retirement village and said it sounded pretty perfect for her too, that she'd give them a call and maybe arrange a visit. Grace found herself offering to take her along to meet her dad one of the days so that she could get a feel for the place. Gladys was someone that she felt she wanted to spend more time with, and this would be helping her too.

She glanced at her watch. 'Gladys, it's been a real treat to meet you and to look round your amazing house. We love it, as you can probably tell. But it's nearly time for Archie's football training and I'm going to have to tear myself away from your beautiful home and do some workings out, and we'll be in touch, if that's OK.'

The moment Grace got in the car, she rang her work and raved to Edward, the agency owner, how much she loved the house, and told him not to show it to anyone else just yet – one of the perks of working as an estate agent. He could hear the excitement bubbling over in her voice but kindly told her to sleep on it and that they'd discuss it when she was next at work.

When she went into the office the next day, they chatted over a coffee and agreed a plan of action. He suggested a low but sensible offer and made the call to Mrs Robinson while Grace waited with bated breath. Gladys wanted to go away and discuss things with her family and said she'd be back to them within a few days, after she'd had time to mull over everything.

In the meantime, Grace couldn't concentrate on a

thing. Her head was full of the house and how it might look once she'd put her stamp on it. Archie had always wanted a navy-blue bedroom, which just wouldn't have been right in their modern build, but Grace thought it could work beautifully in the new house. She had always loved deep, dramatic colours, and because of the height of the rooms and the light that the huge windows let in everywhere, deep colours would be perfect and really make a statement.

The roll-top bath in the main bathroom was simply to die for. She could imagine new tiles on the floor, with underfloor heating. This house had the potential to be magazine-worthy; she had totally fallen in love with it, although she was trying not to get too carried away just in case she was disappointed. But even if she didn't want to admit it, the house had got under her skin. It was even a little closer to the high school that Archie would be going to next year, which was another bonus, and he'd be able to walk home quite easily. There wasn't one thing about this house that she didn't love – apart from the money it would take to get it to be how she dreamed it could be. But there was no rush. If they got it, they'd have all the time in the world, and she'd just have to work harder and gain more commission to pay for the things that it needed.

When, two days later, Mrs Robinson phoned Edward to say that they were happy to accept her offer, Grace couldn't believe her luck. Mrs Robinson said to Edward that she thought Grace was a lovely lady and that Archie was adorable and that she couldn't think of anyone better to move into her home.

Hearing these words, Grace was truly over the moon. This new house would give her and Archie the new start they needed. Maybe dreams could come true after all.

* * *

Two weeks after they'd been to look at the house, Grace and Archie picked up Gladys and took her over to meet her father in the retirement village. She'd told him they were coming, and he'd laid out tea and cakes to welcome her. It was lovely to see her dad with some colour in his cheeks, excited about having guests. Although he could still be grumpy at times, he loved spending time with his grandson and Archie adored his papa. That day, Grace noticed that her dad had on freshly laundered clothes, and she even smelt aftershave. She smiled to herself. He welcomed Gladys with warmth and invited her to take a look around his flat while Grace put the kettle on. He proudly told them all that he'd ordered cakes especially, with his Tesco home delivery. Grace was amazed that he'd bought himself the latest Apple Mac and had been having lessons in the community centre from a young IT professional who was helping the residents get 'on the line'. He'd ought to be clocking up loyalty points based on how much he was spending on his Amazon account.

Her dad was telling Gladys how safe and secure he felt in his new home, how he could be alone if he wanted to and cook his own meals, or how more often than not he went to eat in the community dining room where he didn't have to do any washing up. Grace was delighted to see that her father seemed to have a new lease of life, and Gladys was bowled over by the place, asking Grace if she could arrange an appointment with the manager to find out if there were any free flats. Grace and Archie wandered off over to the main building to see if she could find someone to talk to. The manager came back over with her to her father's flat and, as they walked in, all they could hear was the tinkling of laughter from the lounge.

It warmed Grace's heart and she hoped that

Gladys and her dad would become firm friends if she decided to move in there. Gladys went to view an apartment and returned a short time later with a huge grin on her face, announcing that she would be moving into flat number five as soon as she physically could. Grace was amazed by how quickly she'd made her decision and asked her whether she needed to take some time before committing.

'I've spoken to the family and we had already decided that it was a great idea. I've done nothing but look at brochures of this place since I accepted the offer you made on the house and had pretty much made up my mind. Coming here and meeting your dad and some of the other residents in the community hall has made me realise how I miss company. There's a flat vacant so I'm moving in and I am looking forward to moving on to a new adventure. It must be fate, meeting you and you telling me about this place,' she said, giving Grace a big hug.

Grace adored this little old lady, who seemed to have more energy and positivity than she did. Her father appeared delighted at the prospect of having a new friend close by, and they chatted about what mischief they could get up to when she moved in.

* * *

The sound of a taxi beeping outside Grace's house shook her from her memory, and she took in a deep breath, knowing it was now or never. It was a good job that she'd hardly had to do anything to get ready; it was nice having her hair, make-up and clothes all sorted for her. She'd really just had to grab her hand-bag, touch up her lippy and go. It had been ages since she'd been out properly, and Monica had arranged for them to go to Elizabeth's wine bar in the village.

As the taxi set off, and she'd greeted Monica, who was already sitting in the back, Grace reflected that Little Ollington was the kind of picture-perfect vil-lage that she had always dreamed of living in. There was a duck pond on the green, overlooked by the local church, and a high street with several shops. A few were for tourists, selling knick-knacks that you would never use, but there were a couple of teashops and a few other practical shops, plus the obligatory supermarket. The local forest attracted lots of visitors when the weather was nice, and there were dog walkers and mountain bikers galore on a beautiful sunny day. She didn't know how she'd feel about living in a village when she first moved here, not re-ally knowing a soul, but she'd made contacts through work and school, and some of those had become friends. Now she couldn't imagine *not* living here.

Her parents had lived on the outskirts of Birmingham and they'd never really known much about their neighbours and locality. Despite growing up there, Grace much preferred the countryside to a city, loving the fact that when you went to the local supermarket, you'd bump into lots of people you knew and would have the chance to chat to. And because the estate agency was such an integral part of village life, she'd got to know the other shop owners and locals quite quickly when they arrived. Grace loved that Archie got to grow up in a much nicer, calmer place than she had, where they could appreciate nature and walk around feeling safe and secure.

The taxi dropped them off, and as they walked down the high street, they passed a shop that had been closed down for years.

'One day...' Grace muttered to herself.

'One day what?' Monica asked.

'Christ, can nothing get past you? How did you hear that?'

'Errr, hello! You said it out loud! So come on, spill the beans! What did you mean?' Monica enquired.

'Oh it's just a dream of mine. I can't tell you because that would make it real and I've never admitted it to anyone before.'

A voice came out of nowhere. *Darling girl, if I taught you nothing more in life, it's that through hard work and determination, you can make your dreams come true. You just have to have the courage to follow and pursue them. Don't let dreams just be dreams. Life is short; turn your dreams into reality. But how can anyone help you if you don't help yourself?*

Monica replied, 'You're going to tell me though, right?'

Grace took a deep breath and quickly mumbled, 'I've always dreamt of turning that place into a book-shop, that's all.'

'Well, do it then!' said Monica.

'Don't be ridiculous,' Grace replied. 'Just because I had an idea doesn't mean that I'd ever be capable of turning it into a business. I'd never be able to do that!'

'Why ever not?' Monica questioned. 'You've been brilliant at the estate agency. Clearly you have a head for business. Don't put yourself down. You can do anything if you put your mind to it.'

'Hey, I need to stop you there, hun. Don't you think there's been enough life-changing today?'

Reluctantly, as she knew she'd already put her

friend through her paces, Monica muttered 'Whatever' and dropped the subject as they went into the wine bar. Grace groaned internally, knowing that Monica was just parking this idea for a future conversation.

The bar was modern and pretentious and not the sort of place that Grace would normally choose to go, although she went out so rarely that she didn't know what she did or doesn't like these days. Monica introduced Grace to the barman.

'Grace, meet Mario, Italy's finest barman. He fell in love with a friend of mine called Beth who was on holiday in the Italian Lakes. He missed her so much when she returned home that he got on a flight to the UK, spent weeks tracking her down and when he finally did, declared his undying love. Luckily for him, she owned this bar, and that's why the gorgeous Mario is our wine waiter this evening.'

Mario smiled. 'It is all true. And I met this a-lovely laydee called Monica who is my wife's a-friend. So, beautiful laydeees, what is your delicious pleasure this evening?' Coming from an English man, that would have sounded so cheesy, but it just sounded so perfectly right in a sexy, deep Italian accent. Monica ordered them a bottle of chilled Pinot Grigio, and Mario said that he would bring it over to them, so they took the two tub chairs in the bay window that overlooked the pretty high street. Grace sighed with contentment. She really loved living here.

'OMG! I nearly forgot to tell you. You will *never* believe what happened to me this afternoon,' Grace said, relaying the story of 'Fit Bloke' turning up. Her eyes shone and she lit up with excitement as she described Vinnie.

'OK, madam!' Monica announced. 'You very clearly need a man in your life, so the next thing I am going to do is find you one.'

'No thanks, Mon,' Grace replied determinedly. 'I'm happy enough on my own – well, with Archie and Becks, anyway.'

'Darling, Archie is a child and I hate to be the bearer of bad news, but one day he is going to grow up, become independent and leave you. And as for Becks... Well, I hate to burst your bubble but Becks is a *dog* if you hadn't realised, not a man! And you're hardly going to meet someone when you don't go anywhere. You walk to school, go to work and sometimes venture to your local supermarket. It's not enough though, Grace,' Monica said kindly. 'I know that people invite you places, so please don't tell me they don't. Why don't you go?'

'I just feel that everyone must be thinking there's something wrong with me because I can't find a bloke. I hate going out when people are in couples. I know it's really kind of them to invite me, and they don't understand, but I just feel like a leper being on my own. Do you know, recently I met up with some of the mums from school for coffee and one of them said that her brother had arranged to have a table at a charity event at a local rugby club and she wondered if any couples would like to go. I wanted the ground to open up and swallow me whole. I was mortified. Then when I got home, I realised how bloody rude it was of her to do that! And then I became angry because she obviously felt that it was OK to leave out people who were single and only invite people if they were in a couple. Yet, I ended up being the one who felt awkward. How could I allow someone to make me feel like that?'

'God knows what that was all about. I wish I'd have been there. I'd have bloody said something. I'm sure she didn't mean to hurt your feelings. But darling, that was how *you* chose to feel. Everyone has a choice in how they feel. And you can't change someone else's behaviour. All you can do is change your reaction towards their behaviour. If you felt that she was being rude, perhaps you should have said something at the time rather than come home and let it fester so you ended up feeling doubly bad.'

Grace knew that for all Monica's interference and exaggeration, she was incredibly astute when it came to feelings and that she only had her friend's best interests at heart, always trying to give her confidence from a place of love.

'Anyway, I knew you'd say no, so I've already signed you up with a profile on a dating site.'

Grace nearly spat out her Pinot. 'You've done *what*?'

'Well, you wouldn't have done it yourself so I've done it for you. It's a site where you can write a statement on behalf of your friend. Do you want to know what your profile says?' she asked, getting her iPad out of her handbag.

Grace put her head in her hands, her heart sinking, and sighed loudly. 'Oh, Mon, what have you done?'

'I'm putting you out there, gorgeous. You are much too fabulous to be alone and I've been lovely about you. I'm your friend and I know how amazing you are, so of course it's just fantastic. Just listen to what I put before you say it's not for you. Please, Grace.'

Monica took Grace's stunned silence as approval

and read out the profile that she'd very carefully pondered over for hours before finally hitting the submit button.

'"Vivacious and curvy with a fabulous personality, Grace is my amazing friend who is beautiful inside and out and deserves someone in her life who will love her deeply and treat her like a princess. She's kind, she's generous, she's totally awesome and would do anything to help anyone ahead of helping herself. She's a mum to a ten-year-old, and it's now time that she started to put herself first and have someone wine and dine her and love and respect her for the incredible person that she is."

'See, that's not too bad, is it?' she asked.

'S'pose not!' Grace answered like a truculent teenager. 'But I am so going to get you back for this one day!'

'Oh darling, that's fine by me. I mean every word I say about you. I hate to think of you being alone when Archie is at his dad's. I know how much you hate it and you can't just keep going to bed at eight o'clock at night so that the time goes quicker. And don't even try to deny that!' She held her finger up to stop Grace as she went to open her mouth to speak.

'Anyway, I did this last weekend and I wanted to leave it till today so I could get a fab picture of you all dolled up to put on the site. I used that picture of you that we took today, after your make-over with Bernice and Carlos! Let's have a look at some of the men on there and see if there's anyone you like the look of.'

'Oh God! Must we?'

'Yes, we must, gorgeous!'

'Well, I suppose it wouldn't hurt to take a look, would it?' Grace said tentatively, peering over Monica's shoulder at the list of available men.

'Oooh, he looks nice!' Monica picked out Dave from Essex.

'He looks like he's just come out of prison,' muttered Grace. 'Or is still in there.' The corners of her mouth actually twitched upwards in what was very nearly a smile.

'OK, what about Roger from Nuneaton? Do you fancy rogering Roger?'

They both tittered with laughter and Grace thought that if nothing else came from this experience, at least they'd have had a bloody good laugh.

'They're all old, Monica!' Grace exclaimed.

'I hate to tell you, babe, but you're no spring chicken yourself these days! We could always extend the age range to incorporate toy boys for you?'

'No! Absolutely not! Ooh... what about him? He

looks nice. What does his profile say?' She pointed out the most normal-looking of the men on the page. He looked nice and friendly. The only downside was that his name was Derek.

'It says, "Derek is a self-confessed great bloke. He hates nightclubs and noisy pubs and would much prefer to go out for delicious meals and a good bottle of red. A plumber who is very handy around the house, and very well house-trained, he loves taking on refurbishing projects and going on long walks in the countryside."

'He sounds worth a try, Gracie. You might get your dream bathroom quicker than you thought! And think about the house. You could make a list of jobs you need doing and ask him on your first date if he's capable of doing them. Interview him to see if he's up to the job.'

Grace smiled and thought how nice it would be to actually have someone handy around the house. Mark was absolutely rubbish at DIY and too tight to pay anyone to do it, so consequently they had lived in a state of unfinished jobs which she'd had to pay a fortune out to have finished before she could even consider putting the house on the market.

Within a few clicks, and before Grace could even

think any further about it, Monica had sent a request through to the site to connect with Derek.

'OK, let's see what happens now!'

Grace could not believe that she had been talked into this. Internet dating was something that tons of people had suggested to her and she had strongly protested against. In fact, she'd had a massive row with Hannah about it when Hannah had suggested it'd be a great laugh. 'A great laugh for the people who didn't have to do it,' Grace had yelled at Hannah, slamming down the phone. She'd had to ring back and apologise, realising that she was so scared at getting out of her comfort zone that she'd taken it out on her sister, who Grace knew would never upset her intentionally.

Another friend of hers, Lynne, had suggested that she should go speed-dating and said that she thought it would be great fun. It was OK for her though; she was married, and her husband John even said that he'd go too and choose someone for her! It seemed that their idea of a fun evening out was a little different to Grace's.

Grace temporarily and conveniently forgot their discussion about the dating site and she and Monica slipped back into their favourite pastime of people watching. They loved to pick out people and make up stories about them.

While they were discussing the lives of a couple that they'd nicknamed Doreen and Dave, who had hardly anything to say and sat on their respective phones ignoring each other, there was a commotion at the entrance of the bar and a group of rowdy men came in. When they dispersed to the bar, one of them in particular caught Grace's eye. He had his back to them and was stood on the edge of the group, not really fitting in, seeming quieter than the rest, and, oh boy, he looked like he had a body to die for from the back. He was dressed in smart jeans and a trendy blue shirt and jumper.

For the first time in a long time, Grace thought that he looked like the sort of guy she might like to get to know better, then checked herself and wondered why anyone like that would ever look at her. She was a single mum of a ten-year-old, fat and frumpy, and her idea of an exciting night out was a trip to her local Tesco to buy a new pair of pyjamas. She'd even been invited recently to a food-tasting event by the local manager for being one of their most loyal customers! Even before Monica had thrown away most of her wardrobe, Grace had had more clothes to go to bed in than she did to go out.

'Ooooh! Fitty at ten o'clock! He's lush!' whispered Monica. 'I could see you and Fitty making beautiful babies together.' They giggled just a tad too loudly, feeling the effects of a glass or two of Pinot until 'Fitty' turned round and looked Grace straight in the eye.

It was Vinnie!

He smiled shyly at Grace as soon as he recognised her, seemingly embarrassed by his own loud friends. *God, he really is gorgeous*, she thought. Then he was lost in the crowd as they all started jostling each other and began what appeared to be a drinking competition.

Grace excused herself to go to the ladies' and when she came out, he was just on his way into the gents'. As she passed him, she realised once again that he had the dreamiest blue eyes she'd ever seen.

'Hello again,' he said. 'Sorry about the loud blokes I'm with! Hope they're not spoiling your evening.'

'That's OK,' Grace replied. 'You don't seem to be half as loud as they are, though.'

'I'm not, that's why. But my mate dragged me out.' He looked sheepish but she couldn't help thinking how incredibly handsome he was. She could get lost in those eyes forever. And that *voice*!

'I know that feeling. I'm normally in watching *X Factor* and eating a Chinese in my jimmies on a Saturday or dancing around the lounge to *Strictly*, but I've been dragged out by my friend Monica. She's trying to encourage me to get out into the big bad world more.' Grace smiled, knowing that Monica only had her best interests at heart.

'What about your husband? Is he babysitting tonight? I noticed that you wear a wedding ring and I remember you talking about your son earlier.'

'Oh no, the rings belonged to my mum, I just wear them because they were hers and it makes me feel close to her. No... as for me and my son's dad, we're not together any more.'

Vinnie smiled. 'Oh right. That's good. Oh sorry, I don't mean good. You know...'

'Oy-oy, Vinster!' A tall, friendly looking man came up and patted him on the back. 'Hope you're not chatting this poor defenceless lady up, mate. You know Ellie won't like it!'

Vinnie looked sheepish. 'I suppose I'd better get back to my mates. I can't wait till tomorrow, truth be told, as I normally spend my weekend mornings at the new coffee shop in town. It belongs to my sister Ruth, and I try to make it look busy for her. I always take some work along so I don't look like an idiot on my own, or you can find me in a corner with my nose stuck in a book. I'm a proper bookworm. Probably shouldn't have confessed that,' he said, smiling. 'But you should come along, it's really nice there and the coffee is great.'

Grace loved that Vinnie admitted to reading books. Mark always said she was rude when she read instead of watched TV with him. 'Bye, Vinnie, good to see you. Enjoy the rest of your evening.'

'You too, Grace. And it was really nice to see you again. You look amazing, by the way!'

Grace blushed. She was not used to getting compliments. Vinnie's cheeks also looked a little on the rosy side all of a sudden. Perhaps he wasn't used to giving them out.

As she walked back into the bar, she turned at the same time he did, and they grinned at each other and he gave her a wink. Her heart exploded with lots of tiny fireworks. But then she thought it was just her luck to find someone she finally fancied to discover he was already taken. She wondered if 'Ellie' was the sender of the text message he'd received when he was looking at her garden, the one that had made him frown.

'Monica, you will not believe who that fit bloke at

the bar was.' Grace was flushed as she returned to her seat.

'Ooh, how exciting. Tell me more, you gorgeous creature,' slurred Monica, who had reached the bottom of her large glass of wine and had been up to the bar to fetch another bottle. 'I told you that you looked a million dollars tonight, didn't I?'

'Ha! Only Vinnie, the gorgeous landscaper. He said that his sister has a coffee shop and that I should pop in on a Saturday as he's always there. I probably won't go, though. Anyway, I think he has a girlfriend. His friend mentioned a girl's name and said that she wouldn't like him talking to me.'

'Not going? For God's sake girl, you don't have to marry the guy, he only asked you for coffee! You have to go. Just get yourself out there and start to live again. You can't just live your life for your son. You are so miserable when you're not with him, but this is how your life is now. I just want you to do something for yourself when Archie's with his dad. You can either wallow and have a pity party, or you can get out there and grab life with both hands. Life is too short, and you are too fabulous to be alone!'

'I know life's short, Mon, but I hate not being a mum and being part of a family. It's all I ever wanted in my life, and when I had Archie I felt that my life was complete. When he's not with me at home, it's like the soul has gone from my house. The only thing I've ever been really good at in my life is being mum to Archie and when he's not there I feel completely lost.' Grace tried to explain.

'You're lonely, Grace,' Monica said gently. 'You need to get out more and enjoy some company or you're going to end up a very sad and lonely lady who lives her life for her son. You are such a lovely person and have so much to offer someone. But if you're not careful, you are going to smother Archie and when he grows up and wants to fly the nest, you're never going to want him to leave. You'll have him still living at home when he's forty!'

Grace laughed and snorted wine down her nose and all over her blue jumpsuit.

'Ew sweetie, you're going to have to brush up on your manners if you're going on a date!' Monica laughed.

'I haven't said I'm going yet,' Grace replied.

* * *

Thank heavens for that. No pun intended! I'm so glad I engineered you meeting this nice young man. You need to recognise a good'un when you see one. I wish you could see what I could see, my darling girl. I wish you could see into the future and know that there is someone out there who is perfect for you. Someone who is kind, who is gorgeous, solvent and handy too! But above all, someone who knows how to treat and respect a woman. Now all you have to do is make sure you don't bugger another one up! I love you, Mum xxx

6

The following day, Grace was making her morning coffee and trying to juggle her finances, which were pretty non-existent while she was concentrating on making the house nice for her and Archie, when Monica's face flashed up on the caller display.

'You just can't keep away from me, can you?' Grace laughed.

'Babes, are you doing anything tonight?' Monica asked in a creepy, 'I want something' type of voice.

'No, just a quiet one in front of the TV for me, catching up on *Love Island*,' she replied.

'Actually, hun, you're not. I know Archie has gone to his dad's for two nights this weekend, so you are free, and I just got an email from Derek from that dating website. You're meeting him tonight for a drink at the Duke of Wellington at seven o'clock.'

'But...' stammered Grace.

'Don't you "but" me, young lady! Now, before you even start to argue that you are not going, I can't get in touch with him now, so he's expecting to see you there. It's just a drink, just meet him and see if you like him. If you don't, you'll never have to see him again, and if you do, that's great. If nothing else, it's a night out. Just think of it like you would if you were networking at work.'

'I think I hate you right now, Monica!' Grace said, laughing.

'No you don't, babe, you love me to bits, you know you do. Now be a good girl and go and get your glad rags on. Ring me later or tomorrow and let me know how you get on. Love you. Byeee.'

She'd disappeared before Grace had the chance to protest any more. She resigned herself to the fact that she was going to have to go. What was the worst that could happen?

* * *

Grace walked into the Duke of Wellington and could not see a soul that resembled the picture from the dating website. She went to the bar and asked for a gin and tonic, needing something to calm her nerves. There was a vacant table in the window with two comfy leather armchairs which overlooked the village square, so she smoothed down her long-length blue top over her jeans, hung her linen jacket over the back of one of the chairs, plonked herself down in it and pulled a book out of her handbag. As an avid reader, she always made sure she had a book with her. It made her think of Vinnie, who'd said he was a bookworm. In fact, there was nothing that made her happier than clean bedclothes, some new pyjamas and a great novel.

She checked her watch; it was twenty-five past seven. She was just considering whether to stay or not when a guy who looked like the father of the man in the photo and half the height appeared at the door. She looked him up and down and took in his scruffy attire. He'd clearly come straight from work because he had on a logo'd polo shirt and combat trousers with a tool belt attached. He came bowling over to her and said, 'Please say you are Grace.'

'I am,' she said as she stood to greet him. She towered over him and she only had a pair of mid-height kitten heels on.

'Derek,' he announced and shook her hand. 'Back in a sec!' And he disappeared again.

She wondered whether she could sue the dating site for misrepresentation. That was clearly a *very* old photo. She went back to her book for the moment, vowing that she wouldn't go on first impressions and would give him the benefit of the doubt when he came back. He might be nervous too.

Ten minutes later, he appeared with a pint of Guinness and threw himself into the other armchair.

'Just had to go to the loo! Been dying for a poo all the way back from Liverpool! You know what it's like when you just have to go?' he laughed, too loudly, and a couple who were sitting at the bar turned round at the noise. She smiled an apologetic smile at them, wanting the ground to open up beneath her.

'Oh right!' She raised her eyebrows in surprise at his familiarity. Poo conversations normally waited until you knew someone a little better. It also really annoyed her that he'd got himself a drink and hadn't bothered to ask her if she wanted one. He hadn't even apologised for being late either.

She packed her book back in her handbag wishing he'd just bugger off and leave her to finish her drink and read in peace. She couldn't believe she'd left her comfy sofa at home for this, but she couldn't bring herself to be impolite, even if manners seemed to escape him.

'So, I expect you'd like to know all about me, wouldn't you?' he asked.

'Oh, OK then. Why not?' She was trying to work out different ways to kill Monica when she saw her next. She was in for *such* a bollocking later.

'Well, I'm a plumber, as you know from my profile and this.' He pointed at the logo on his shirt. 'The picture was taken ten years ago but it was my best ever photo so I thought I'd use it. And I've really not changed that much.'

Yeah right, thought Grace as she took in the huge bald spot and tufty grey hair, the bit of hair that he did have left.

'So I'm thirty-five...'

Grace tried not to raise an eyebrow at this – if he was thirty-five she was Kylie Minogue!

'...and I have my own business. I'm very successful. Well, it's my dad's business but he's practically handed it over to me now. I have one of those Mitsubishi trucks that cost loads of money, but I can fit all my work stuff in. I live with my mum and dad. I play rugby every Saturday and when I'm not playing it, I'm watching it. I'm a bit of a lad, if you know what I mean.' He winked as he said that last bit. Grace groaned to herself. 'I earn shit loads of money and am a pretty good catch, even if I say so myself,' he finished. 'What else would you like to know about me?'

She resisted the urge to say 'nothing at all' but again her tendency to be polite took over. 'How long have you been on the dating site, Derek?' she asked.

'Just over three years,' he replied. 'So not long really. I've been on eighty-seven dates so far but have still not yet found the girl of my dreams. There's been something wrong with every single one of them.'

What a surprise, thought Grace.

'Most of them have got kids, too! What's that all about? Little horrors just take up all your money and suck the life out of you. Why would you want kids in this day and age? I can spend my own money, thanks very much, don't need anyone else doing that for me.'

Oh God! She wondered how long she had to stay before she made her excuses and left. She knew it was a mistake coming tonight. She'd had a bad feeling. And she really was going to kill Monica, probably with her bare hands.

At this point, his phone started to ring and he answered it in a loud, booming voice that the whole pub could hear. 'Diggers! How you doing, buddy? Great to hear from you.' He wandered outside to take the call, totally oblivious to Grace, who shrank back even further into her seat.

Her own phone rang. It was Hannah. 'Hey, my beautiful little sister. How's things with you?'

Grace was so happy to hear her sister's friendly voice. 'H, you must be psychic! If I told you, you wouldn't believe me.'

'Try me!'

'I'm on a date that bloody Monica arranged. He's a nightmare! So far, he turned up late and hasn't apologised, disappeared to the loo for a poo and didn't come back for ages, then got himself a drink and has talked about himself for the last twenty minutes. I'm delighted that one of his mates just rang and he's gone outside to talk to him.'

'Get out of there right now,' Hannah said assertively.

'I can't just walk out, that's rude,' Grace replied.

'No, love, what's rude is what he's done to you since you met him. What a knobhead. You need to just leave and go home. Go on, do it. He won't even notice if he's on the phone. Pick up your things, walk out of the door and get in your car. Drive home and call me back. For once in your life, stop being nice to people who are not being nice to you!' She hung up.

Grace's heart began to beat really fast as she actually considered doing what her sister said. In her head she heard a voice say, *Go on, Grace, just walk out the back door to the car. He's not for you! Just go!*

Grace got up from the table. Her hands were shaking, but she picked up her handbag, glancing at Derek who was pacing around outside the pub with one hand down his trousers, totally oblivious to anything but whoever he was chatting to on the phone. He wasn't even looking at her. She walked towards the back door, on the way out to the car park, then doubled back and went to the bar and asked the barman if she could borrow a piece of paper and a pen. He handed them to her with a grin on his face as if he'd been watching the whole debacle.

She went back to the table and scribbled a note, putting it next to Derek's glass. As she walked past the barman, he high-fived her and told her he'd never treat a woman as beautiful as her that way. She blushed but smiled as she left by the back door, practically running to her car. She started the engine as fast as she could and raced out of the car park like Lewis Hamilton on Red Bull. She smiled to herself, imagining his face as he read the note she'd left for him.

> *Derek, here's a tip from me. On your next first date, treat your lady like a princess. Turn up on time, be nice to her, buy her a drink, ask her about herself and don't talk about poo. Maybe, just maybe, if you follow this advice, one of these dates might just work out for you. Good luck with that! Grace*

Grace drove home realising that everything that had happened that night was the reason she had never wanted to do internet dating in the first place. It had been a disaster. She fired off a quick text to Monica telling her that she was in deep trouble due to a disastrous night out. *If this is the calibre of men available,* Grace thought to herself, *I'd be happy to stay in every night!*

7

Grace was so excited about being in their new home, even though the whole renovation process was excruciatingly slow when you were on your own and trying to budget. But the three months since moving day had flown by. She'd spent lots of time on Pinterest, putting together mood boards for each of the rooms in the new house, and loved the idea of stamping her own taste on her dream home. At the back of her mind though, she worried a bit about Archie and how he was adapting to yet another new home. He seemed OK, but he had gone a bit quiet lately, although they'd also had a talk about puberty at school recently. She'd been lucky that because she'd had Archie through C-section, she'd always been able to cheat when telling him where babies come from, because he came out of her stomach. But now he'd realised that winkies and fufus had a whole different type of relationship, and he seemed a little traumatised by some of the things he'd learned.

He was closer to his father right now than he'd ever been before, perhaps because there were lots of things about boys and men that Mark was able to talk to him about. While she felt a little jealous of his developing relationship with his father, she knew it was important for him to have a good male role model in his life, and Mark obviously knew way more about how the male body worked than she did. A book about growing up had been recommended to her, so she'd left it lying around so that Archie could look at it without embarrassment. Archie did pick it up from time to time and she'd found him tittering away at some of it. She wondered how different things would be if they were all still together and whether they'd done the right thing by going their separate ways.

Why, oh why, do these sweet children have to grow up? she wondered. She wished she could wrap up Archie in cotton wool and protect him from everything, but she knew she couldn't. She was finding it very difficult to give him more independence. The last time she had been round to measure up at the house before they moved in, Gladys had said something that really stuck with her. She said that it was the job of a parent to prepare their child for their next level of life and to raise a child who is comfortable and independent enough to leave them. Grace had never quite thought of it like that before. She hated the thought of Archie getting a partner and eventually leaving home but knew that it was not his responsibility to make his mum happy. He'd been through such a lot of changes since the split and moving to yet another house. She knew though that their new home would be a place where he would feel safe and secure. As they faced the next stage of their lives, Archie would grow up to be more independent and eventually would leave home and go off on his own adventure. She shook off that thought before she got even more morose.

* * *

'Have you forgiven me yet, gorgeous?' asked Monica when she rang Grace the next morning.

'Nope! And I'm not sure I ever will!' Grace sulked back at her.

'Oh, babes, you have to try these things, you

know. I'm sorry it was such a disaster but at least you've done it now and popped your internet-dating cherry, so to speak. Anyway, what are you doing today?'

'I've just got back from taking Becks for a lovely long walk over the forest, and I'm just going to make myself a great big cup of coffee and have a read and make the most of my Monday off before Archie comes home from school.'

'Wrong! I want to know every detail about Derek, so you're going to jump in your car and meet me at the little teashop in the high street. I'll be there in ten minutes. So go comb your hair, put some lippy on and get down here and meet me. I'll be waiting.' The phone went dead so there was no way that she could argue.

Grace smiled to herself. She knew that Monica was only trying to help her, but she was just feeling a tad sorry for herself. As the weather was particularly warm for the time of year, she quickly put on a strapless elasticated-top sundress, grabbed her denim jacket from the banister, picked up her car keys and slammed the door behind her before she changed her mind.

On her approach to the teashop, Grace, as always, said a little parking prayer up to her mum in heaven, asking for a nice space right outside the door. *Perhaps if I didn't do this, and parked a little further away from everywhere I went and walked that little bit further, I wouldn't be such a lardy arse.* Lo and behold her wish was granted, but as she looked through the café window, Monica was nowhere to be seen. Pushing open the café door and looking around, Grace confirmed it – Monica wasn't there. It was bizarre. It was very unusual for her to be late.

'Errr, excuse me, you must be Grace.' She turned towards the timid voice to be met by a man who looked around the age of fifty-five to sixty, wearing a dark green jumper over a shirt and stripy tie that looked like it belonged to his granddad, a pair of what could only be described as 'slacks' and brown shoes with Velcro fasteners.

Confused, Grace nodded. 'I am, and you are...?'

'Malcolm, dear. Monica has told me all about you. I love the idea of a website where a friend arranges the dates for you. It's very clever. I was so delighted when you said you'd meet me here for a cup of tea.'

'Erm, I'm sorry! You said that Monica said I'd meet you here?' she asked inquisitively.

'Yes, dear. I've been waiting for half an hour. I wanted to get here early because I was so excited.

When I saw your picture on the website, you were the prettiest girl I'd seen for ages and I clicked on your profile. I plucked up the courage to get in touch and when your friend replied and set up this date, I was over the moon.'

Grace smiled politely, but inside she was thinking that she was going to kill Monica the minute she laid eyes on her. Her phone signalled that familiar harp sound to say she had a text message and when she excused herself to Malcolm and looked at it, it was short and sweet, from the traitor herself.

> Have fun babes and ring me later.
> Mon x

The only wringing that would be done later would be that of Monica's neck when Grace got her hands on her.

'Come and sit down, dear, I've already got us a pot of tea.'

Oh God! Grace thought to herself. *Am I really doing this? I'll just stop for a quick cup of tea to be polite.* There she was again, being polite and pleasing everyone else. It really was the story of her sad little life.

'So tell me about yourself, Grace. I want to find

out everything about you.' Malcolm smiled at her as he put the tea strainer on the cups and started to pour out the tea. She looked closely at him. He wasn't an unpleasant-looking man, she supposed, but he was quite old and, well, a bit square. His hair was receding and the bit he did have was in a comb-over. He just looked a bit careworn but unfortunately not in a shabby-chic way. Even when Bridget Jones met Mark Darcy, you could see that underneath that awful Christmas jumper there was a glimmer of gor-geousness just bursting to get out. But Malcolm was no Colin Firth, more's the pity. Shaking off her thoughts, Grace decided to give Malcolm a chance. She knew that first appearances could be deceiving.

'No, you go first, Malcolm.'

'Well, I've been a vicar now for just over fifteen years. I'm at St Cuthbert's church in Camberdown Village at the moment, been there for twelve months, and apart from my parishioners I don't really know anyone around. I've held a fair few cheese-and-wine evenings in the vicarage but they're a funny lot in our village. It's only really the old dears that come along, and they just come for the wine, I think, and a bit of friendly company. No one my age ever comes along.'

Grace thought what a bundle of fun it must be at the vicarage cheese-and-wine parties and reminded herself never to go along if she was offered an invitation. She checked herself and realised that Malcolm probably had more fun than she did – at least he wasn't stopping in most nights in his jimmies with a dog for company.

'Mother says that I'm trying too hard to make friends and that I'm too nice to people. But I'm a vicar, that's what we do!'

'Where does your mother live, Malcolm? Is she local?'

'Oh, she lives with me, of course. I lived with her until I was given my first parish and vicarage, and then I could repay the favour so I invited her to come and live with me. We rub along nicely. She's a good old thing. She cooks and cleans for me still, won't hear of me doing anything like that, bless her.'

She didn't quite know what to say next. 'Do you have any pets, Malcolm?' she asked, casting her mind to some topic of conversation where they might find some common ground.

'Oh yes, we have three cats. I'm a huge cat fan. And I collect pottery that is cat themed. Every time Mother has a few days away somewhere she always manages to bring me something back to add to my collection. Do you like cats, Grace?'

Even though she really wanted to reply, *No, I can't*

stand the bloody things. They creep into my garden, crap and creep out again, she didn't feel that it was appropriate to say 'crap' to a vicar.

'More of a dog person, myself,' she replied, now quite nervous that she might swear in front of him – even more so because she was trying so hard not to. 'I have a chocolate labradoodle called Becks, named after David Beckham. He's adorable.'

'Oh, David Beckham, isn't he that footballer fellow who used to be the captain for England? I think I know of him, although I don't have a television so I don't watch much sport. I'm more of a Radio 4 man myself. Going back to dogs, I got bitten by a dog when I was seven and I've been scared to death of them since,' he replied.

'Do you mind me asking how old you are now?' Grace was shocked at her direct question but thought she'd grab the opportunity to find out, assuming he was at least fifty-five. She picked up her tea and took a sip.

'Forty-two,' he replied.

Grace swallowed and coughed at the same time and a massive hiccuppy, burpy-type noise came out as she sprayed her tea over the table between them. Malcolm jumped out of his chair and patted her on the back.

'Oh, I'm so sorry, that went down the wrong way,' she explained, wanting to shout out, *Forty-two! No fucking way!*

When she looked at him, she realised that he was deadly serious. It was no wonder there were no younger people going along to his evenings at the vicarage. They all thought he was about twenty years older than he actually was!

She kept up the coughing, making it appear much worse than it was so as to cover up the shock she felt that he was only a few years older than her. As she got up, the leg of the chair caught on the bottom of her dress and before she knew it, the elasticated top came down and she flashed both her ample boobs at Malcolm.

'Oh my God! Oh shit... I'm sorry for saying God! And now I've said shit too!' Could she dig a bigger hole for herself? 'Good grief, I'm so sorry Malcolm, but I'm going to have to cut this, erm, date short. I suddenly feel quite unwell and am going to go home immediately. I really am so sorry.' She took a deep breath, adjusted her dress, popping herself away, grabbed her denim jacket from the back of her chair and shook his hand before he could realise what was happening. The teashop door was opened by a new customer coming in, so she ducked under their arm and bolted as fast as she could. She made the mistake of turning round and Malcolm was just staring at her quite bewildered and just a little bit red in the face, although not as red as her, whilst other people in the café were hiding their laughter behind their hands. She felt mortified at what had happened, and bad for leaving so abruptly – but not as bad as Monica was going to feel when she got hold of her.

Grace jumped in the car and got her phone out of her handbag and dialled Monica's number. She answered after two rings and Grace didn't wait for her to speak before she started a tirade of abuse down the phone.

Monica let her ramble on, then when Grace had run out of swear words, got everything out and quietened down, she said, 'Go home, put the kettle on and I'll be round in ten minutes.'

When Grace pulled up on the drive, she saw Becks through the window. He had ultrasonic hearing and could always tell when her car pulled up, and he had clearly jumped up onto the windowsill. As she opened the front door, he jumped up, gave her a big sloppy lick and knocked her to the ground.

'Aw, Becks, why can't I meet someone who's just like you but human?' She laughed as he rolled over for his tummy to be tickled. She heard a car door slam, and she turned. Monica was walking up the drive waving a white hanky above her head. She couldn't help but laugh and let in her bonkers friend.

'If I'd told you, would you have gone?' Monica asked.

'Of course not.'

'I rest my case!'

'Point taken, but next time you set me up, please make sure it's not with someone who looks like Hugo off *The Vicar of Dibley* or his dad... I flashed the bloody vicar, Mon!'

'What the...?'

Grace's mouth began to twitch at the same time that Monica's started to turn up at the corners. They laughed, then they laughed some more. Between giggles, Grace related the story, which caused them both to dissolve into a laughing fit. Monica's mascara was now running in big black streaks down her cheeks, and Becks didn't know what was happening and started to jump around the place, barking, which made the women laugh even more. Grace realised that it had actually been ages since she'd laughed so much that she cried, and she made a mental note to make sure she did it far more often. It felt really good!

'God, I hate you, Monica,' Grace said as she gave her best friend a hug. 'Promise me, you will never set me up on anything like that again! If you do, I swear I'll dump you as my best friend as fast as lightning.'

'I promise.' Monica hugged her tightly, crossing her fingers behind her back. 'Now, go make me a coffee.'

* * *

Oh darling. That was hilarious. A vicar! If there is one thing I cannot imagine you as, it's the wife of a vicar! Monica is certainly entertaining me so far with her choice of dates. She's a terrible judge of character, although how I love that she's changing you from a dull, drab caterpillar into a beautiful emerging butterfly, so I have to forgive her. I wish I could reach out and touch you. I wish I could make you realise how wonderful you are and what a fabulous mother you are to Archie and how beautiful you are on the inside and the outside. I just wish you could see what I see. Now, go out there and grab that life and have some fun. I love you. Mum xxx

8

The two disastrous dates so far had led Grace to make another important decision about her life. When she was with Mark, he always used to grab her 'love handles' and call her 'chubster', supposedly as an 'affectionate' term. She knew she had been putting on weight, but she was so unhappy in her relationship and Mark was such a time thief that she had been overeating to fill the loneliness and never had the opportunity to do any kind of exercise. He took all the time that was in their relationship to do stuff for himself. And then he had the cheek to complain that he never had any 'me time'. *God knows what going to the rugby, going to the gym and going to the pub was then*, Grace thought, frowning at the memory. It was Grace who'd never had any 'me time' as she tried to work, bring up Archie, keep on top of the housework and make sure that the meals were cooked. Stupidly, she had thought that when they had a child, parenting would be a joint responsibility. How naïve she'd been.

But that was in the past and she had shown herself recently that she could step outside of her comfort zone and have some time to herself, so she decided it was time to lose some weight. She really wanted to try to lose a few pounds before the stupid awards event that was constantly looming over her, and as the date drew closer, her anxiety about the awards was rising.

So far, Grace had tried every excuse she could think of with Melanie and Edward to get out of attending the awards, but they'd covered every single one. First she said that she couldn't get a babysitter, so they offered their teenage daughter for the night. Then she said that her dad needed taking somewhere that night, so they offered to pay for a taxi. It didn't look like she was going to be able to get out of it, whatever she tried. At the back of her mind she had rather hoped that one of the dates she'd been on might have turned out to be someone that would be worthy of inviting along, but sadly not. So now she was going to feel out of her comfort zone as well as dateless, while all her work colleagues enjoyed the free bar with their partners.

However, one night a week she was now alone while Archie was at Mark's, so she decided to pluck up the courage and go along to the local slimming club. It took a lot of guts for her to go, especially on her own. Totally mortified, she bumped into one of the teachers from Archie's school. They nodded at each other, clearly making a silent pact that they would never speak of the incident again.

There was nothing shameful in wanting to drop a few pounds, but unfortunately it seemed that Barbara, the club leader, had a way of making them all feel like they were the lowest of the low but that with her help, they could become someone worthy. After being weighed for the first time and finally admitting her weight and agreeing a target for the next few weeks, Grace sat with everyone in a semicircle while Barbara shouted out the names of the people in the group and either congratulated, reprimanded or humiliated them, depending on whether they'd lost weight, stayed the same or had a gain.

The thing that annoyed Grace most was that people seemed to have no respect for anyone else and just had their own conversations while Barbara was chatting. Although, listening to the woman, a little bit of Grace could actually understand why. They were probably trying to drown out the sound of her irritating, patronising voice.

Grace drifted off, wondering if anyone had ever set up a slimming club for busy people. There must be hundreds of people out there who would go to something like that. A club that offered real advice on diet and exercise with helpful encouragement, rather than trying to sell their own 'low-fat' ready meals which were in actuality full of E numbers. Maybe advice on healthy eating would be more beneficial and just a check-in on weight each week too?

Grace had a tendency to stress about the smallest of things and make them huge. She was definitely getting better but still had a way to go. Everyone told her she needed to chill more, but she found it so difficult to do that. She'd tried to meditate once because she'd thought it would be good for her but she just couldn't switch off, lying on her bed, thinking about putting the washing on, how the windows needed cleaning and making a mental to-do list. She didn't think she knew how to relax any more, apart from reading. She tried from time to time to listen to podcasts and webinars but got so fed up with the introductions that she gave up on them. She didn't want to know what the narrator had been doing or the background behind everything. She was always shouting at them to get to the important bit.

Monica had got so exasperated with her always running around that she'd used one of her trained skills, personality profiling, to assess Grace's character traits, and her results had been most illuminating. And no wonder, in a way, that she and Mark didn't gel properly. When they discussed his attributes, and answered the questions from Mark's perspective, it was clear they were poles apart in their personality types and were both too stubborn to acknowledge that the other one was different; they just didn't agree on anything and both thought they were the ones in the right.

Grace's profile showed that she was the sort of person who liked the sociable side of life, loved chatting with people, loved coming up with ideas but wasn't particularly hot on detail. It showed that she detested lateness and saw it as a total lack of respect. It also revealed that she was blunt and liked other people to get straight to the point and not, as she called it, 'fanny about'.

When she chatted to Monica about Mark and how incompatible they were, it showed that he was dominant, keen on analysis, critical and big on detail. Total opposites. Monica said that sometimes these opposing personality types complement each other, but sometimes they clash.

It was a standing joke in their relationship that when Mark was looking for a new car, he'd spend hours researching it, telling her all about the horse-power (whatever that was) and the engine size. All Grace used to ask was what colour it was. If she liked the colour, that was her decision made. Since talking to Monica, and doing her character profiling, she'd worked hard on trying to be more sympathetic to other people's personality types and understood now that was just Mark's way. That was how his brain dealt with stuff. It was just that their differences in personality types worked against each other instead of together.

Grace put most of her impatience and inability to relax down to having a busy life as a mother. There was *so* much to do. When Archie was little and fell asleep, she never knew whether to wash up, put a load of washing in, clean the house, make a coffee, have a bath, wash her hair, catch up on the TV pro-grammes she'd recorded or read. She just always seemed to have so much to do and would put herself under pressure to get it all done without any help.

She didn't understand how some people just seemed to be able to just 'be'.

Consumed by her own thoughts, Grace was brought out of her trance abruptly as Barbara yelled her name.

'Grace! And we'd like to give a huge warm welcome this evening to a new member – Grace! Let's all give her a round of applause for finally realising that she's a fattie and joining our group to lose weight.' Grace went as red as a beetroot and wanted to crawl up her own armpit.

Everyone who had lost weight was rewarded with a sticker, like Archie used to get at nursery, a round of applause and Barbara's favourite phrase: 'Well done, dearie, you are cooking on gas!' If Grace had heard it once in that first session, she'd heard it a hundred times. In fact, at one point she was so bored that she started a mental tally sheet for each time it was said. So far she'd counted twenty-seven times. Grace was sure that if she ever heard that phrase again, she'd shove Barbara's face in a cooker and show her what cooking on gas really meant.

She quickly realised that this group wasn't for her. The last thing she wanted to do with her precious free time was to pay to come out and be publicly humiliated.

She really did want to do something about her weight but she hadn't the time to waste; when she'd arrived she'd waited in a queue for over half an hour to be weighed while the two ladies who were on the weigh-in desk finished their little chat, because clearly they couldn't weigh people at the same time as talking. Grace was tapping her feet in frustration and getting more annoyed by the minute. And then the next hour was spent listening to everyone else's stories, which without wishing to be rude, she wasn't really interested in. This group just wasn't the right way for her to lose weight.

A light bulb went on in her head. If the group that she wanted to go to didn't exist, why didn't she just create it? Then it went off again as she heard Mark's voice saying, *Don't be ridiculous. Why would people want to come along to something you've created?*

As she drove home, she pondered the idea and it wouldn't go out of her head. A busy person's slimming club! When she arrived home, she got a fresh new notepad out of her stationery stash and started to make a list of all the things she would and wouldn't do, and it sounded better by the minute. If she hated that group she'd attended, there must be loads of others who did too. She knew people who didn't go to slimming groups because they didn't want all that unnecessary malarkey that went with it.

If it was her club, she'd stick to the basics and get to the point of being there quickly.

She'd made up her mind. She wasn't with Mark any more and he couldn't tell her what she could and couldn't do and what she was and wasn't capable of. She was capable of anything she wanted to do. Her mum had instilled in her as a child that she should dream, make a plan and make those dreams come true. She didn't know where down the line she'd stopped believing in herself. But she felt now that it was time for her to dream again.

She'd put the word out there about her idea and test the waters, and if she got a positive response, she'd get the club started. She would need a venue, though. She racked her brains trying to think of somewhere.

Since Grace had split up from Mark and had her coaching from Monica, she'd become a real 'doer'. She decided on a course of action and did it. When she was with Mark, she was a grey, dithering person, never making a choice because either she didn't want to risk upsetting him or because he'd laugh at it, belittling her. Now she didn't have him questioning her every move, she'd changed into a black-and-white decision-maker. You either did something or you didn't. Why spend hours pondering? She just didn't get it! She couldn't understand people who weren't doers and, in truth, they really got on her nerves. But she knew that she needed to make more effort in getting to understand that people were different from her, and it was something that she was trying to do.

Someone once told her a great way to make a decision – to count down from five and then, if it felt right, go with your first instinct. It was now the way that Grace made all her decisions, from deciding what to cook for dinner to the new shade of paint to use in the hallway.

She thought back to her old college friend Saffy, and asked herself what Saffy would say about the idea of setting up a slimming club for time-poor people. Making decisions often brought Saffy to mind as they always used to talk things through, from boyfriends to which new top to buy for their Saturday night out. She knew that Saffy would tell her to go for it. So she would. Decision made. And damn, it felt good to finally be in control of her own decisions and not have someone tell her that she was ridiculous, or not capable.

Grace felt that she'd come a long way even in the last couple of months and that her life was truly changing for the better. She was challenging herself way out of her comfort zone; she couldn't believe that she'd even considered internet dating, let alone gone along and actually met people. And she felt that her life was getting way more interesting than it had been for a long time. She'd noticed that she was excited to get up in the mornings, actively looking forward to the days and weeks ahead, instead of just whiling away the time while Archie was at his dad's.

* * *

Finally, darling, I am seeing a change in you. You are back to the Grace that you used to be years ago before Mark dulled your sparkle and suppressed your personality. You now have an idea – run with it. Before, you'd have mentioned it to him and then he'd have told you why it was such a rubbish idea and you'd have gone back into your little cocoon. Now you are finally getting back to the person you used to be: the person that never saw an obstacle as an obstruction, just something you have to work out how to get over, round or through. I love that you are finally getting that sparkle back! My little caterpillar is becoming a bright, brave, beautiful butterfly. I couldn't be prouder of you, my darling. I love you, Mum xxx

9

'Just one more, Grace, and then I promise I'll never, ever, ever arrange a date for you again. But this one I'm sure is the one for you. He's gorgeous, he's single, he's got no children and he's asked to take you out. I have a photo of him – look! He looks really nice and normal and quite hot, too. You have to go. Just think if you said no and he's "the one"! You could be missing out on the opportunity of a lifetime.'

'Oh Monica, do I have to? It's so bloody demoralising going out on dates with crappy men. I'd rather stay in and read a good book.'

'Yes, darling, I know you would, but I just want to see you with someone who is going to turn your world upside down and inside out. Someone who loves you as much as I do. God, if I was that way inclined you'd be my ideal partner. But as you know, I like cock, so there's no chance of that!'

'Monica!' Grace admonished, but she couldn't help but smile at her friend's way with words.

'Just one more, Gracie? Go on. For me, pretty please.'

'*One* more! Just one. Then that's it. But here's the deal: after this date, you promise to delete my profile from the site if that's what I ask you to do. Deal or no deal?'

Monica winked at her. 'Deal, Noel Edmonds! And keep your tits inside your dress this time, you floozy!'

Grace arrived at New Street Station in Birmingham, a bit of a jaunt for a date with it taking around forty-five minutes on the train, but Monica insisted that she needed to be looking further afield. She saw a man standing there in a black leather jacket and jeans. She had a feeling that this was him. He turned round and it was.

Mmm, not bad, she thought. For once, someone who looked like their photograph. That made a nice change.

'Grace?' he asked tentatively as he wandered over.

'That's me,' she replied nervously.

'And even prettier in real life than in your picture. I'm Tommy, it's lovely to meet you.' He reached across and kissed her on both cheeks. 'There's a lovely Caribbean restaurant just down the road, I thought we could go there. Is that OK with you?'

'That sounds lovely.' *Quite decisive then,* she thought. *That makes a change from spending wasted time saying 'I don't mind' and never actually going anywhere.*

They walked along chatting easily about their respective days. Tommy worked for a mobile phone company in Stoke on Trent so he was quite a long way from home, but had arranged to meet her here as he'd been working in Birmingham that day. He asked her lots about her job and what she liked to do in her spare time.

When they reached the restaurant, The Rum Shack, they were shown to their table and Grace took in her surroundings. The walls were painted bright yellow, green and red and there was a real Caribbean beach bar feel to it, helped along by the reggae tracks which were playing in the background.

They were shown the menus and Tommy asked her if she'd like a cocktail. She chose a Reggae Rum Punch for old times' sake. Barbados sprung to mind, and a little trip down memory lane to a holiday with Saffy, whose very kind, wealthy father had paid for them both to go on holiday when their college course had ended. After a day on the beach, they arrived back at their hotel each evening, perched in the rocking chairs on the wooden porch, watching the sun go down over the beach, putting the world to rights, planning their futures and dreaming. One night they were so tiddled that they didn't actually get out for dinner as they'd planned, just about managing to stagger back to their room and fall asleep in a drunken stupor. It was an incredibly relaxing and recuperating holiday, which was exactly what they had both needed at the time after all that hard work they put into passing their exams.

Grace had surprised herself that holiday. She had snorkelled and swum with turtles and scuba dived for the first time, experiencing the most incredible underwater world including lion fish and puffer fish and real life Dorys and Nemos. She had even jumped off the deck of a booze boat into the Caribbean Sea. These were things that she'd never imagined herself doing before she went.

She remembered this Grace before Mark, the Grace who would try new things, the Grace who was brave and adventurous and didn't have a care in the world. A Grace who seemed like a very different person to the one she was today, but a Grace that she was working on getting back again.

As Grace reminisced, she realised how sad she was that when Saffy's relationship took her to Australia around the same time that Grace met Mark, they'd eventually lost touch. The wonderful memories that came flooding back to her just from being in this restaurant made her resolve to look up her long-lost friend on Facebook and make contact again after all these years.

She heard a cough and looked up to see Tommy staring at her. 'I'm so sorry, I was just back in Barbados for a second or two there. It must be the reggae,' she explained.

He smiled at her. 'It was obviously a good memory as you had a really contented smile on your face.'

Grace explained what a fabulous holiday they'd had as they looked through the menu choices.

Grace chose chicken breast in a creamy jerk sauce, plantain, rice and peas. Her mouth was watering just at the thought of it. Tommy chose shrimp and mango curry with rice and peas and a flatbread, and they shared a side order of sweet potato fries. The breadth of choices on the menu got them talking about food and cooking. Tommy explained that he loved cooking but didn't get the chance to do it very often and couldn't really be bothered to cook for himself so just heated up ready meals more than anything else. The conversation flowed easily and for the first time since Monica had started setting her up on these dates, Grace felt herself relax and enjoy the evening.

Grace watched Tommy closely as he talked. He was really very good-looking in a tall, dark and handsome clichéd way and was what her mum would once have called a 'bit of a charmer'. He seemed like a genuinely nice guy and she thought that perhaps she'd just been unlucky with the first eejit Derek and then the vicar. Perhaps Monica could be right. Tommy could be the one that changed her opinion of internet dating.

'So, it says on your profile that you've never been married and don't have children. Does it bother you that I have a child?' she asked. She may as well get this bit over and done with early, she thought.

'No, not at all. I've always quite liked children but I've just never found the right woman to settle down with and have a family. It's not that I've never wanted to, it's just that the opportunity has never arisen and so I suppose I just threw myself into work and the years just passed me by. Sad, really.'

The more time she spent talking to Tommy, the more she liked him. He just seemed to be normal, a good conversationalist and actually interested in her and what she had to say, which, after Derek the Dickhead and Malcolm the Vicar, was exactly what she was looking for.

Grace looked at her watch and realised that she only had about twenty minutes before the last train home. The night had gone so quickly and really had been rather lovely.

'So, this isn't something I've ever done before, but I really feel a connection with you, Grace. I'm stopping in a hotel just round the corner so you don't have to go home, you know. You could always come back with me and we could start with a nightcap.'

Grace's heart stopped. There was a teeny tiny bit

of her that thought, no one need ever know... She'd never had a one-night stand before and perhaps she should just throw caution to the wind and get on with it. But the sensible side of her knew that she wasn't ready to get her clothes off in front of someone new and be intimate with them yet. She knew that, because the thought of it scared her witless. She nervously smiled and said, 'It's a lovely thought, Tommy, but I have to get back. Maybe another time, if that's OK?'

They swapped numbers while they waited for the bill, which Tommy insisted on paying. They both said how much they had enjoyed the night and that they would like to do it again, soon. When they arrived at the train station, Tommy tenderly took her face in his hands and kissed her gently on the lips before waving her off.

As she sat down on the train, she realised that Archie had a match in Stoke the following day, although Mark was taking him – what a coincidence. She sent a quick text to Monica:

Finally a normal one! Tommy is really nice, I like him a lot. We're going to see each other again. You were right – but I still haven't forgiven you for the other two dates! X

Then she got her latest book out of her bag and settled down for the journey home, buoyed by the memory of the tender kiss Tommy had planted on her lips. She tried not to get her hopes up, but she knew deep down that she couldn't wait to see him again.

* * *

The first call that came into the estate agency the following morning was from Mark, telling her that she would have to take Archie to football that night as something had come up. She wasn't doing anything else that night, not that it would have mattered to Mark, but she stomped around work for the first half an hour, annoyed with him for dumping on her yet again. But it did mean that she'd get to spend more time with Archie, so after another latte from the machine in the kitchen, she calmed down and stopped winding herself up. She'd got better at this over the years, when she realised that the only person who was suffering was herself. Mark didn't give a damn. He'd already moved on once he'd ended the call. She'd learned to choose her arguments.

Football after school was always a rush, getting back from work and making sure Archie had enough food in him to give him energy but not enough to make him feel sick, and in plenty of time for them to get to the venue too. She loved it when the matches were at home as it was only a fifteen-minute drive, but there were other times like today when the match was nearly an hour away. Sometimes it was a relief to arrive early and have a bit of time to catch up with herself while Archie was training. Being a single mum was something she was getting used to, but from time to time it could be demanding. It was always her who had to do everything. It might be nice just once in a while for someone else to put the bins out, make sure there was food in the fridge, take the dog for a walk, make sure the washing was done, or even flick the duster round. Sometimes it would be nice for someone to just make her a cup of tea.

She'd never thought that she'd be in this position when Archie was born; she just wanted to be loved and needed and always thought they'd be a family.

At least Becks needed her when Archie wasn't around.

There were thirty minutes till kick-off, so she waited at the nearby sandwich van, making small talk with the woman in front of her in the queue, while Archie went to warm up with his team mates and discuss their game strategy. The way they discussed tactics was serious stuff, even if they were only playing on an under-elevens team! Grace smiled to herself as she wondered whether Cristiano Ronaldo's mum used to stand on the touchlines and watch him play.

She joined the other football mums and they caught up since the last time they'd met. They'd both found it tough when Archie first joined the team. All the boys knew each other both at football and outside of it as they attended the same school, whereas Archie was at a different one, so he'd felt a real outsider but had tried really hard to make friends. Grace didn't know any of the parents either, and she'd found it really hard to mix, especially on match days when most parents came in couples, along with their other children. She'd made a real effort to speak to the other parents over recent weeks though and broke the ice when she was able to give some advice to one of the mums who was looking to put her house on the market. It was harder making friends when you were older, but she had definitely started to think of these people as a new friendship group and now she looked forward to catching up with them while Archie was on the pitch. They were a really nice bunch.

The lady who was in front of her in the queue came and stood near Grace, and they laughed at the fact that they were both either side of the halfway line, on opposing teams, but were close enough to carry on their friendly conversation. The woman kept checking her watch because her husband was supposed to be there and hadn't arrived yet. She said that she was waiting for him to take over at the match so she could go home and cook their celebratory nineteenth wedding anniversary meal. As they chatted and watched, Archie yelled for the ball and it was passed to him.

Grace yelled, 'Come on Archie, shoot!'

He ran with it, weaving past a defender and looked the goalie straight in the eye as he flicked the ball up and over his head into the goal mouth. Shouts of *Goal!* and *Yes!* could be heard around the ground, and there were lots of calls of *Go Archie!* from the parents and coaches. She was so proud. He turned to Grace with a huge grin spread across his

face and she laughed as the whole team did a celebratory floss dance.

She turned to the nice lady she'd been chatting
to, who now appeared to be having a full-on snog
with her husband who'd just turned up. *Lucky cow*,
Grace thought. The couple pulled apart and there,
standing in front of her, was Tommy. Despite everything he had said just last night, he seemed to be
very happily married with children. And clearly a
big fat fecking liar.

'Are you OK, love?' the lady asked. 'You've gone as
white as a sheet!'

Grace looked at Tommy whose jaw had dropped
open and who clearly didn't know where to put himself. She composed herself and drew herself up to
her full five feet five inches of height.

'I'm fine, thanks. Your husband just really reminded
me then of someone I once knew. Someone I thought
was a really nice bloke and wanted to get to know more
but turned out to be a complete fake. Your husband
must be his doppelgänger. How strange. Anyway, enjoy
your anniversary dinner, it was nice to meet you.' Grace
composed herself and smiled at his wife, feeling incredibly sorry for her. As she walked past Tommy she muttered under her breath for his ears only, 'Arsehole!'

She held her head high and walked towards the other end of the supporter's group, leaving the pretty lady staring after her and Tommy looking like he'd developed a facial twitch.

At half time, Grace went to the car and rang Monica. She was still shaking with shock. 'Right, that's it,' she yelled down the phone. 'Take me off that bloody site and do it now!'

'OK, OK, keep your knickers on! What on earth has happened?'

Grace told her what had transpired and Monica was just as flabbergasted as she was.

'What a tosser, and what a shame for his wife,' she sympathised. 'She sounds so lovely too. I'm going to report him to the dating site tomorrow and make them remove him. I do wonder how many other lies he's told to other women. I'm so sorry, babe. I promise I'll do that first thing and will remove your profile right now.'

'And don't ever think about setting me up with anyone again. Do you hear me, Monica?'

'I promise you I won't.' And this time she wasn't crossing her fingers. 'But at least you've pushed your comfort zones a bit and can say you've tried internet dating now. You can't say we're not triers.'

'You, Monica, are extremely trying, and it's a very good job that I love you as much as I do! Bye!'

She wished her mum was still around. Even after so many years, she still wanted to pick up the phone just to hear her soothing voice when something was getting her down, or pop in for one of her special hugs. Sometimes – and thankfully, more often these days – she remembered her mum with fond memories and a smile. Other times, the grief rose up from nowhere and just sucker-punched her right in the gut.

She swallowed down a lump in her throat, wiped a tear from her eye and threw her phone onto the passenger seat as she went back to watch the second half of the match from a viewpoint as far away from Tommy as possible.

* * *

I'm so sorry that you've had a tough few weeks and some disastrous dates. I'm really not sure that Monica is the right person to be choosing them for you. I wish I'd realised the truth about Mark while I was there on earth but he was always so charming around your father and me. It was only towards the end of my life that I started to see cracks in your relationship and how forced your smiles were. They didn't reach your eyes and didn't come from your heart. But at that point, I didn't have the energy to do anything about it. I'm sorry, sweetheart, but I was so tired of fighting that blasted cancer attacking my body. I know you thought that I should fight to stay around for you forever, but I'd fought it on and off for ten years and I was so exhausted. I know that for a while after I'd gone you were angry because you thought I didn't love you enough to fight for you. But I did and I do. I couldn't have loved you more if I tried.

I just wish I'd told you that I knew how things were with Mark. That you didn't have to pretend around me. I know you felt that you were letting me down, but you weren't. You could never let me down. All I wanted for my girls was for you both to be happy.

Please don't think that mine and your father's relationship was always a bed of roses. In our day you wouldn't have been able to do anything about it, that's all, so you had to stick it out. And I'm bloody sure that if your father had died before me, I'd be out having a whale of a time, kicking up my heels and really living. I know he's your father and you obviously love him, but sometimes I could kick him up the bum for sitting and moping around. I'm not ready for him up here yet and he's got plenty of living yet in him. Let's hope he starts to live again in his new home.

And you too, my darling: you need to live and be happy. I wanted to make sure you knew what I wanted for you before I left you, but I ran out of time. You think you have time, you see, even when you are dying, but you don't.

I want you to learn from life that you have to do the things you want to do, live every day to the full, don't save anything for best, because you just don't know how much time you have left on earth. So eat the damn cake, wear the best clothes and drink from your crystal glasses.

I love you, Mum xxx

10

The week after what she'd now named 'the disastrous dates' and after many conversations with Hannah and Monica – whom she had only just forgiven for setting her up with Derek, Malcolm and Tommy – Grace decided that she needed to put it all behind her and throw her energies into setting up her potential slimming club. She was charged with excitement as she got ready to check out the new café in town to see whether it could be a possible venue.

Grace touched the aqua aura crystal she wore on a chain around her neck for luck, took a great big breath and pushed open the door of Coffee Heaven and looked around. She'd never been in a coffee shop without planning to meet someone else, so she was extremely nervous and her palms were slightly sweaty. She'd dressed up for the occasion, to give herself more confidence, another little Monica trick, but now wondered whether the turquoise silky top, skinny jeans and brown knee-high boots were actually 'her'. Perhaps she'd have felt better if she was wearing something she'd had for ages – that nice black top she always wore and her comfy old jeans, for instance. But then she knew that Monica would have killed her.

Monica was now like a little devil on her shoulder every time she got dressed. She'd had more compliments lately than she'd ever had before in her life though, so perhaps Monica had done her more of a favour than Grace gave her credit for. Yet it had still been pretty harsh when she'd walked past the charity shop in the village the other day and thought how frumpy the clothes in the window display were before realising that most of them were hers. At least no one could accuse her of looking like Archie's granny any more. She was so determined to never go back to that point in her life.

Grace noticed him the minute she walked in. He was sitting on a leather settee, tapping away on his laptop on the low table in front of him, looking studious, with his glasses perched on the end of his nose. He was a man of many looks and they all suited him. When she had first seen him, he was in his gardening clobber, then he'd been looking smart on a night out, and now he looked deliciously casual in jeans, a snug fitting t-shirt (yum!) and smart trainers.

Grace's first reaction was to turn around and walk straight back out again, but she remembered Monica telling her that she had to change the way she approached situations that made her nervous, so she took a deep breath and walked over to the table.

'Ahem.' She coughed nervously when she got there, trying to pluck up the courage to say hello and wondering whether he'd remember her.

'Grace! How lovely to see you.' Vinnie beamed at her and stood up, and they had one of those awkward moments when you don't know whether to shake hands, or kiss once, or even twice. So they did nothing.

'What brings you to my sister's fabulous café today then? I do hope you are going to join me,' Vinnie said, packing his work away.

'Wow! So this is her shop? It's lovely. And only if I'm not dragging you away from your work.'

'That's more than OK. I'm just sorting out some

invoices and it's truly dull, so I don't need any excuse to stop. It's lovely to see you. What can I get you?'

While Vinnie went over to the counter to order her a skinny latte, she found herself grinning as she realised that she was properly checking him out. She quickly averted her eyes as he returned before she started staring at his crotch. She looked up at his face instead and realised that she had forgotten how devilishly handsome he actually was.

'So what have you been doing since we met last? I did try to find you in the bar when I spotted you that Saturday night, but you'd disappeared,' he said.

'Yes, we decided to head off for some Chinese food. We'd had a busy day.'

'Shame, I was so fed up of being with my idiot mates, I was desperate for some normal company. When I couldn't find you anywhere I sneaked off home, much to my mates' disgust. It really is a lovely surprise to see you here today, you know.'

'Thanks, Vinnie. I'm glad I came now. It's nice to see you too!'

'There are some people you just don't forget, Grace,' he said, and then he immediately blushed.

'Here you go, little bro!' said a cheerful, pretty lady in a vintage flowery apron, putting two huge mugs of coffee before them. 'Aren't you going to introduce us?'

'Grace, meet Ruth. My very annoying but adorable and *much* older sister!' The two women shook hands and smiled at each other.

'Nice to meet you, Grace, and nice to see my little brother with some female company for a change!' She winked at Grace and perched her bottom on the arm of the sofa. Vinnie glared at her.

'Alright, I'm going!' Ruth replied, getting up. 'I know where I'm not wanted. I know you only want me for my coffee. And it's about time you settled your bill, Vincent. I'm not a charity.' She winked at Grace and smiled as she collected the empties from the table next to them and returned to the counter.

Grace could see that they had a relaxed and easy-going, loving sibling relationship. It made her heart twang a little as she realised how much she missed Hannah. While she could never have stopped her emigrating to the US and living the life of her dreams, she still wished that her big sister was closer than a huge ocean away.

Grace and Vinnie chatted easily while drinking copious amounts of coffee and devouring an enormous slab of a divine coffee and walnut cake, which tasted just like the one her mum used to make. Ruth had sent it over on the house, which was so kind of her. Probably not going to do her diet any good, but the cake was so delicious that she didn't care.

They talked about their jobs: Vinnie had been working in the world of landscaping since he studied horticulture at college and had worked his way up from the bottom. He now had his own business and could work from anywhere as long as he had an internet connection, so he was lucky that his sister, Ruth, had reliable Wi-Fi in the coffee shop.

'The only thing wrong with working from here so much is that I'm now addicted to Americanos – and cake!' Vinnie chuckled.

Grace told him about her job as an estate agent and how difficult she had found getting that job after being a stay-at-home mum for so long. She also shared with Vinnie her ambition to one day own a bookshop café. She didn't know why she told him that, because it was a dream that she hadn't shared with anyone else apart from Monica, but he was so easy to open up to. She felt like she'd known him for years. In turn, Vinnie told her about his dream of living by the seaside. They agreed that there would be nothing better than a walk on the beach every day to ground you, get some sea air in your lungs and feed your soul.

Glancing at her watch, Grace realised that she'd been there for well over two hours, and that Archie would be home soon.

'Perhaps we could meet up again. There's a new bistro in town that I was thinking about trying. Do you fancy coming with me, Grace?'

'Erm, yes. That would be nice.'

She wasn't sure if he was asking her because he was going anyway and wanted company or whether he was asking her on a date, but they decided to meet up on the following Wednesday evening. He flipped open his wallet to take out a business card with his personal details on it and she noticed a photo of a blonde lady, but she couldn't look at the picture properly as he saw her looking and immediately closed his wallet again. She wasn't quite sure how to say goodbye – was it too formal to shake his hand? – so she awkwardly went for a quick peck on the cheek, but as she did that, he turned slightly and she ended up planting a kiss on his nose.

'OMG! I'm so sorry!' she said as she went as red as a beetroot.

Vinnie blushed and then they both started to giggle, which calmed Grace's heart a little, because it was really thumping in her chest. She waved at Ruth, who was busy serving customers but yelled, 'Lovely to meet you and really hope to see you again, Grace!' across the room.

Grace walked away from Coffee Heaven with a big smile on her face and a warm, fuzzy feeling in her heart, which she hadn't felt in a very long time. She kicked herself when she realised that seeing Vinnie there had completely distracted her from the fact that she'd gone there to size up the venue for her slimming club and she'd forgotten to ask anything about that. Smiling, thinking about Vinnie again, she then remembered the picture in his wallet, and her heart sank a bit as she wondered who the mystery lady was. She was probably jumping ahead of herself and it likely wasn't a date after all, even though Ruth had implied he didn't have anyone. Crikey, she was so jaded with what had happened with first Mark and then Tommy, she wondered if she'd ever trust anyone again.

* * *

I'm so glad that you finally met up with a lovely man, even if I did have to try really hard to make it happen. I've worked it out, now. If I want you to think something, I just have to stay really close to you, making sure that you make connections. I'm really rather clever, you know.

I just have to concentrate my mind so much that you know what I'm thinking and then those thoughts become yours. I shall be working hard to send you little messages to steer you in the right direction. I just hope that you follow my clues. I love you, Mum xxx

11

Grace walked through her front door and was leapt upon by four big brown paws and a big sloppy lick. 'Ew, Becks! You are such a monster.' She laughed as he practically wrestled her to the ground because he was so excited to see her. She giggled. 'Come on, sausage, let's go and have a nice long walk'.

Not far from Grace's house, there was a stunning forest, where the world and his wife walked their dogs. From the moment she got Becks, Grace had had to learn about a whole new doggy code of conduct: that when you have a dog it's OK to stop, chat and pass the time of day with people you've never seen before. This was something that rarely happened if you went for a walk on your own. Luckily,

Becks was a friendly soul and the perfect ice-breaker, and walking around her village had introduced her to so many people that she might not otherwise have ever crossed paths with.

She was still in her little happy bubble, thinking about seeing Vinnie on the following Wednesday and wondering if it actually was a 'date' and who the mysterious lady in the picture was, when her phone rang. Her heart sank when she saw it was Mark. She wondered which Mark it would be today.

'Need a word!' he said in his normal abrupt and patronising manner. Oh OK, it was *that* Mark today. Being a head teacher made him think that he could speak to everyone like he spoke to the parents and children at the high school he worked at.

'Hi, Mark, what can I do for you?' said Grace. She had given up asking how he was a long time ago because a) he normally went into a long story about how tired he was all the time because he had such a busy job and she wouldn't understand, and b) she didn't actually care how he was.

He had changed so much since becoming a head teacher. It was almost like the power had gone to his head. She remembered the days when he was such good company, caring and compassionate, when as a teacher he worried about the pupils he taught, always putting Grace first, as well as work. That was the Mark that she'd fallen head-over-heels in love with. When life with Mark was good, it felt like it was all she'd ever wanted and more, but when it was bad, it was horrid.

She was jolted back to the present.

'It's my weekend to have Archie next weekend but something's come up and I need to go abroad instead to help someone out with something.'

'And...?' She waited for him to ask her if once again he could swap dates when something more important than his son came up.

'You need to have Archie because I won't be here, obviously,' he replied.

'Do you mean, would I mind altering my arrangements to accommodate you?' she asked.

'Well, I can't have him so you'll have to.'

She was used to his brusque manner and the way he spoke to her when he was in one of his moods.

'OK, that's fine,' she replied, her first thought being, *Yay! I get to spend more time with my boy!* She couldn't understand what could be more important to a parent than spending time with their child, which was why she found it so tough that her relationship with Mark had not worked out, meaning that they had to share their son.

She sometimes felt that Mark had only ever gone for shared custody so that he wouldn't lose face at school and damage his reputation as head teacher, rather than because he wanted to spend time with Archie. Although when he was in one of his good moods, he was the perfect dad, treating Archie to new football boots just because he wanted to. But when he was in one of his supercilious moods, he would keep pointing out to Grace that he had a '*very important job*' and that she wouldn't possibly understand as she only had her fluffy little job in an office.

Her 'fluffy little job in an office', along with the pittance of maintenance that Mark paid her each month, was what paid the bills and kept a roof over her and Archie's head, but Mark couldn't seem to understand that. Not to mention the fact that she loved her job! Estate agents often got a bad rap, but Grace could honestly say that she only had her clients' best interests at heart and loved nothing more than finding someone their forever home.

'Good, that's sorted then!' he said and ended the call.

'Thanks, Grace,' she mouthed to herself sarcastically as she rolled her eyes.

Despite Mark's attitude, she brightened up as she

thought about what she'd organise for her and Archie to do the following weekend.

Her phone rang again. *Oh no, what have I done now?* She immediately thought, expecting it to be Mark again, and was really pleased to hear Monica say, 'Hey, babes, how was the coffee shop? Is it suitable for the busy people's slimming club?'

'Oh, Mon,' she said in a dreamy voice. 'You'll never guess who was there?'

'Donald Trump?'

'You are ridiculous!'

'Lady Gaga?'

'Not even close.'

'OK, last guess. Prince Harry?'

'Remember Fit Bloke – the landscaper? Well, it's only his sister's café. I'd completely forgotten that he'd said she owned one.'

'And...?'

'Well, he saw me and asked me to join him. I was there for over two hours. It was just... well, just lovely.'

'Gracie's i-in lur-ve! Gracie's i-in lur-ve!' Monica sang.

'Oh, you're so childish!' Grace laughed.

'Yep, I sure am. But you love it! So, are you seeing him again?' Monica asked.

'I am actually, we're going out for a dinner on Wednesday night,' Grace replied.

'OMG, you are *so* going to get a seeing to on Wednesday. You'd best dust the cobwebs off your lady garden, Mrs. As they say at the fair, "Buckle up, baby, this could be the best ride of your life!"'

Grace's heart dropped to the floor. It had been so long since she'd even found a man that she fancied, she hadn't even thought about going that one step further until she went out with Tommy. She shivered at the thought of what might have happened if she'd gone back to his hotel room and then found out he was married. Mortifying. And really! How could she possibly let someone who wasn't Mark see her body naked? She was so conscious of the fact that she'd put on weight that she didn't even look at herself in the mirror any more. And she didn't think she'd shaved her legs for six months. Even Archie had started commenting on her legs looking like a hairy monkey. Despite everything that Monica had done on the outside, she still felt old, fat, frumpy and unattractive on the inside.

'Oh crap, Mon, I hadn't even given that a thought! I'm going to have to call him at once and cancel. I can't possibly go through that.'

'You will do no such thing! You will be well prepared, de-fuzzed, sparkling and beautiful and you are gonna knock his socks off!'

'It's not his socks I'm worried about.' She sighed. And then she remembered the picture in his wallet. Maybe she might be worrying for no reason. Maybe this wasn't a date after all.

12

The week did not start well. She'd had to battle that morning with Archie to get ready for school on time, having to wrestle the iPad from him at one point, which resulted in him having a huge meltdown. Then, after school, two of his school friends knocked on the door and asked if he could go to the park with them to play football.

'Can I, Mum? Can I?' he'd begged her, pulling on her jumper.

'I'm sorry, Arch, but I really don't think you are old enough.'

'I am though, Mum. I'm ten and you let me walk home from school now. How's this any different?'

It didn't matter how many times she explained to

him that she wasn't happy about him going to the park in the evening with boys she knew from school, but didn't really know anything else about, he was still cross. They'd have main roads to cross and while she knew she had to let go of him sometime and increase his independence, this was not going to be that day.

He stomped off upstairs into his room and refused to come down for an hour. He seemed to have morphed into a teenager over the last few weeks. The only thing that brought him out of his room was the fact that they were going to visit Papa, who she hoped might talk some sense into him.

They drove the five miles to the retirement village in near silence, with Archie staring out the window and giving one-word answers to any questions she asked. She left him in the lounge with her dad while she went to make a cuppa for them all, and as she returned and stood outside the lounge door, she heard them talking.

'But Mum never plays football with me any more, Papa. She's always too busy cooking, or cleaning, or decorating. She never has time for me. *And* she never lets me go to the park with my mates, either.'

'But you're not really old enough to go to the park on your own yet, son. I know it's hard when you see other kids doing it, but all your mum is trying to do is to keep you safe.'

'If Dad was still with us, he'd be able to share jobs and then Mum would have more time for me.'

'Your mum is working her socks off so that you can have all your fancy stuff. If you want Z-Boxes and aPads, someone has to pay for them, son. And if she doesn't do the cleaning and cooking, who will? I don't suppose you help her, do you?'

She looked through the gap in the door as Archie shook his head.

'You need to cut your mum some slack. She's trying her best. Now come over here and give your old papa a man-hug.'

'I'll try, Papa. I promise I'll try.'

Grace promised herself that she'd do her damnedest to make more time for Archie, even if it meant having to stay up later to get the housework done. Who needed sleep, anyway? She'd already rocked his world by splitting with his dad. It was her job as his mum to protect him from hurt, and she already carried that guilt around with her, so she had to make sure that he didn't end up resenting her.

* * *

Wednesday evening arrived. She'd told Mark that she was going out at six thirty and he did his normal trick of not arriving to pick up Archie until six forty-five, blaming the traffic. She knew he did it on purpose and had often thought he probably sat around the corner, deliberately waiting till he was late before arriving at her house. She used to get really wound up by his tardiness and say that perhaps he should have left a bit earlier, but it was obvious that he got a real kick out of winding her up, so now she took the high road and never mentioned it, much as she had to grit her teeth.

Grace always prided herself on being able to make pleasantries with everyone she met – even if she was busy or stressed. She knew that being kind and open cost nothing and got the best out of people. But Mark could wind her up in a way that no one else ever could. She wondered how someone could go through life constantly challenging people and being argumentative. It must be exhausting. She was quite sure that Mark could have an argument if he was in a room by himself. She wondered how he'd ever got the job he'd got, looking after the welfare of hundreds of children and countless staff, and how he actually got through a day at work. Unless he had a personality transplant every morning when he walked through the school gates? She spent her life trying to make sure that Archie didn't adopt some of his father's quirks and showed people respect. Luckily so far, he seemed to have far more of her in him than his father.

Mark walked into the kitchen and started rummaging through the post on the counter, seeming not to care that it wasn't his home. Spotting the invitation, he raised an eyebrow. 'You've been nominated for an award. Brilliant.' He laughed and flung the invitation back down on the side.

Why couldn't he say he was proud of her? They might not be together any more, but surely, as the mother of his child, he didn't have to put her down all the time, especially in front of Archie.

'Although, if you do go, I'm actually free the weekend after next, Grace, so I'll come with you as your guest. It'll be good for me to be seen at a local business event. I've always wanted to meet the Lord Mayor too; I could tap him up to come and present awards at the school, which will go down well with the parents. I'll put it in my diary.'

Half of her wanted to smack him in the face for being so arrogant, while the other half of her thought that it might be good to go with someone, even if it *was* Mark. And he could be charming when he wanted to, able to make small talk with a whole host of people. It was only when he'd got that ruddy job that he had changed, turning into the arrogant man she saw in front of her now.

Grace knew Mark would be lovely to all the other people there, even if he couldn't bring himself to offer the same courtesy to her. And at least if she went with him, she could stop worrying about finding someone to go with, which had been really stressing her out. She would need to find someone else to have Archie, though, as Mark was her back-up plan. Edward and Melanie had offered to pay for a babysitter but there weren't many people she'd be comfortable leaving Archie with. If she could sort that bit out, she could be an adult for a night and grin and bear it. Another problem sorted.

She glanced at her watch. *It's a good job I'm not actually going out until seven thirty*, she thought to herself as Mark drove off with a smirk on his face. She'd learned to adjust the times to suit herself months ago but hadn't shared that with him. She was still reeling from her conversation with him before he'd left.

Looking intently at her, he'd said, 'You've changed your hair.'

Archie had butted in, saying, 'Of course she's

changed it, Dad! Didn't you notice? D'oh. She's had it all cut off and it's a different colour now!'

Mark had muttered something about it looking nice, before hustling Archie out for a quick exit.

When they were together, on the rare occasions that they did go out together, and she'd really made an effort to look nice, she'd ask him if she looked OK and he always used to answer, 'You'll do,' without even looking at her. And that was when Mark had been her partner, so she was shocked that he'd noticed her change today. But she had no time to think about what it all meant, as she was nervous as hell for her meet up with Vinnie. Running upstairs, she quickly got changed into the teal wrap dress that she and Monica had picked out from their recent swishing trip. Her hands were shaking as she carefully applied her make-up the way that Fiona had shown her and, when she finished, she slipped her feet into a pair of grey wedges that she'd carefully chosen to go with most of her new clothes stash.

She heard the deep hum of an engine outside her house, and as she waited for the doorbell, she sprayed herself with her Jo Malone Lime, Basil and Neroli perfume, a present from someone she'd recently done a house deal for. When the bell rang, she grabbed her grey cashmere cardigan, took a deep breath, exhaled and went downstairs.

'Wowsers!' Vinnie said when she opened the door. 'You look fabulous, Grace.'

'Why thank you,' she replied and blushed slightly as she looked him up and down. He looked bloody gorgeous too, simply dressed in a black cotton t-shirt – which fitted him in all the right places, skimming over his abs like a second skin – a pair of dark blue jeans, a smart black jacket and black boots. Her very own Milk Tray Man. His dark hair was slightly gelled, his face looked sun-kissed from working outdoors and his short beard was perfectly groomed. As he turned and walked down her drive towards his car, Grace pulled the door shut behind her and couldn't help but look at his backside, which was pert and perfectly formed. She grinned to herself. All her good intentions to not even think about having sex seemed to go out the window and she strongly resisted the urge to grab him by the lapels, snog his face off and rip his clothes off there and then. Date or not, she knew a mighty fine-looking man when she saw one.

She was struggling with the whole 'is it a date?' dilemma. He hadn't exactly said it was a date; he'd just said he wanted to try out a restaurant and asked her to go along. Did that constitute a date? Or was it just two people who needed to eat going out and eating together?

They had the most perfect evening. The sun set in the distance over the countryside as they sat outside the restaurant, and they once again very comfortably chatted about their respective weeks so far. Vinnie was a great conversationalist and storyteller; he was quick-witted and just delightful company. The meal was delicious, too. The restaurant belonged to a couple who Vinnie knew from university and they made them feel really welcome and special, recommending all their signature dishes and making a real fuss over their guests.

When they'd finished their meal and said goodbye to Vinnie's friends, thanking them for such a fabulous meal, he opened the car door for her and she climbed in. She was pleased that he had a nice car. She didn't want to seem petty or materialistic but she remembered years ago going on a date with a guy who was six feet five and very good-looking, but when he picked her up, he had a bright green Fiat Cinquecento that he had to unfold himself from and she was mortified. Vinnie's flame-red BMW X5 certainly met with her approval.

During the short ride home they chatted like old

friends, and when they pulled up outside her house she dithered a little about whether to invite him in or not. But before she'd thought about it too much, he said, 'I've got to be up early to drive to Southampton, so even if you were going to invite me in for a coffee I'd have to decline.' He grinned and she couldn't help but smile back at him because she knew he could sense she was unsure.

'However...' He hesitated. 'I've had a wonderful evening, Grace, and if you're free at the weekend, I'd love it if we could see each other again.'

'Oh, Vinnie, that would have been lovely, but I can't do this weekend as I'm taking Archie away, but I am free on Monday or Tuesday evening, if you're free then?' she replied. She hoped she hadn't blown it.

'Well, let's make it Monday then because I don't think I can wait until Tuesday to see you again. How about going to the cinema? Do you like films?' he asked.

'Yes, it'll make a change to watch something that's not got a PG certificate.' Grace smiled. 'I normally get nudged all the way through a kids' film as I have been known to get way too comfortable and nod off.'

'Then it's a date. I'll check the film times and text you what time I'll pick you up, if that's OK?'

Aha! So the next one definitely was a date then.

He turned to her and there was an awkward moment where they didn't know whether they should kiss – and if so, whether cheeks or lips. They went for a kiss on each cheek, continental style. She opened the door and climbed out and raised a hand in a wave and said she'd see him on Monday. He waited until she'd opened the front door and turned and smiled at him with a little wave as she closed the door. She appreciated that he'd made sure she'd got inside safely before driving away. A gentleman. She loved it.

She did wonder if she'd done something wrong though, as he hadn't kissed her, apart from the little peck on the cheek. She wondered if he'd just had a nice night but wasn't that into her. But then why would he ask her to go out again? *And* he'd said the D-word. He couldn't possibly have a girlfriend if he was asking her out, surely? Perhaps she just needed to go with it and see what developed, if anything at all. It was all so blooming confusing.

All these thoughts were going round her head when there was a soft knock at the door. She opened it and to her surprise, there stood Vinnie.

'I'm sorry, Grace, but there was something really important that I forgot to do.' He took a step inside the door, reached down and cupped her face in his hands. 'I really have loved every minute of this evening, Grace, and I've wanted to do this from the very first moment I stood on this step that Saturday afternoon.' She closed her eyes and their lips met, and he kissed her slowly, tenderly, yet with an incredible passion, and she felt like she was going to float away on a cloud. She didn't know that a kiss could feel so sensual. His soft short beard gently grazed against her chin.

He pulled away and smiled at her. 'Thank you, I've wanted to do that all night!' He turned and walked down the path and when he reached the car, blew her a kiss.

He waited until she shut the door to make sure she was safely tucked inside again before he drove away. She leant up against the door, touching her lips with her fingers. *Christ!* she thought. *If he makes me feel like that with a kiss, how on earth am I going to feel if I ever have sex with him?*

She floated around her bedroom in a daze, getting changed into her pyjamas and taking off her make-up, when her phone pinged to say that she had a text message.

> Thanks for the lovely evening. That kiss will keep me going until Monday. Can't wait! Goodnight, sweet dreams. Vinnie x

Vinnie's gorgeous face was the last thing she saw in her mind as her head hit the pillow and she dreamt those sweet dreams.

* * *

Sleep well, my darling. You looked so beautiful this evening and I'm so pleased that you both got on like a house on fire. I knew you would. He's lovely! Just enjoy the time you spend with him and concentrate on yourself for a while. Let that smile that I saw this evening, which hasn't been around for a long time, be a permanent fixture on your face. It's so lovely to see you so happy. I love you, darling. Mum xxx

13

After lunch the following day, Grace was slightly concerned to see the name of Archie's school showing up on her phone's caller display. They only ever phoned if there was a problem.

'Mrs Beam?'

'Miss Carnegie, actually, but yes, I am who you are after.'

'Is there any chance you could pop in to see the head teacher for ten minutes just before you pick Archie up today, please? There's been an incident at school that we'd like to discuss with you.'

'An incident? Is Archie OK?'

'He's fine. We'll explain when you come in. We don't like to discuss matters like this over the phone.'

'Certainly, I'll be there just before pick-up.'

Wondering what on earth had happened, Grace spoke to her boss and asked if she could leave slightly earlier than normal and said that she would make up her time at home later. They were a really easy-going company, thank heavens, allowing flexible working, so it didn't really matter when she rearranged things slightly. It was one of the main reasons she'd taken the job in the first place. That and the fact that she loved helping people to find a new home. It was almost like a dating agency, but you just had to match the person with their ideal house instead of another person. Much less trouble.

She arrived in the school reception as agreed and was invited to take a seat in the head teacher's office. Grace liked Mrs Kelly. She was strict, but fair, and if there were ever any issues, she was always able to sort them out without making the parent feel like a failure.

'Grace.' Mrs Kelly greeted her with a handshake. 'Thanks so much for coming in. I'll get straight to the point as I know it's nearly end of school time and Archie is in the library at the moment but will be heading down this way shortly. Archie punched a boy in the face today.'

Grace's heart hit the floor. This was totally out of

character for him. A hundred questions ran through her head in one go, blowing her mind. She didn't know whether to feel angry with him, worried for him or embarrassed about what he'd done. '*What? Archie did? My Archie? I can't believe it. What on earth did he do that for? Who did he hit? Are they OK?*'

'It is totally unacceptable behaviour, and extremely unusual for him, but even so, it cannot be allowed. As it happened at lunch break, I've kept him in here with me since, but he won't tell me what instigated it. I think it best if he takes the day off tomorrow and has a think about his behaviour. If he apologises to the other boy, then I'm prepared to overlook the matter, but it will go down on his records.'

Grace was mortified. Her Archie was not the type of boy to go around punching others. But Grace knew that he was growing up and ten was a difficult age, with testosterone starting to surge around. There had been a couple of occasions recently when he got angry for no major reason, mainly when she asked him to stop playing on his Xbox, but this was totally unacceptable.

Mrs Kelly spoke kindly to her. 'This is most unusual for Archie and because it is so out of character,

I thought it would be prudent to talk to you first. May I suggest that you take him home – the secretary has just gone to fetch his bag and coat and grab him from the library – and not mention anything until you get home and see if he'll open up to you in his own surroundings. There is obviously something very serious bothering him.'

'Thank you.'

Archie appeared at the door, his eyes red. He'd clearly been crying. Despite what he had done, Grace's heart went out to her son; still so very much a child, but wanting to grow up. She held her hand out to him, and for once he took it, but he kept his head down all the way home and didn't say a word. Grace found it very difficult not to ask him about it but heeded the head teacher's advice.

When they walked through the front door, he flung himself at Becks and burst into tears.

'Archie, are you OK?' she asked tentatively.

'Yep. Just brilliant,' he shouted as he stomped off upstairs and into his room, slamming the door behind him.

She thought she'd best give him a little space, but after fifteen minutes she really thought it was time they spoke about what had happened, so she made herself a cup of coffee, poured a glass of milk and put some cookies on a plate. She knocked on the door lightly and asked if she could go in. There was no answer so she opened the door and saw Archie sitting on his bed, staring out of the window. When she walked towards him, she could see that he'd been crying again.

'Sweetheart, whatever is the matter?'

'I can't tell you. Dad said not to.'

'Oh, darling, you know that you can tell me anything. You mustn't bottle things up and get angry. Please talk to me. You know that I'll try to sort out anything that's upsetting you.'

'I can't, Mum.'

'You also can't be getting yourself into a state like this, darling. It's not good for you. Now, please tell me. I can't help you if you don't tell me what happened.'

'I'll tell you but you have to promise not to tell Dad I told you. Promise?'

'OK, I promise.' Grace hated it when Archie made her promise not to tell Mark things. It made life very difficult when he was upset and things needed sorting out, issues that needed a dad and a mum to work through them together.

'Dad says that someone from school saw you last night with your new boyfriend! The person who told him has a girl in my class and she was singing "Your mum's got a boyfriend" at me. George joined in and he wouldn't stop and said that now you've got *him* you won't love me any more. He was right in my face and wouldn't stop saying it and I was so angry that I punched him.'

Oh great, she thought. *Thanks so much, Mark!*

'Darling, I don't know why Dad said that to you because it absolutely is not true. Yes, I did go out for a meal with someone last night. It was someone I met recently. He's a nice man and he's just a friend at the moment. Surely you don't want me to sit in on my own when you're not here and be lonely, do you?'

'How can you be lonely, Mum? You have Becks.'

'Yes, but Becks is a dog, darling, and he's a bit stinky at times, too.' Grace saw the crack of a smile forming on Archie's face. 'I was going to tell you when and if there was something to tell you. I met someone who invited me out for dinner and I went. That's it, really. I promise you.'

'Are you going to go out with him again, Mum?' he asked as he looked up at her with those baby blue eyes that always made Grace's heart swell.

'I'd like to. He seems like a very nice man. But I'll only go with your approval, my darling. You always have been and always will be the first priority in my life. From the moment you were born, you stole my heart. Between you and Becks, there's only a bit of room – and time – left for anyone else, anyway. It is just nice for me to have some adult company when you're not here, love. That's all.'

'OK, Mum, but I'm not sure I even want you to have a boyfriend.'

'How come it's OK for Dad to have a girlfriend but not for me to have a boyfriend, out of interest?' she said gently to Archie, realising that she would have to tread very carefully.

'Well, that's clearly very different, isn't it?'

Grace raised her eyebrows at her son's statement.

'I just wish that you and Daddy were still together and we all lived in the same house. Then I could be like some of the other people at school. But I suppose if that's not going to happen right now, then I think I'd like to meet this friend of yours as soon as possible as I have a lot of questions that I'd like to ask him. I wrote them down at lunchtime at school today.'

'Oh, OK, honey, that's... er, really great.' She squirmed inside. Who knew what Vinnie would think about being interrogated by someone else's child? He'd probably run a mile.

'Now, I know you're upset about this, but you

can't go round punching people for taunting you. That's just not on.'

'This big rage came over me, Mum, and I didn't know what to do. Before I knew it, I'd hit him. I am sorry, Mum, really, I am.' He was still crying but getting the words out through his tears.

'Well, tomorrow we're going to have a day at home. Mrs Kelly has said that you are not allowed to go back to school until you apologise to George so you must do that the day after. We'll tell Daddy that you have tummy ache tomorrow. But you have to promise me that you'll talk to me about anything like this in future. Violence is not acceptable in any way whatsoever. Understand?'

'OK, Mum.' He hung his head in shame.

'Now, give me a great big hug and eat your milk and biscuits.'

'OK, Mummy. Can it be a big heart hug?'

They'd had lots of rituals over the years, one of them being their heart hugs, but Archie had grown out of them a couple of years ago. Grace had to kneel down so that she was Archie's height and then they could hug tightly with their hearts right next to each other. They had to hold the hug for at least the count of twenty. Apparently it was a proven fact that a hug lasting for twenty seconds or more releases happy endorphins into your body and lowers stress, blood pressure and heart rate. It was something they'd done since he was old enough to hug her.

He clung on to her like he was never going to see her again, but when they separated, he smiled and said, 'I don't ever want you to not love me. That's why I was so annoyed at the thought that you'd replace me.'

'Impossible. That, my darling, would never ever happen.'

'Are you sure?' he asked. 'Not even if David Beckham asked you to marry him?'

'Mmm, now that is a toughie! Let me just take a minute to think about that.' She rubbed her chin, pretending to think it over.

'Mummy!' he warned. 'Make sure you get the right answer.'

'OK! Not even if David Beckham asked me to marry him!' she replied.

'Yes!' shouted Archie as he fist-pumped the air. 'The right answer!'

* * *

Grace stood at the kitchen sink, swilling some crockery around and pondering what had happened.

She'd only been on one date with Vinnie and it had already caused a massive issue for Archie, and when all was said and done, Archie was more important to her than anyone. She really liked Vinnie, but was getting involved with someone new worth upsetting Archie for? And what was going on with Mark? He had actually been quite nice to her last night, even complimenting her. Was he jealous, or was it just a case of him not wanting her but not wanting anyone else to have her either? Grace was so mixed up. She knew that in an ideal world, Archie's family would be complete and they'd all be together. And in fairness, that's all she had ever wanted, but having that shouldn't mean putting up with someone who had disrespected their family unit and cheated on her. God! It was so hard being a single mum. All this was making life so complicated.

'Oh, Mum. I can't tell you how much I wish you were here to chat through stuff with. I can't believe it's been so long and that I still miss you so much.' A tear rolled down her cheek as she contemplated her life while she finished the washing up.

* * *

My sweet boy. I love you, my darling beautiful Archie. I know I never met you in person, but I've watched you since the day you were born, and even before that when I used to lay my hands on your mummy's tummy when she was pregnant. You know that I am around you all the time. I know you feel it. I see your smiles, and I get all the kisses you blow to me in heaven. And I know you saw me that time when I stood in the lounge doorway and Mummy asked you who you were waving at. I will be your nanna for the rest of your life, even though I'm up here and not physically there with you. I will do everything I can to guide you in the right direction and will always be around. I will make sure that you and your beautiful mummy will be very happy in your lives. Goodnight, my sweet little angel. I love you. Nanna xxx

14

Mark came round at four thirty on Friday afternoon to see Archie before he went away on his weekend to Spain and before Grace and Archie headed off to Wales. He was suspiciously nice for a change and gave Grace a hug as he came in. She was thrown by that and offered him a cup of coffee, immediately kicking herself because she didn't normally give him any reason to stay. He spent some time playing with Archie on the floor, something she hadn't seen him do for a long time. A tickling competition ensued, and soon both were properly belly-laughing. Grace felt a pang of regret for all the good times they'd had.

Looking at Mark and their son smiling together made her heart flutter. It was times like this that all the bad things about her ex were flung out of the window and all the good things that they had shared came flooding back from her memory bank. Grace got up to walk out of the room, as the feeling was quite overwhelming.

'I love it when our family is together. Come on, guys, let's have a family hug.' Archie didn't give either Mark or Grace the chance not to be involved as he grabbed a hand from each and pulled them in for a hug. Mark gave her a wink over the top of Archie's head, making Grace blush. She felt a real pang and wondered whether she should have tried harder. If she began a relationship with Vinnie, would that mean she was turning her back on the possibility of them ever being a family again?

She hadn't mentioned anything about the incident at Archie's school. She didn't want to betray Archie's confidence, and Mark didn't mention her evening out. Archie seemed happy so she thought she'd leave things till the next time she saw Mark. She didn't want to upset the apple cart while he was in a good mood. Perhaps she'd speak with him about it when Archie wasn't around, if she still felt it necessary. The last thing she wanted now was to get into another slanging match with her ex. She knew that she had to pick her battles, and right now she couldn't cope with this one.

* * *

Grace was so delighted she'd decided to look up Saffy on Facebook. They had agreed to get together and Grace had been thrilled to accept Saffy's invitation to stay at Bendigeddig House, her home in Wales.

After a two-and-a-half-hour journey to the North Wales coast, Grace and Archie arrived at the imposing double-fronted house. It was located in a pretty little coastal village which boasted views of glorious mountains from one side of the house and a stunning sea view from the other. Saffy greeted them with open arms. She and Grace hugged deeply and when they parted, there were tears in both of their eyes for their lost years. Grace couldn't wait to catch up with her friend and find out every detail about her life since they'd last been in contact.

'I'm so glad you got in touch, Grace. It's something I've been meaning to do for so long, but when you're busy, life just passes you by and you don't always get round to doing it at the time, and then another year comes and goes. It makes me so happy to see you.'

'I was on a date – that's a story for another time – but I was thinking of you, and the memories were so lovely and precious that I knew I had to try to find you. And being with you now, even for just a short time, feels exactly the same as it did all those years ago. I'm so glad we're back in touch. I didn't realise just how much I'd missed you and all that blooming great advice you used to give me.'

After a cuppa and a piece of home-made cake, Grace and Archie chose a pair of wellies each from the boot room, which contained wellies of every pos-sible size and colour, and headed for the beach. As Archie and Becks ran ahead, splashing in the waves, Grace and Saffy caught up on some of what had been happening in their lives, and Grace felt so happy to have this fabulous friend back.

'So when you talk about Vinnie, you light up, Grace, but when you talk about Mark, you frown. That says such a lot. So why are you even doubting a relationship between you and Vinnie?'

'I suppose I'd forgotten just how charming Mark can be. And when I see him and Archie together having fun, it feels so wrong to keep them apart from each other. Plus, the fact that I've been on a date with

Vinnie and really like him has already made Archie wobble. Do I really risk what I have with Archie over someone I don't even know very well?'

'I learnt when my parents split up when I was Archie's age that it's better to have two parents who are happy apart than two parents who are constantly trying so hard to be nice to each other around their children, then sniping at each other when the kids are out of the way. My mum was so much happier when my dad left. It was like a physical weight had lifted from her shoulders. It taught me that everyone has a right to be happy. And that's what you deserve too, Grace.'

Grace nodded, but she still felt selfish, thinking of her own happiness instead of her son's.

Lots of long leisurely walks on the beach collecting shells, tons of fresh air and time spent chatting with a good friend over a glass of wine really felt good for Grace's soul. Both she and Archie felt sad to say goodbye to Saffy on Sunday, but they promised to get together again when they both had the chance. The break had really recharged Grace's and Archie's batteries, and they both felt great when they returned to school and work on Monday morning.

* * *

Mark knocked on the door at four thirty on the Monday evening, with two gift bags in his hand. He was having Archie that night, to make up for not having him over the weekend.

'Hello, you two,' he said cheerily. 'I've brought you both presents.'

He gave Archie a huge bag of sweets and Archie ran off to the kitchen to put them in his sweety drawer.

'And this is for you!' he said, and he leant forward and kissed Grace on the cheek as he handed her a silver gift bag. She peered inside to see a bottle of Daisy by Marc Jacobs. Only last week when he'd been picking up Archie, there was an ad on the TV for it, and Archie had commented to his mum that it was the one that she'd tried on recently when they'd been shopping. Mark had obviously taken note, and Grace was shocked at his thoughtfulness.

'It's to say thank you for dropping everything at the last minute again so that I could go off and do what I needed to do. I do appreciate you being so amenable; I know I don't often show it. And I certainly haven't shown it in the past. You really are an angel, Grace. I don't know what I'd do without you in my life.'

Ha, she thought. *If only he had paid me half this*

attention when we'd been together, we might actually have made it work, despite our differences. But he'd torn them apart when he went off with Lorraine, the floozy of a school secretary. What a cliché! Grace had walked in on them on a Wednesday evening in June two years ago when she had gone to surprise him and take him out for their anniversary dinner after work. Only Grace was the one that had got the surprise when she'd found him embracing Lorraine behind his desk. They'd jumped apart instantly, and he'd tried to bluster through it and brush it off as nothing important. But it was quite obvious that there was a lot more to it than he'd admitted, especially when she saw how upset Lorraine looked when Mark told Grace she meant nothing to him. Grace even felt a little sorry for her, looking at her crestfallen face; she'd obviously fallen for Mark's charming demeanour and lies, and of all people, Grace understood how that felt.

Agreeing to put the incident behind them, Mark had tried hard to win Grace and Archie back with days out, home-cooked meals and a willingness to really throw himself into family life. For the first time in a long time, Grace had felt that she had the happy family life she'd always craved. Then all of sudden Lorraine had started appearing everywhere they went – in the supermarket, in the coffee shop, in the bank; Grace became accustomed to spotting her when they were out and about. It eventually came to a head when Lorraine rang her up and gleefully told her that she and Mark had been having an affair for six months.

Grace had struggled with what she should do, wondering whether it was something that they could get through, or whether this was the end of their family as they knew it forever. She'd felt lower than she'd ever felt before. While she'd been busy trying to build a family, he'd been tearing it down. He had betrayed everything they had; the vows they'd taken to be faithful to each other had been destroyed. Her self-esteem had hit rock bottom. What could Lorraine offer him that she couldn't? He was enough for her, she loved him, even with his moods, and she wouldn't ever dream of looking outside of their marriage for someone else.

She'd talked it through with Hannah, and through tears and anger and sadness, after arranging for Archie to have a sleepover at Hannah's house, she had gone back to their home, where they'd lived since before they were married, and packed the majority of Mark's clothes into black bin liners. She rang him and told him to come and collect his things and said that she was changing the locks. When he'd turned up at the house, he was in a rage that she'd never seen before. He'd told her she was being completely unreasonable and that she'd be hearing from his solicitor and that he'd take her to court for custody of Archie. This threat had done exactly what he intended it to do and terrified her more than anything else he could have said, but for once in her life Grace knew she had to stick by her morals and stand up for herself. He had totally disrespected her and their family unit. He was the one in the wrong, not her, and she knew she had to remember that, no matter how tough it got.

To hear Mark talk now, it was as though none of it was his fault and he clearly thought that he could just be nice to her and everything would be OK. He was still with Lorraine now, even though every couple of months he'd make a comment that he didn't love her after all and was just with her because Grace wouldn't have him back and being with Lorraine was better than being on his own.

Grace jolted back to the present as Mark reached out and gently brushed her cheek with his fingers.

'I think we should try again, Gracie. I know how much you hate being away from Archie. Just think. You could be with Arch all of the time. Just imagine how that would make you feel. Don't you think you owe it to Archie to have our beautiful family back together again? What do you think?'

'What about Lorraine?' she asked, pulling away from him.

'What about Lorraine?' he asked.

'You live with her!' she said.

'She's never meant to me what you have, babe, you know that. I'd break up with her tomorrow if I thought you and I had a chance. You and Archie were the best thing to ever happen to me, you know that. I was an idiot to throw it all away. A total idiot.'

'You are quite unbelievable, you know,' she said, not intending it as a compliment.

'Just think about it. You know I'm right. Just say the word and you know I'm yours – and we could be a happy family again, for Archie's sake.' He turned and walked towards the front door.

Archie came bounding down the stairs and flung himself into her arms. 'I love you, Mummy. See you after school tomorrow.'

'Bye, darling. Mummy loves you to the moon and back.' She kissed his head.

It wouldn't be that much longer that he'd let her do this. He was growing up fast. And she was noticing things every day, like when she tried to hold his hand, he'd hold hers for a second and drop it; and when she told him she loved him on their walk to school, he just ran in without looking back. She wondered if she'd ever get over the feeling of missing him so much every time he went to his dad's.

As she waved them off, Grace wondered, not for the first time, whether she should say yes to Mark and mend their broken family.

15

Vinnie was arriving at seven thirty to take her to the pictures. She was really looking forward to seeing him again, even though she had such a lot on her mind this evening. He seemed to have such a calming and comfortable effect on her. She didn't feel quite so nervous about seeing him this time. He knocked on the door at seven thirty on the dot, and it made her smile; she loved the fact that, unlike Mark, he turned up at the time he said he would. She hoped that this wasn't just the good behaviour that everyone displayed when they first started dating someone.

She glanced in the mirror, wondering if her jeans and sparkly top looked OK, grabbed her linen jacket from the bottom of the banister and opened the door with a big grin on her face.

'Hey, beautiful,' he said as he kissed her cheek. They walked to the car where he held the door open. 'Your carriage awaits.' She went to get in the car, but he stopped her. 'Just one minute, lady, not so fast.'

He leaned forward, closed his eyes and kissed her, long and hard, on the lips. 'Mmm. That's better! I've been waiting for that all weekend.'

As he closed her door and walked round to the driver's side, she touched her lips, which seemed to be on fire, and beamed from ear to ear. He climbed in beside her and she had to tell herself to stop grinning like the village idiot, but she really felt that the time she spent with Vinnie was definitely better than that without him. She was determined that despite the conversation she'd had with Mark earlier, she was going to forget about everything else and relax into a lovely evening with Vinnie.

'So, as I'm not sure what sort of films you like, I'm going to give you a choice of two and let you pick if that's OK? We could either see that new Melissa Mc-Carthy comedy or the new Tom Cruise action film. Which would you prefer?'

Grace knew that she had to stop comparing Vinnie to Mark but, on the very rare occasions that they'd ever had a night out at the pictures, he'd told her what he was going to see and she was asked if she wanted to go along. To have a choice was a real treat.

'Being a massive Melissa McCarthy fan, that would be my choice, if you don't mind, that is.'

'To be honest with you, Grace, I'm really glad you said that. I can't bloody stand that little short-arse! I just thought I'd give you the option in case you had a crush on him.'

He grinned at her and her heart skipped a beat. He was looking so handsome tonight. The blue of his t-shirt set off his twinkly cornflower-blue eyes perfectly. *God, he'd make beautiful children*, she thought, suddenly reining herself in as her mind worked overtime.

They chatted comfortably about their respective weekends. He'd enjoyed some time with Ruth and her family, and Grace told him about their weekend in Wales. He seemed to be really interested in finding out more about Archie. He had two nieces and a nephew and talked about how much he loved spending time with them, so he certainly wasn't a stranger to having kids around. Always a good point when you were single and had a child. Before they knew it, they'd arrived at the cinema.

'My treat,' Vinnie said as he paid the cashier before Grace even had a chance to get her purse out of her handbag.

While Mark had been generous, he'd also always made her feel that she should be grateful that he kept them clothed and housed, despite the fact that Grace was looking after their child and felt she earned it. But with Vinnie, she had the feeling that he was just trying to be a gentleman. Grace loved the fact that now she was working, she had money of her own to spend. She was still getting used to that after being a stay-at-home mum for the biggest part of Archie's life.

'Well, in that case, I insist on buying the popcorn and the drinks,' she said.

The film was hilarious. They both laughed till tears streamed down their cheeks and chatted about it all the way back to Grace's house. This time, when Vinnie pulled up, she asked him if he had to be up early or whether he wanted a coffee. It was only just after ten o'clock.

'And I do mean coffee, young man!' she said jokingly when his eyebrows raised cheekily.

They'd had such a lovely evening but the thought of anything more at this stage, even though she really liked him, just made her feel sick with nerves.

'Go on then, I'll have a quick one,' he said.

This time Grace raised her eyebrows at him, and as he realised how wrong that sounded, he blushed. Grace laughed at him as they headed into the house. It felt good to laugh and she realised again how comfortable she was around Vinnie, even after just a short time.

While the kettle was boiling, Vinnie stood close to her and her nerves were tingling. She bit her lip as his head bent down towards her, and his lips were what seemed like a millimetre from hers when her mobile rang. After a second or two he stepped back, and she grabbed her handbag and fished her phone out. It was Mark.

'I'm so sorry but I'm going to have to take this. It's Archie's dad.'

'Of course. Can I just pop to your loo?'

She pointed to the doorway at the side of the kitchen.

'Mark, is everything OK?' she breathed into the phone.

'Not really, no!' Mark replied. 'Archie has got a really high temperature, said he feels sick and he's just crying and crying and saying he wants his mum. Can you pop round?'

Grace sighed. She knew that Archie would have

to come first. 'Of course I will. I'll leave straight away,' she said.

Vinnie walked out of the toilet and caught the tail end of the conversation. 'Do you need to go?' he asked.

'I'm so sorry, Vinnie, but Archie needs me. He's really poorly.'

'That's OK, love, I understand that your son comes first.' He sounded really dejected. 'But will you ring me later and let me know how he is? I want to make sure you're both OK.'

'Sure will, and I'm so very sorry, Vinnie, I've had such a great evening again. I hope we can meet up again soon.'

'I'd love to if you would,' he replied. 'Let's speak later and sort something out. It doesn't matter what time you phone me, I'll be waiting for your call.' He took her face in his hands and looked deep into her eyes, then kissed her long and lingeringly on the lips.

'Mmm...' She heard a low guttural moan then realised that the noise was coming from her.

'Until next time,' he said, walking her towards the front door.

She picked up her car keys and handbag and headed for her own car, waving as he pulled away.

It took ten minutes to get to Mark's house. As a

family they had originally all lived in a new-build on a development, which Mark had chosen and she'd thought she liked. It wasn't until after they'd decided to split up and sold the house that she realised she'd never really felt at home there. She could go for days without seeing a soul. Most people left to go to work in the morning and returned home without conversing with the neighbours, keeping themselves very much to themselves. That was hard when she was at home all day with a small child and no friends.

Mark now lived on the fourth floor of a modern apartment block, which was nearer to his work, and she had to park miles away from the front door. She rang the intercom and he kept her waiting for at least five minutes, and she had to ring three times before he clicked the latch.

Why didn't he just open the door if he knew she was on the way up? But then she realised that it was part of his controlling behaviour. He liked to keep people waiting; he did it all the time. He was still trying to control her, even now. She wasn't even sure he realised that he did it, but she figured it was part of his self-important persona.

Mark opened the door and stood back, letting her in. The room opened straight into the lounge, and Grace spotted Archie sitting on the sofa bed. Mark's apartment had only one bedroom so when Archie stayed over he had to sleep on a sofa bed in the lounge, which meant that he never got to go to bed very early. For a head teacher, Mark's own parenting decisions often left a lot to be desired. Grace always wondered how he had the nerve to question the parents in the school and make judgements about their parenting styles.

'Hey, Mum!' Archie said as she walked straight over to him. 'You OK?'

'I'm OK, darling. More to the point, are you?' she asked him.

'Yes, I'm fine thanks. I felt a bit sick but I think it was because Dad made me eat something I didn't like for tea. I feel fine now though. And Dad's turned the heating off so I'm not so hot any more! What are you doing here anyway?'

'Your dad asked me to come. He said you were crying and wanted me,' she said, glancing at Mark suspiciously as he walked into the kitchen.

'Did he? That's strange. I told him not to disturb you because I knew you were going out with your friend tonight,' he said, with emphasis on the word 'friend'.

So that was what it was all about. Mark just

wanted to spoil her evening. It seemed like every time she planned to do something nice in her life, he spoilt it. He'd been doing it for years. He was like a naughty selfish child who didn't want anyone else to have anything nice.

'Where's Lorraine?' Grace asked, following Mark into the kitchen.

'She's staying over at her friend's tonight so they can have a drink,' he replied. 'But while she is out of the way, have you thought any more about what I said earlier about us getting back together?'

'No, I haven't, Mark.' Grace raised her voice at him in frustration. 'You can't just expect an answer from me to a question like that! It's something that we would both have to think very seriously about before even considering it.'

'Well, I know it's what *I* want. When you realise it's the right thing to do for our son, our son that you're supposed to love with all your heart, our son that you'd do anything for, then perhaps you'd like to let me know.'

Mark had always managed to rile her. He was such a contradiction. Sometimes a self-obsessed, patronising jerk who frustrated her beyond words. If she didn't agree with him, she was wrong. If she had an opinion, she was having a go at him. If she asked him to do something, she was nagging. But then there was nice Mark, the one who charmed the pants off her the moment she met him, who wined and dined her and won her over and proposed when they were expecting a baby. The Mark who said he'd love her forever.

The trouble with people who were constantly manipulative but nice from time to time was that for some reason, you remembered the nice moments more than the nasty ones. Human nature, she supposed. But it didn't help when trying to make an important decision.

She walked back into the lounge and kissed Archie on the head, and he looked up at her with his baby-blue eyes. 'Mum, can I come home with you? Now you're here I just want to be with you.'

She looked at Mark. 'Go on then,' he said. 'Take him back with you, as long as it's not going to spoil your evening.' He smirked at her.

'It's a bit late for that, as you very well know,' she said through gritted teeth. 'Come on, sweetheart, pop your dressing gown and your slippers on and let's get you home.'

Archie went into the bathroom to get his slippers. When he returned, he threw his arms around his dad and Mark ruffled his hair and kissed the top of his head.

'Bye, Daddy.'

'Love you, son.'

This exchange between father and son was another tug at Grace's heartstrings.

16

When she got back, she settled Archie into bed as quickly as possible, as it was now nearly eleven o'clock and it was a school night. Remembering her promise, she texted Vinnie to say that she was home. Within seconds, her phone rang and his name flashed up on the screen.

'Hey you!' he said, and just hearing his gorgeous, smooth velvety voice made her feel safe and calm again. 'So how's your boy?'

'Nothing wrong with him, it was just his father being difficult,' she replied.

'So what's the score with you two then? We've not really talked about that, have we?' Vinnie asked gently.

'Nothing really to say. Like so many couples, I suppose we just outgrew each other. He can be a great dad to Archie when he tries but can make my life quite difficult if he feels like it.'

'Can I ask you something, Grace?'

'Anything you want.'

'Is there ever any possibility that you'll get back together, do you think? I really, really like you Grace, and I think and hope that you really like me too, but I don't want to come between you and him if there was a chance that you might become a family again.'

Grace thought about what he had said. Did she want to be a family again with Mark, to give Archie another chance to have his mum and dad under the same roof?

'Vinnie, I can't deny that sometimes in the past I've got lonely and thought about what might have been and how good it would be to have my son with me all the time and not to share him. But, although Archie sometimes says that he'd love us all to be back together again, I know I don't want to go back to the life I had.'

'OK, so it's alright for us to carry on seeing each other? Because, Grace, I have to tell you, I really feel that we have something special. I've not felt like this about anyone for a very long time. When I think about you, I get a goofy grin on my face and I think that means that I like you. A lot!'

'I like you too, Vinnie,' she said softly. 'I know we've not known each other long but I want to know more about you. I want to know everything about you. I feel like we're going to enjoy getting to know each other.'

'Me too, Grace. And perhaps tonight had to happen for us to have this conversation. Now get yourself off to sleep and let's speak tomorrow night. How does that sound?'

'That sounds really good, thanks, Vinnie. Goodnight.'

'Goodnight, Grace,' he whispered and disconnected the call.

Grace realised this was the downside of dating when you're far past your flighty early twenties; the people that you enter into relationships with have 'baggage'. She tried to put herself in Vinnie's shoes, but she didn't know how she would cope if the roles were reversed.

* * *

Ooh, I could bloody kill that Mark with my bare hands sometimes. If he loves you, he needs to show it all *the time. I do hope you don't let him spoil things for you! You have some important decisions to make, darling. I hope for everyone's sake you find it in your heart to make the right ones. I wish I was there to talk things through with you. You have to think about yourself, not just Archie. It has to be right for all of you. Just take your time and make the right decision. Love you, Mum xxx*

17

Grace had an hour to spare the following day between house-viewing appointments, so she popped into Coffee Heaven for a change of scenery. It was really quiet and there was no sign of Ruth, so she ordered a gingerbread latte and, although she looked at the cakes, she was quite pleased with herself when she decided not to have one. The young girl who took the order said that she'd bring it over to her, so she took a comfy armchair by the window to watch the world go by.

'Hi, Grace darling, how are you?' She looked up to see Ruth smiling down at her.

'Oh hey, Ruth, I'm great thanks. I didn't think you

were here today when I didn't see you behind the counter.'

'I was just out the back with the delivery driver. Ooh, that sounded worse than it actually was – I should be so lucky! Are you on your own or meeting someone?'

'No, just on my own. I had a house-viewing appointment but it was just cancelled. The couple have split up. I suppose it's a good job they've done it now rather than after moving in together. So I thought I'd come in here and grab a coffee. Are you too busy to join me?'

'I'd love to, if you're sure. I know when you're a mum you don't get much me time, so I don't want to spoil your peace and quiet.'

Grace laughed to herself as she remembered that when Archie was a toddler he used to ask her if she'd like a 'piece of quiet'. 'It would be nice to have some company,' she responded.

'So, I may as well ask at the start rather than building up to it,' Ruth said as she sat on the opposite armchair and put her drink down on the coffee table. 'How's it going with my bro? I hear you went out for a meal and then out again to the pics last night.'

'We did indeed.' Grace could feel her face light

up as she talked about the evenings she'd had out with Vinnie. 'He's lovely, isn't he?'

'Well, obviously he's my brother and I'm not going to say he's an arse, even if he was, but he's actually not! He's so lovely. I worry about him all the time. He works too hard, but it's been so lovely to see him with a spring in his step and a glint in his eye since he met you, Grace. You seem to get on so well together, and I'd love to see more of you too. I think he's a little fearful about your ex and whether he's going to get caught up in the middle, and that's my concern too, to be truthful. So I do hope you don't mind me asking what the score is on that front?'

'Mark and I knew each other at school and we went out briefly just before we went to university. He'd always wanted to be a teacher and I'd always wanted to work in interior design. At university it was clear we were moving forward in two completely different directions. I wanted a family and the life that comes with that. I come from a very loving family and my parents had been married for over fifty years when I lost my mum, and it tore us to pieces. We were all devastated.

'We split up then and met up again a few years later. He'd done his time at uni and was a qualified teacher. He moved back to our hometown and we started dating and fell in love all over again. I'd been off living my life and having holidays with my friends and was ready to settle down, and so was Mark.

'A couple of years later, I found out I was pregnant. Mark wasn't overjoyed, but then when Archie came along he changed and became the model father. We got married and were so happy, but then as Archie grew up, he changed again, especially when he became a head teacher. It was as if he was jealous of his own son. He started to resent the time I was spending with Archie. He was a baby, for goodness' sake, he couldn't do anything for himself. When Archie was a toddler, I found out that Mark had been cheating on me with a woman at work. You can imagine how gutted I was. I felt like I'd been cut open with a knife and had my heart torn out.

'I realised that he just didn't want to settle down, but I couldn't split my family up. Even after everything he'd done, I couldn't take my boy away from his father. So we muddled on.

'Then eventually it all came to a head when I found out that he was still seeing her. He'd promised me after the last time it was all over. He said he'd given her up and that we were all he wanted, but then I found out it was happening again. And that was the last straw for me. I knew that we should be worth more to him than that, so we went our separate ways.'

Ruth nodded in agreement. 'It's tough, isn't it, when you know what you should do but feel that you can't.'

'It's really tough, Ruth. You're a mum and you know you'd do anything for your children, wouldn't you? So I thought it was something I had to put up with. So I learned to live that way,' Grace said sadly. 'He didn't love me the way he should. We lived separate lives but in the same house. It was no life for either of us to be honest and certainly not for Archie. People used to think that I was a single mum, even before I was one for real.

'When I look back at our relationship, Ruth, I was unhappy for so long, and since we split up I feel like I've really found myself again. I've realised that I have a right to be happy and I've actually been happier on my own than when we were together. I hate the times when I'm not with Archie, but I've learned to accept them and fill that time with things for me. I've worked out that I'd rather be alone and happy than in a relationship and miserable. Life is just too damn short.

'I hope he is more settled with Lorraine,' Grace continued, trying to forget the fact that Mark had said he would dump Lorraine if Grace would only take him back. 'I don't want him to be unhappy, and I clearly wasn't making him happy, but it's taken me till now to realise that some people don't even know what happiness means to them, so how can they possibly achieve it if they don't know what they're looking for?'

'You're so right, Grace. I know a lot of people who seem to have the perfect life but they're constantly searching for something or someone better. Has there been anyone else since Mark, if you don't mind me asking?'

'I don't mind you asking at all. There hasn't. I've not felt like I've needed anyone in my life up till now, and until I met Vinnie, there was no one that I'd felt really drawn to. Does that sound a bit soppy?'

'I'm a big believer in fate, Grace, and that people come into your life at the exact time and for the exact reason that they are meant to. I really hope that's what's happening with you and Vinnie. You may have gathered by now that I love him to bits, even if he is a pain in the neck from time to time.' She laughed. 'Working here, I do a lot of people-watching and I'm very observant, I'll have you know. I notice that when you speak about Mark, you seem to shrink inside yourself, yet when we talk about

Vinnie your whole face lights up and you smile from ear to ear, and that fills my heart with joy and warmth. Now, the other thing that warms my heart, but sadly ends up on my backside, is cake, and I have cake galore, which needs eating up before I throw it out. Let me bring some over.'

'Oh dear, that's not going to help when I go to fat club later! But it's cake and I'd rarely say no to cake, although I did decline earlier.' Grace groaned. 'I hate fat club but I need to go.'

'Why do you go if you hate it?' Ruth asked.

'I need to lose some weight and this seems to be the only way I can do it, although the woman who runs the group is a nightmare. I'd love to set up my own group but it's knowing where to have it and how to do it. Just a little dream of mine. I'd love to do a meals-on-wheels-type service, too, for people who are working but would love home-cooked food that follows the fat club principles but haven't got the time or ingredients to do their own. Perhaps it should be called something to do with laziness! I'd love to run a book club as well. But that'll have to wait till I get my dream bookshop. Perhaps I can do my fat club there. I have too many ideas running around in my head all the time. It's why I don't sleep well.' She laughed.

Ruth looked thoughtful. 'You could always do it here. With me.'

'Well, to be honest, when I came in the other week, I came because I was looking to find a venue,' Grace replied, delighted that her little daydream might actually come true.

'Well, here is perfect, isn't it? My café is closed at five p.m. You could do a fat club here. There's plenty of room and maybe those who came would come back as customers at other times, so it would be good for my business too. And I'm a trained nutritionist and chef. I'm bloody wasted here.' She laughed. 'Let's do it together, Grace! Life is too short not to grab opportunities as they come up. I've been looking at different ways to get new customers and didn't think of your idea. It's genius. There's times in the day that I have nothing to do and I'm just twiddling my thumbs waiting for customers to come in. I could be in the kitchen cooking up some of these meals if you give me the recipes. Then people can order and either pick them up or we could eventually even do a delivery service. Between us, we could really make this work!' said Ruth, clapping her hands with excitement. 'I think people would bloody love it. They can have a cuppa for free when they get here, then pay for any additional food or drinks. Oh, Grace, I love this idea. Please say we can do it.'

Grace laughed. 'I'd really love it, Ruth. Are you sure, though? We've only just met really.'

'We have but I have a really good feeling about you, Grace. I like you a lot and even if things don't work out with you and Vinnie, I'd like to think that we could be good friends. And this is a great idea. I'd love to be a part of it.'

Ruth glanced over to the counter where a big queue was forming and jumped to her feet. 'I could sit here and talk to you all day, Grace, but the daggers that Beth is throwing at me tells me it's time my coffee break is over! Can we talk about it soon and get some dates in the diary? This is going to be great, Grace, I just know it. Let me bring you another coffee over and you can get your notepad and pen out. I know you don't go anywhere without them, Vinnie told me! You can put your thoughts down and we can discuss them later.'

Grace sat and smiled and got out her latest hand-stitched notebook and her fountain pen. Apart from her stationery fetish, she was a big journal writer and had recently started to write a gratitude journal again. This was something she had always done as a child, but when she was with Mark, he ridiculed her and dismissed it, saying that all the 'hippy shit' was addling her brain and she needed to get in the real world.

She once bought a yearly book where she could write down all her goals and dreams, and Mark just laughed at her and threw it away, saying that she hadn't the time to follow her goals and dreams as she had him and Archie to look after. So once again, to keep the peace, she'd stopped keeping her journals. One of the best things about being single and following her own whims was being able to start up her gratitude journal again and work out her goals and desires, without someone trying to pour scorn onto it.

She was so grateful to Ruth for providing the venue for this new club that she'd been thinking about. The ideas just wouldn't go away, constantly niggling at the back of her mind. She'd wanted to do it but hadn't known where to start. But now she had a venue, someone fabulous to do it with, and she was really looking forward to getting this idea off the ground. She loved her job but felt that something was missing from her life, especially the times when Archie wasn't around. She knew she was going to enjoy organising this club and was really glad that she'd mentioned it to Ruth. Who knew that just saying the words out loud would make some of her dreams come true?

Ruth came over with her diary and Grace left the café after agreeing dates for the rest of the year. They had to start somewhere. They had no idea who or how many people would come along or whether they should charge, and if they did how much. But they agreed that Grace would set up a Facebook page for the group and they would share it, asking their friends to share too, and she knew that Monica, her biggest cheerleader, would spread the word with some of her clients. It was all getting quite exciting. Ruth also suggested getting up some posters in the café to promote the meetings. They would just see what sat right at the time and how the group and the idea evolved. It was really all in the hands of heaven above.

* * *

I do love that Ruth. She's helping my girl's dreams come true. Grace, I was willing you to share your hopes and dreams with Ruth. You just need a push from time to time. You've got some fabulous ideas but just need the self-confidence to follow them through and make them happen. I know that you can do anything you set your mind to and now you've got these amazing people in your life, I know you're going to go from strength to strength. I wish you just had that faith in yourself that others have in you.

But I can see your light starting to shine again from within. You have that sparkle back in your eyes and a fire in your belly and an enthusiasm for life that I've not seen for a long time. I never want you to have that sparkle dulled again, and I know that Vinnie is someone who will encourage and inspire you to do great things in your life. That's what being in a relationship should be: two people, wanting to make the other happy and inspiring each other to achieve their goals and dreams and making an amazing future together full of memories.

Because let's face it, memories are all that's left after you've gone. Possessions break, pictures fade, but hopefully memories will remain in your heart long after a person has left your life. I hope I left my girls some wonderful memories of me. I think I did! I certainly tried to be the best mother that I possibly could. I was strict but fair... although you two might not agree! But I loved you both with all my heart and you knew it. And I made sure I told you every single day. I even remember lying in my hospital bed, just before I was taken, and telling you both how much I loved you. I needed those words to be the last you ever heard from my mouth. And I know that you haven't forgotten.

I love you. You'll always be my little girl even if you're nearer forty than four or fourteen and I'm always watching you, just giving you a gentle shove, or a bloody great big one, when you need it.

Love you, Mum xxx

* * *

Saturday night had come round quicker than Grace thought possible. While she knew she'd made a lot of progress in the last few months, with a number of changes in her life, including getting a job, buying a house and renovating it on her own, thinking more positively, changing her hair and her clothes, she still had the same insecurities. She supposed years of allowing someone to make her feel not good enough for them, despite trying to do everything she could, had rubbed off and it was those feelings that she was trying so hard to shake now.

Belinda turned up at six thirty armed with DVDs and popcorn ready to sit with Archie for the evening while Grace went to the awards ceremony. Belinda wolf-whistled at Grace and told her she'd never seen her look so beautiful.

Mark had said he wanted a drink so would get a taxi to Stafford town centre and meet her at the entrance at ten to seven. Grace had agreed readily, feeling that the less time she had to spend with him the better.

She felt a million dollars in the turquoise cocktail dress that Monica had talked her into on their swishing trip, the colours of the dress blending beautifully with her aqua aura crystal necklace. As the taxi pulled up, she noticed that Mark was waiting on the steps of the town hall. She watched him through the window; he looked handsome in his tuxedo, and her mind flashed back to when they were younger and very much in love. He didn't look that much older now to be honest, just greying around his temples, and a little stouter, but it suited him. A lump formed in her throat and she swallowed down a twinge of regret for everything that had once been. It took her breath away how two people who had so much promise for the future could now be living such separate lives.

She paid the driver and turned to Mark, who whistled and winked at her and took her arm as they made their way into the building. The next person she bumped into was Edward, her boss, who was looking out for her. She introduced Mark to him, and Edward shook his hand.

'You look stunning, Grace, really stunning,' he

said as he kissed her on her cheek and introduced Mark to his wife and business partner, Melanie. Grace loved Melanie. She was fun and bright; a real pleasure to work with. Once again, Grace thought about how lucky she was to have found a job with such a friendly and supportive team. They immediately started chatting as they headed over to their table where the rest of the team were already seated. They all greeted her and Mark warmly, and Grace smiled at them all, trying to quell her inner nerves. Not only was she was worried about the prospect of having to get up on stage – not that she really thought she was in with a chance – but she'd found the whole dressing up thing so stressful. She might have had a major make-over and felt a long way from the old frumpy Grace who wanted to hide from the eyes of the world, but she still found it all quite nerve-wracking.

The meal was probably lovely, but Grace was so discombobulated about the whole evening that she could hardly eat a thing. The first few awards categories and the winners were announced and then it was time for the Business Superstar award. She didn't think for one minute that she'd win and believed it was a complete mistake that her name was even included. Part of her had been expecting someone to get in touch and tell her that they'd make a mistake, so she didn't really know why she was feeling nervous. There were so many other local businesses that she'd heard of in the local press, so she was flabbergasted when the nominations were called out, and the winner's name announced – it was hers! She really couldn't believe it. She was actually delighted and felt a little gobsmacked. Edward and Melanie beamed at her.

The Lord Mayor asked Edward to join them on stage and suggested that he'd perhaps like to say a few words about why he felt Grace deserved the award.

Edward got up and offered Grace his arm, and they made their way to the stage, Grace slowly and precisely, praying silently that she wouldn't trip and make a tit of herself. She arrived unscathed and was helped up the steps by Edward.

'Melanie and I couldn't be prouder of Grace than we are of our own children at a school awards evening.' The audience laughed and Grace relaxed a little. 'She has come such a long way since she joined our family estate agency a year ago, and she's brought her light and her sparkle to the team and we adore having her around. She's amazing at her job, the customers love her and she's a pleasure to work with.

'When Grace started, she joined us as a part-time member of staff but made a role for herself that we could never do without now. She came up with an idea of videoing houses, which our house buyers love and which makes both vendors and buyers come to us. She's hit way above her sales target and been a mentor for many of the younger staff coming through the ranks.

'Thank you, Grace, for being you. I couldn't think of a better person to work alongside, apart from my good lady wife, of course.' He winked at Melanie and blew her a kiss. 'Huge congratulations on your award, Grace.'

What an amazing speech. How on earth could she follow that?

In a timid little voice, she started to speak. 'After being a stay-at-home mum for such a long time, it was really hard to get back into the workplace.' She looked up and saw lots of faces smiling, and it gave her the boost she needed and her voice became more confident and louder. 'But Edward, you and Melanie gave me a chance. A chance to prove myself, and for that I shall be eternally grateful. I absolutely love my job, love that you allow me to fit it in around my son and I would like to thank everyone for voting for me to win this amazing award. Thank you all so much.'

Loud applause broke out in the room and whoops of delight could be heard from their table as she and Edward left the stage. Melanie got up and kissed her on both cheeks, then Mark stood up and hugged her. He kissed the top of her head.

'I'm so proud of you,' he said.

It felt like such an intimate moment, one that hadn't happened for such a long time. Grace felt stunned by his response.

'You must be very proud of your ex-wife, Mark,' Edward said as he returned to his seat.

'Yeah, of course I am.' Mark grinned. He raised his glass of champagne to Grace and toasted her. The table joined in and he smiled at her, his eyes lighting up.

As the event drew to a close, Mark walked Grace to the taxi rank and suggested that they go back to hers for a coffee. He winked at her and said that Lorraine was out this evening at a club in Birmingham so he wasn't expected to be home for a good couple of hours yet, and he suggested they have a nightcap with their coffee. He nuzzled into her neck, in that special place that always used to make her spine tingle. And he knew it.

She hated the fact that she knew she should say no but felt she would be rude if she refused. Despite herself, she found herself leaning into his embrace, but she swiftly thought of Belinda and made an excuse that she needed to get back to the babysitter.

As the taxi pulled up at her house, she quickly said goodnight, gratefully thanked the driver, flung a tenner at Mark for her share of the cost and got out as quickly as she could. When she got in the house and shut the door behind her, she was grateful for a lucky escape.

* * *

On Sunday morning, Grace's heart gave a little flip when she noticed Vinnie's name flash up on the caller display of her iPhone, and she smiled as she answered. They'd been texting each other every day and she knew he'd had a really busy week at work. She hadn't mentioned that Mark was going to the awards with her. Not because she wanted to lie to him, but because it wasn't important to her.

'Hey, you!' His voice was warm and comforting and made her feel like someone had wrapped a big fleecy blanket around her shoulders.

'Hey, you!' she said back. 'What a nice surprise. I thought you were ringing tonight.'

'Well, I was but I thought, what the hell, I'm too old to play games, Grace. I wanted to hear your voice so I called. I hope that's OK. And obviously I wanted to find out how your awards event went.'

'It's more than OK, Vinnie, and I won. Can you believe it? Little old me, who has never won anything in my life, won!'

'Ah congratulations, Grace, that's such wonderful news. I'm so proud of you.'

Her heart gave another little flip. This was someone that she hardly knew telling her she'd done well. She was over the moon.

'I saw your lovely sister recently. I think I've become addicted to the coffee that she serves.'

'She found it in Italy. I went over there with her when she decided to set up the café as she wanted to show me a hotel she'd stayed in once which had an incredible coffee shop attached to it. It was her dream to have a coffee shop exactly the same over here. The hotel is just incredible. I'd love to take you one day and show you.' He realised he was getting a little carried away. 'Erm, if that's an option, that is!'

'What a lovely idea. I've only ever been to Italy once and I don't have good memories. I went for a drink in a bar and needed the ladies' and they gave me a key, led me down a lane and across a courtyard and into a shed where there was just a big hole in the floor! It really freaked me out and put me off ever going back!'

Vinnie laughed and it filled her with joy. His laugh was deep and sexy and she loved hearing it. 'I promise you that there are proper porcelain toilets in the place that I stay. It's a stunning little boutique hotel, and the owners are amazing. You wake up every day to the smell of freshly baked bread and pastries and freshly roasted coffee, and the patio is just through the double doors and overlooks glorious lush green mountains on one side and stunning turquoise sparkling sea on the other.'

'Stop telling me, Vinnie, you sound like an advert on their website. You've already sold it to me. It sounds divine and I want to go there right now!' She laughed. *Wouldn't it be fun to just hop on a plane and do something so spontaneous?* she thought.

'Don't tempt me! Anyway, the reason for the call, as well as the fact that I wanted to hear your voice, was that I wondered if I might have the pleasure of your company on Saturday evening, madam? Lady Ruth has invited you and me round for dinner, if that's not too much too soon.'

'Aw, that would be fab. I really like Ruth and I'd love to meet her hubby too. We've just decided that we're going to do a fat club together. Do you want me to meet you there or pick you up so you can have a drink?'

'I know all about it. She's already told me how excited she is to be working with you on this project. No love, that's fine. I'll pick you up. I'm not much of a drinker and if I change my mind, I can always leave the car and we can grab a taxi back between us.' It was nice to be with someone who wasn't a drinker. Mark liked a drink, and when he drank he became a person she really didn't like, belittling her by saying that she needed to loosen up and have fun. He had always been repentant the next morning, but the damage had been done.

They chatted for another ten minutes, just laughing and joking, really at ease in each other's company. Grace realised that she'd never had this before. She always felt as if she had to be on her best behaviour with Mark in case he didn't like what she said and snapped; yet with Vinnie, who she'd not known that long, she felt really comfortable and knew that she didn't have to put on any airs and graces and could just be herself.

Becks started to bark at her and she realised that

she hadn't taken him out yet. She had a thought. 'What are you up to today, Vinnie?' she asked. 'I'm just going to take Becks out for a walk to the forest. With Archie at his dad's, because we've swapped days around, I'm home alone so thought I'd get out. I don't suppose you fancy joining me, do you?'

'Do you know, I'd really love that. I've sat at my computer since six this morning and I'm going googly-eyed. A walk in the forest sounds perfect. We can grab a cuppa at the café to celebrate your award win.'

'OK, shall I pick you up? It's probably easier because Becks is likely to run off into the streams and get filthy and smelly and at least I can stick him in the boot of my car, which is already quite mucky. Can you be ready in about half an hour? Oh, and by the way, have you eaten? I could put a quick sandwich together and a flask if you like?'

'Sounds perfect, gorgeous, I'll text you my address. I'd better flick the duster round before you come just in case I can entice you in for a coffee afterwards. It's the stuff my sister sells...'

'Ooh, I bet you say that to all the girls. Cool, see you in half an hour then, and don't dust on my account, Vinnie. Housework is for people who don't spend their lives having fun!' She laughed as she disconnected the call.

She realised just how much she'd changed recently. The old Grace, when expecting visitors, would have been running round the place like a thing demented, spraying polish into the air so it least smelt like it was clean and shoving things in drawers and storage boxes to give the illusion of a clean and tidy house. It was amazing how quickly you could get housework done when you knew someone was about to descend upon you. But with Vinnie, Grace had the sense that none of that mattered.

* * *

Grace picked up Vinnie exactly thirty minutes later. He was dressed casually in jeans, walking boots and a navy long-sleeved t-shirt. He looked incredibly sexy and Grace smiled to herself.

As he jumped into the passenger side of the car, he turned round to the back and said, 'Hey, Becks!' as naturally as if it was one of his mates. 'I love walking, but you feel such a jerk on your own, don't you?' he said. 'I've always wanted a dog but it's difficult when I work such long hours, wouldn't be fair on one. I'll have to borrow Becks next time I fancy a walk.'

'You can, or you're welcome to join us anytime. I

know what you mean though about walking on your own. I would never have dreamt of doing that before I had him. I always wanted to but never had the courage to go out on my own.'

'How long have you had him?'

'Just under a year. It just seemed like the right time and he's great company for me when Archie is at his dad's. Saves me talking to myself, anyway!' Grace laughed.

They pulled up in the small car park and she grabbed a rucksack out of the boot as Becks jumped out. They walked briskly for around a mile as Becks sniffed every blade of grass he came across, and weed up most of the trees, before they found a picnic bench and decided that it was time for a pit stop. Grace poured coffee from an aluminium flask into two plastic mugs and opened up a big plastic box which revealed a whole host of savoury food: sausage rolls, chicken bites, satay sticks, scotch eggs, pork pies and crisps.

'Blimey, Grace, you know how to put on a snack. I'll be the size of a house if I keep walking with you guys.'

'Then you'll just have to come to our fat club, won't you?' She laughed. 'I take after my mum. She was a feeder too.'

The walk had made them both ravenous and after they'd polished off the lot between them, they started walking again.

The closer they walked together, the more they touched each other and each touch felt like an electric current soaring through their bodies. Vinnie suddenly stopped walking and Grace stood still too, puzzling over why he was standing still. He swept up a big section of her hair to one side which had blown into her face, tucked it behind her ear and kissed her gently but fully on the lips. He smiled and carried on walking and she caught up with him. He grinned at her, took her hand in his, kissed it, tucked it under the crook of his arm and then didn't let go. Neither of them seemed to be able to stop smiling.

'I don't think I've ever felt this comfortable with anyone before, Grace. Just walking side by side, we don't even have to be talking, it just feels right to be here with you. Does that sound a bit mad? Am I scaring you with too much too soon?' he asked.

'Not at all, I love it!' she responded. 'It just feels good and right and I feel like I've known you all my life, if that doesn't sound too forward.'

They smiled at each other and a kind of deep understanding passed between them. They'd got to the end of the walk and were nearing the car park again.

'What are you doing for the rest of the day, Grace?' Vinnie asked.

'Not much planned to be honest. I have to be back by six as that's what time Archie is back but apart from that, nothing.'

'So can I persuade you and Becks to come back to mine and curl up on the settee and watch a film, do you think?'

'Are you sure you want that furry smelly monster in your house? He needs a good wipe down first.'

'Well, I've got some old towels and a sponge knocking around in the airing cupboard. I'm sure we could give him a bed bath!'

'Ooh, he'd love that! Not!'

'He'll be fine, won't you, mate?' he said to the dog while ruffling the fur on his head. Becks licked his hand and raised his head in a look of complete adoration.

'See, he's my buddy! Leave it to me.'

'OK, if you insist, but don't say I didn't warn you.'

When they got back, Vinnie went into the house first and grabbed some old towels and a sponge. He kneeled down by the front door. 'Come on then, boy,' he said as he patted his knees. Becks bounded up to him and jumped up, nearly knocking him over. Where Mark would have hit the roof, Vinnie just laughed and rolled around on the floor with him, Becks licking his face. Then Becks sat obediently and did everything Vinnie told him to while he gave him a wash down and dried him.

'Amazing!' said Grace. 'I definitely think you have a new best friend.'

'Come on, boy, let's see what we can find you for a treat,' he said, opening and closing cupboard doors. 'What can I give him?' He looked at Grace for advice.

'This might sound a bit mad, but do you have any carrots?'

'I do. They're in the fridge. Will that be OK? I've never heard of a dog eating carrots before. Are you sure?'

'I hadn't either, but they're good for their teeth apparently and it'll keep him quiet for a while.'

He gave Becks the carrot and walked over to where Grace was standing, putting his hands on her shoulders and kissing the top of her head. 'Fancy a cuppa?'

'Mmm, please,' she responded. 'Can I do anything?'

'No, sweetheart, all under control. Why don't you go in the lounge and see what films we can watch.'

Grace walked into the room that Vinnie had indicated and took a look around. It was obvious that it was a man's room. It had a black leather suite and there was a footrest with some car and men's health magazines on it. His Apple Mac sat on a low black glass-topped table in the far corner and there were very few knick-knacks around. As she looked around the room, her eyes caught a photograph on the mantelpiece of him and Ruth together and another of him with his arms around a beautiful young woman, standing on the side of a mountain, bathed in sunshine. It was the lady whose picture was in his wallet. Vinnie looked like he adored the very ground that she walked on. You could see the love in his eyes. Her heart caught in her mouth.

She picked up the photo and looked at it in detail. The woman was tall, slender, blonde, beautiful, young, vibrant and full of life. She was wearing a white skimpy vest and very short shorts. She was quite simply stunning. Grace was gutted. Her heart sank to the bottom of her boots. She felt green with envy and could feel jealousy surging through her body. This girl couldn't be further away from herself – she was everything that Grace wasn't. Grace was short, curvaceous and dark, and she couldn't help but wonder who this beautiful lady was. She was obviously someone very important to Vinnie, if the photo was still on the mantelpiece, yet everything she knew about him told her that he was single.

'Ah, you've seen the photo then,' Vinnie said as he walked into the lounge balancing a tray in his hands while Becks danced around his ankles.

'Yep!' Grace looked at him.

'I should explain,' he said as he put the tray down and took the photo out of Grace's hand and touched the glass, stroking the girl's face tenderly. Grace felt sick with jealousy.

'This is Meredith. I loved her so much. She's stunning, isn't she?'

'She is indeed,' replied Grace, wondering what on earth was going on and why he was telling her about how much he loved another girl.

'My beautiful brave girl,' he said, his voice catching on his words. He took a deep breath.

'Are you OK, Vinnie?' Grace asked, wondering about his emotional reaction.

'Yes thanks, I might just need a hug though.'

Grace stepped over to him and hugged him, even though she was confused as to why she was comforting him when he was clearly so devasted about an ex-girlfriend. Especially one who was stunning to look at!

'Perhaps I'd better tell you about my Meredith.'

Sit down, Grace.' He sat on the sofa and patted the seat next to him. 'Meredith was the most incredible girl I've ever known. Full of life, full of adventure and full of love. She meant the world to me. I loved her so much.'

Grace couldn't move; she felt compelled to listen even though she knew he was about to say something she really didn't want to hear.

'She was just twenty-one when she died of leukaemia. It was discovered way too late and the illness was short and over quickly and we could do nothing to help her. I've never felt so helpless in my life. I loved that girl with all my heart. I still can't believe that my little sister was taken away from me!'

'Your sister? Oh my God, Vinnie, your sister? How awful.' She hugged him tightly, knowing that it was hard for him to have to explain. She wanted to kick herself for being such a jealous bitch, but she really had thought it was an ex. Now that she knew the truth, she felt dismayed at her initial jealous reaction, and empathy for this man, having to go through the pain of losing a sibling. She couldn't imagine how that must have felt and she vowed to ring Hannah as soon as she could to tell her how much she loved her.

Vinnie wiped his eyes. 'God, I'm so sorry! I'm not

normally so open. I've shielded my heart for so long because I thought it would never mend after Meredith had gone, but I feel like I can – and need to – open up to you, Grace, and let you into my life. What have you done to me?'

She put her hands on either side of his face and wiped away his tears with her thumbs. She kissed the place where the tears had gently rolled down his cheeks. 'I am *so* sorry that you went through this Vinnie,' she said. 'I couldn't even begin to imagine how you could get over something like this.'

'But it's strange, Grace, because for the first time in a very long time, I actually feel like I'm ready to move on from this part of my life and start a new chapter. It's almost like she's willing me to do it. Meredith leaving us hit Ruth and me really hard, but we know that we can't continue to live in the past, wishing that she was going to walk through the door, because it's never going to happen. I know it's time to move on. We'll never forget Meredith but we have to learn to live our lives without her.

'Since I met you, Grace, I feel like I finally have something special to look forward to. I feel like I can finally start to see some light at the end of a very dark tunnel. I haven't had anyone special in my life for a long time. I suppose what happened with

Meredith broke my heart and I just didn't want to put my feelings out there again to be bashed around any further.

'I don't know what the future holds for you and I but I have a good feeling, a really good feeling, that we could have something really special together and I'd like us to explore that. God, I hope that's not too heavy for a Sunday afternoon. I sound like a big girl's blouse and a stalker rolled into one!'

Grace laughed, realising that she was relieved he'd acknowledged the fact that there wasn't anyone else in his life. 'You don't sound like those things at all, you sound like a wonderful human being who adored his little sister. I do know what you mean about us, though. I know we've not known each other for long but this just feels so right. I know it's early days but I also think we have something special, and I'd love to see where this goes. How does that sound?' She kissed him long and lingeringly on the lips and gave him a hug that said lots of things. Becks started barking and jumped up excitedly, which made them both laugh out loud. 'Now, are you going to pour that coffee out or not?'

They sat side by side on the sofa watching a comedy, which lightened the mood somewhat. Becks crept up onto the sofa and put his head on Vinnie's lap. Grace went to move him off but Vinnie said he was happy for Becks to join them. He rested one hand on Becks's head and the other held Grace's, as she snuggled into his shoulder and realised that she never wanted to move from that spot. They stayed like that until Grace realised the time; she needed to head home soon as Mark would be bringing back Archie. Grace felt that this afternoon had been a pivotal point in her and Vinnie's relationship and that they had shared something incredibly special. She hoped that it would be the first of many special moments.

Vinnie popped to the loo, and his phone was on the coffee table. It pinged to say there was a message and she couldn't help but look at it. It was from someone called Ellie and it simply said:

Ring me, it's urgent.

Her heart sank and she had a really bad feeling in her tummy. She knew it could be something, and she knew it could be nothing.

When Vinnie came back downstairs, he quickly looked at the phone, frowned and put it in his back pocket. Grace kissed him on the cheek and drove home, her mind full of what ifs and maybes.

Would she ever learn to trust someone again? Perhaps she was better off with Mark. At least she already knew he was a shit sometimes. At least she wasn't trying to get the measure of someone all over again. Perhaps it was a case of better the devil you know.

18

She arrived home and was just getting Becks out of the car as Mark and Archie pulled up. Archie ran up to her and flung his arms around her as if he hadn't seen her for days.

'Hello, gorgeous, how are you?'

'I'm better now I'm with you, Mummy,' he replied. 'Can I go on my Xbox?'

'Oh, OK, but only for half an hour,' said Grace, wondering how she was going to have tea and get Archie in the bath, and get some of his school reading done, all before bed, once he'd got on the Xbox. And it would have been nice for some snuggling up on the sofa time before he went to bed.

'You're too soft on him. You can say no to him,

you know.' Mark laughed as he saw her brain whirring, and Archie ran upstairs to his room.

She laughed back at him and was glad that things between them had been better lately. They seemed to have reached a truce and it was all quite a relief.

'OK then, Archie, say goodbye to Daddy,' she shouted up to him. 'We've got lots to do so hurry up, sweetie.'

He ran back downstairs and hugged his dad goodbye, and she said a cheery goodbye herself and shut the door, feeling relieved that her world was now complete again now her boy was home, where she felt that he belonged.

'Do I have to go to Dad's all the time, Mum? You know I'd rather be here with you instead. It's so boring at his house. I don't have my own bedroom and he and Lorraine are always yelling at each other. I think sometimes they forget I'm there. All Dad does is watch TV or work. I even asked him if he'd listen to me read earlier and he said he hadn't got time, but then sat and watched the Chelsea match on the telly.'

'Dad would miss you so much if he didn't see you darling, you know that.'

'I don't think he'd even notice whether I'm there or not,' he mumbled as Becks suddenly realised that his buddy was home and came running towards Archie, giving him a great big lick. Archie's frown disappeared and his beautiful smile returned when he saw his furry friend. Becks rolled over on his back and let Archie tickle his tummy.

'Come on, gorgeous, I baked your favourite chocolate brownies this morning. I think you deserve one!'

'Just one?' he asked with a cheeky grin that he knew wrapped his mother around his little finger.

'We'll see. You don't just bat your eyelashes at me and get your own way,' she replied, and he grinned back at her and fluttered away, knowing that he absolutely would get his own way, like he always did.

'What have you been doing today, Mummy? Have you had a nice day?'

'I have, darling, thank you. Do you remember I told you that I had a friend called Vinnie?'

'Mmm?' Archie said suspiciously.

'Well, I was taking Becks for a nice long walk over the forest and Vinnie asked if he could come with me, so he did. We had a bit of a picnic, then I went back to Vinnie's house for a cuppa and watched a film, then Becks and I came home as we were looking forward to getting our boy back.'

'Mummy, is Vinnie your boyfriend?'

'I'm not sure what to call him,' she replied honestly. 'I do like him though, he's a very nice man. I like him a lot. I think I'm a bit too old to call him a boyfriend.'

'So when can I meet him?' he asked.

That was unexpected!

'I'm not sure, darling, would you like to meet him?'

'Mummy, are you for real? This is someone who you spend time with when I'm not here. Of course I want to meet him. I want to make sure he's nice to you. I know that Dad sometimes isn't and I do tell him that, you know! I tell him that he's not to upset you, that you are my mummy and that I don't like it when he's nasty. I need to ask this Vinnie man lots of questions, so can you arrange it as soon as possible? Can you ring him now and ask him over one of the days this week?' Sometimes, it amazed her just how grown up her son was for a ten-year-old.

'Oh, OK love, I'll give him a ring soon. But for now, we need to sort tea and you can do some of your reading while the bath is running.'

Her heart pounded. She needed to know exactly what she had with Vinnie before she introduced him to Archie. He said all the right things, and when she was with him she felt that he only had eyes for her –

but she couldn't help but think of the feeling that she got when she saw that text message. Women's intuition, they called it, and she was definitely feeling something odd. Perhaps Vinnie wasn't the man she thought he was, after all. But then, it could be totally innocent. God, this dating lark was really hard.

She and Vinnie hadn't discussed him meeting Archie yet, and she wondered how he would feel when she asked him to meet her son. She knew now that she'd have to broach the topic with him when she next spoke to him. She knew that she'd have to mention the text message that she'd seen at some point, but when did you bring up something like that? It had already played on her mind constantly since she'd come home, so she knew that it should be sooner rather than later and vowed to do it the next time she spoke to him before she chickened out.

She didn't have to wait long. While Archie was splashing around in the bath, and she was sitting on the toilet seat reading to him, the phone rang and Vinnie's name flashed up on the screen.

'Is that him?' Archie asked.

'It is!'

'Speak to him, then!' Archie said, grinning from ear to ear.

She answered the call and took a deep breath. 'Hi, Vinnie, how are you?'

'I'm good, Grace, thanks, are you? Just wanted to say thanks for a lovely afternoon. I'm glad we talked about Meredith. I didn't really know how to bring it up in conversation. It's not really the sort of thing you just drop in, is it?'

'I suppose not, but I'm glad you told me.'

Grace walked out of the bathroom.

'Ask him, Mum, ask him!' Archie shouted from the bath. 'Please, please, please.'

Grace took a deep breath and decided that she would keep her fears to herself for now. 'Vinnie, I'm sorry but I have a very impatient little man here who says that I have to ask you something. I hope you don't mind.'

'Go on...'

'Archie would like you to come round so he can meet you. Are you free one day this week at all? Perhaps you could pop in for a cuppa one night, I'd love the two of you to meet.' She waited apprehensively for his response. She didn't know when the right time would be to introduce a new partner – if that's what he was – and her child to each other. It wasn't a problem she'd ever had to consider before and she squirmed a little, finding herself out of her comfort zone.

'I'd love that, Grace, I really would. When would be good for you?'

'Oh, erm, how about Tuesday evening, around five. Would that be OK for you?'

'That's definitely good for me. Perfect, in fact. Thanks, Grace, I'd really like that. I can't wait to meet him. I hope he likes me!'

Grace smiled, hoping that Archie and Vinnie got on too. They chatted for a few more minutes before it was time to get Archie out of the bath. He said he wanted to go into his bedroom as he had some 'private stuff' to do, so she left him for fifteen minutes before calling him down for dinner. When she asked him what he'd been doing, he said 'nothing much'. She was well aware that as Archie was growing up, he needed a little private time. She'd had to get used to the fact that he needed space. She hoped that through his teen years they'd still have the fabulous relationship that they'd always had and that he wouldn't withdraw from her.

After dinner, they finished Archie's reading sat on his bed, snuggling up. Grace's mind kept wandering off to the text message that she'd seen. Was it something to be worried about? Was it too early to be introducing Archie to Vinnie? Oh God! She really hoped she was doing the right thing.

* * *

Tuesday came round and Grace felt on edge all day. She was so nervous about the two very important men in her life meeting each other. Archie raced upstairs when they got home from the school run, shutting himself in his room. When the doorbell rang at five, she walked towards the front door, yelling at Archie to come downstairs. He stood halfway down the stairs apprehensively and as she turned to look at him before she opened the door, she noticed that he was no longer wearing his school trousers and polo shirt but had changed into a shirt and tie. She smiled as she let Vinnie in.

'Hi, Grace,' he said breezily as he kissed her on the cheek, and she stood back to let him inside the hallway.

'And you must be Archie,' he said, leaning up towards him, holding out his hand. 'I've heard so much about you from your mum.'

Archie looked him up and down before shaking his hand as firmly as a ten-year-old can. 'I am. And I'm the man of the house.' Grace's mouth twitched as she tried not to smile. 'So, you must be Vinnie...' he said in a voice that was much gruffer and deeper than his normal voice.

'That's right, I am,' Vinnie said as Becks ran up to him and gave a little bark as if to say hello.

'I've brought you a little something, Archie. I hope that's OK,' Vinnie said, handing him a carrier bag.

'Oh!' said Archie as he peered into the bag. His deep big man's voice was soon forgotten as he squealed with joy. 'Oh wow! Mum, look! It's FIFA 18 for the Xbox! I've wanted this for ages. That's awesome. Did Mum tell you? Thanks so much, Vinnie.'

Vinnie and Archie high-fived each other. 'I don't know how it works though, do you?' Archie asked.

'I do, I play it all the time, and yes, your Mum told me you are an Xbox addict and had some of the older FIFA games when she saw my Xbox at my house,' Vinnie replied.

'Really? You do? Mum, could Vinnie come up to my room and show me how to work it?' he asked.

'Erm, does Vinnie mind?' Grace asked.

'I'd love to, mate!'

'Fab, come on then, follow me!'

Vinnie winked at Grace over his shoulder as they bounded up the stairs and she went into the kitchen and flicked the switch on the kettle. She didn't know whether she needed a cup of coffee or a glass of wine. Her nerves were in tatters.

Whoops of joy and lots of laughter could be heard from upstairs as she made a cup of tea, but as she walked up the stairs with the drinks, the room went quiet and she heard Archie say to Vinnie, 'I hope you don't mind but I've made a list of some questions that I'd like to ask you. Would that be OK?'

'Sure it would, mate, fire away.'

Grace tiptoed closer and peeked round the door.

Archie grabbed a piece of paper from under his bed. This must have been what he was doing the night before when he told Grace he had 'private stuff' to do.

'How old are you?' Archie asked.

'Thirty-five,' Vinnie replied.

'Ever been married?'

'Nope, have you?'

Archie giggled. 'No. There is a girl at school who I quite like, but I'm not sure I'd like to marry her.'

'Ah, well perhaps you need to get to know each other. You never know what the future holds, do you, mate? Is she pretty?'

'She's very pretty and she wears glasses so she's *very* clever too.'

'That's good, beauty and brains. You'll be a lucky boy if you win her heart.'

'Do you like my mum?'

'I do, I like her very much.'

'Do you like Becks?'

'I do, I think he's really cool.'

'Do you ever get drunk?'

'No, mate, I like a glass of wine from time to time but I'm not a big drinker at all. How about you?'

Archie giggled again. 'I don't think I'm ever going to drink alcohol. My dad and his girlfriend drink lots of red wine and I don't like it because they get really loud and shout at each other and it scares me.'

'Oh, mate, I'm sorry to hear that. I did get quite drunk once when I was really young but I didn't like it so I've never done it again.'

'Are you very rich?'

'I do alright. How about you?'

'I have about ninety pounds in my piggy bank right now. Do you have more than that?'

'A little bit more than that.'

'Ah, OK! Who is your favourite football team?'

'Aston Villa of course! Who else?'

'Oh fab! They're my favourite team too. I'd love to go and see them one day.'

'Well perhaps we could go together one day, mate?'

'Sick! I like the sound of that! Do you have any children?'

'I don't. I wish I had but I don't.'

'Do you like children?'

'I do. I'm an uncle to two brilliant girls and a boy. Bella is twelve, going on twenty-one, Rebecca is the same age as you and George is six. I adore them and spend as much time as I can with them when I'm not working.'

'But you'd like a child of your own one day?'

'It would be really cool, but if I don't, that would be fine too. I have lots of lovely children in my life. And now I've met you too so if you don't mind, I could add you to my pretty-cool-children buddies too.'

'I think I'd like that, Vinnie, thanks. On a scale of one to ten, how pretty do you think my mum is?'

'Wow! What a question. I think she's off the scale, to be honest. She's *very* pretty so I'd say around three million four hundred and seventy-one.'

'Good answer! And do you think that one day you might love my mum?'

Grace, listening at the door, exhaled a big breath that she didn't realise she'd been holding in, then tuned in again to hear Vinnie's voice. 'I like your mum. I really like your mum a lot. And I hope that your mum quite likes me too. I'd like to spend more time with her, and perhaps one day that like could turn into love. I think I'd like that very much. But only if that was OK with your mum and you, of course. I'd never want to do anything that might upset her and certainly not you either. I know that you are the most important person in her life.'

Archie pondered on this for a few seconds then said, 'I love my mum *so* much. Do you think you'd love her more than I do?'

'Do you know what, buddy? I think that the love that a mother and her son have between them is extremely special and no one could ever love their mother in the way that a child can. And no one could ever come between that love. And I don't know your mum very well yet, but I can tell that she loves you more than she probably would ever love anyone. But love can come in different shapes and sizes. I think love is about looking after someone and making sure you do things that make them happy as much as you can. I'd like to make your mum happy, but in a different way to the way that she feels about you. Does that make any sense at all?'

'So you wouldn't love her more than me, just different to me?'

'Yep, that's about right!'

Archie pondered on that for a few seconds, judging by the silence.

'Then, yes! That's fine by me. Do you think you might marry my mum?'

Vinnie took a sharp intake of breath. 'I think it's very early days yet, buddy, but I'm not against marriage if two people really love each other.'

'So if you married my mum, would that make you my new dad?'

'No, mate, not at all. You only get one mum and one dad. If, and that's a big if, I was to ever marry your mum, I would be your mate, we'd do super-cool stuff together, but I'd never try to be your dad.'

'So you'd never tell me off?'

'Ah, that's a tricky one. Why, are you planning on misbehaving?'

Archie giggled again. 'Not really, but sometimes Dad makes me stay up really late and I get really tired and a bit grumpy the next day. Then he shouts at me and says I'm horrible and naughty.'

'Oh, mate, I'm sure he doesn't mean it. Perhaps he's just a bit frustrated sometimes and maybe tired himself. Adults get a bit grumpy sometimes if they're tired.'

'But you wouldn't shout at me, would you?'

Grace thought it was about time she intervened and put down the tray she was carrying, wiped away the tear that had trickled from her eye, smiled and knocked on the door. She walked in with the tea tray and a plate of biscuits. 'Not too many for you, young man,' she directed at Archie. 'It's teatime soon.'

'Can Vinnie stay for tea, mum? Please.'

'Vinnie's very welcome to stay for tea if he'd like to.' She looked at Vinnie and he winked at her and her insides turned to mush. Luckily she'd made enough lasagne to feed an army so she was delighted when he said he'd love to stay.

Archie punched the air and high-fived Vinnie and they continued their game. Grace felt a little surplus to requirements but at the same time was truly thrilled that this first meeting was going so well.

'Mum, can you call us when tea's ready? You can go now,' Archie said, dismissing her from his bedroom. 'We're playing FIFA. It's not for girls!'

Vinnie grinned at her over her son's head as she backed out of the room, leaving them sat side by side on Archie's cabin bed. All she could hear was laughter. It was a lovely sound. She noticed when she reached the bottom of the stairs that she had the biggest smile on her face that she'd had for a long time.

* * *

'Guys, dinner's ready!'

Archie and Vinnie came running down the stairs and Archie made Vinnie go into the downstairs toilet and wash his hands, which made her smile. He really was taking his man of the house duties very seriously.

They sat on the stools around the breakfast bar in the kitchen and tucked into lasagne, garlic bread, sweet potato fries and salad.

'My mum is the best cook in the world.'

'I can see that buddy, this is delicious, Grace.' He smiled at her across the table, and her heart melted just a little bit more.

'Can you cook, Vinnie?' asked Archie.

'I can, actually. When you live on your own, you either learn to cook or eat rubbish, so Ruth, my sister, made sure she gave me cooking lessons so I could eat healthily and not just buy stuff that I throw in the microwave.'

'Perhaps one day, Vinnie, Mum and I could come to your house and you could cook tea for us?'

Grace rolled her eyes and mouthed *Sorry!* over Archie's head. Vinnie shook his head.

'Do you know what, mate, I'd really love that. I'll sort that out with your mum.'

After they'd finished tea and Grace was loading the dishwasher, she glanced over and noticed that Archie couldn't have sat closer to Vinnie if he'd tried. Even Becks was at his feet.

'Oh, and Grace, the guys want to come next Monday and get those trees sorted out for you.'

'Yes, that's fab. Can't wait to get some sunshine back into my life.'

'Well, I'm glad to help on that score!' said Vinnie.

If only you knew just how much you already have, thought Grace. Since she and Mark had split, this was the first time she had felt that she could truly look forward to the future.

Vinnie left around seven thirty, leaving Grace to her night-time routine with her son. They snuggled up on Archie's bed and he laid his head on her chest while they read together. She couldn't believe that one of the things she'd learned from helping to set up a reading group at school was that there was a huge percentage of children who never read and were never read to.

Her and Archie's reading time was so special.

Completely magical. He sat so close to her, snuggling in to her ample chest, so close that she could smell the apple-and-melon shampoo that he'd used in the bath earlier. This time of night was their time to put the world to rights, for them to chat about things which had happened during the day and talk over their hopes and dreams for the future. And now Archie was growing up, busy with school and football, she cherished these moments of closeness more than ever, where she could still see her baby in the face of her young handsome son.

'I like Vinnie, Mum, I like him a lot,' he whispered to her. 'I'm happy that you have someone to be with when I'm at Dad's now. I don't want you to be on your own. I'm glad that Vinnie is going to look after you when I'm not here to look after you.'

'Thank you, darling, that means such a lot to me. I love you, my angel, good night and God bless.'

'Good night my beautiful Mummy, I love you too.'

Grace kissed the top of his head, as he snuggled down under the duvet, feeling that her heart could explode at any moment. When he was tired he had a tendency to revert to being much younger.

'Mummy, can I have just one more cuddle please?' he asked.

'Sure can.' She leant over the rail of his bed to get to him. He snuggled right into her and said, 'I love your cuddles so much, Mum, they're the best in the world. I could cuddle you all night.'

'Now that is a lovely thought, darling, but you have school in the morning and need to get some sleep, so just you go to sleep and imagine my arms are around you and you're safe and snug as a bug in a rug.'

'Oookaaay, Mum.' He yawned and within seconds he was snoring, snuffling and dribbling like a pot-bellied pig.

19

When Grace's phone rang the day before dinner at Ruth's, and Mark's name appeared on her screen, her heart slumped. She didn't know why after all this time she still had a very strange 'oh no, what have I done now?' feeling going on right in the pit of her stomach whenever she saw his name on her phone.

'Grace! I need you to have Archie tomorrow night.' No 'please', no asking, just a statement. Experience had taught her that it wasn't worth getting into a prolonged argument about it, so she bit her tongue, saying sweetly, 'OK Mark, what time do you want to drop him off?'

'Oh!' he said, clearly not expecting this response.

'Are you sure that's OK? It's just that Archie mentioned you were going out. I was hoping around six.'

'OK great, see you then. Must fly, I'm just going out. Byeee!' She ended the call. Now all she had to do was tell Vinnie that she wouldn't be able to go to Ruth's for dinner. She called his number but his answerphone kicked in so she left a message explaining what had happened and how sorry she was that the plans for the following evening would have to change.

Five minutes later the phone rang and Grace was delighted when she recognised the voice on the other end.

'Grace, darling, it's Ruth. I've just had a text from Vincent, saying that your ex has changed your plans for tomorrow night. I'm so sorry my love but your plans most certainly have not been scuppered. Just bring Archie with you. My little guy and girls would love to have another playmate. They'll make him feel at home. Bring some jim-jams with you and if he falls asleep you can stick him in one of the spare beds and then take him home when you're ready. How does that sound?'

'Oh, Ruth, you are a love, are you sure? I don't want to put you out at all.'

'Grace, another child when you already have

three doesn't make a blind bit of difference. I'd planned for the kids to have party food in their den while we eat in the dining room, so it's no trouble at all. I insist!'

'That would be lovely, I was really looking forward to coming so thank you for letting me bring Archie.'

'I'm glad he's coming, because it means that our children can meet each other and have some fun. Win-win all round. So we'll see you at seven then? Must fly. I think one of my children is about to murder one of the others! They are lovely, really. Honest! Ta-ta for now!'

Nothing seemed to faze Ruth. She was completely awesome and like a breath of fresh air. Grace really liked her and hoped they would become good friends. She had lots of other friends in her life but had really felt the loss of a sister-character in her life, ever since Hannah had moved to Florida. She got the same warm feeling from Ruth that she did from her big sister. She beamed as her phone beeped to say she had a message.

Sorry I couldn't respond, I'm in a meeting. I've texted Ruth to ask if it's OK to bring Archie tomorrow night. I don't know why I asked really as I knew the answer would be yes! She's going to call you. I'll call you when I'm out of my meeting. Hope you are having a lovely day. Can't stop thinking about you. Vx

Grace's heart did a little leap, reading the words on the screen. This man seemed too good to be true – she just hoped that he was all he appeared to be.

* * *

She didn't know why, but the prospect of going to dinner at Ruth's with Archie made her feel a little apprehensive. When Mark dropped off Archie, Grace stood at the door and didn't invite him in, hoping that he would take the hint and leave.

'Sorry if it's spoilt your night.' He smirked. 'Archie had mentioned that you were going out.'

'Not spoilt my night at all, Mark,' she replied. 'Just means that Archie can come with me, so it's all worked out really well actually.'

Mark's smirk disappeared. She realised that once again, this was just a little game of his and that he'd done it on purpose. She smiled sweetly and dismissed him quickly. 'Come on, darling, say bye to Dad.'

As she shut the door, she exhaled a big sigh.

'You OK, Mummy?'

'OK, Arch? How can I not be OK when the most important person in my life is right here, right now?'

'I love you, Mum.'

'Love you more, sweetie! Now, go and see if there's anything you want to take with you to Vinnie's sister's. We have about forty-five minutes before Vinnie arrives to pick us up. I've put some smart clothes out on your bed so if you can pop them on too, that would be great. I'm just going to put some make-up on and try and make myself look respectable.'

'You don't need make-up, Mum, you're beautiful anyway!'

'Thank you, but I'm a bit sweaty this evening. I'm really hot.'

'Yes you are, Mum!' He giggled.

'You are such a smoothie, Archie.' She smiled, secretly very proud of her beautiful boy who one day would make someone a most fabulous husband.

* * *

'Mum, Vinnie's here. Can I open the door?' Archie had been waiting with his arm around Becks at the lounge window for the longest time, eager to see Vinnie again.

'Yes, darling, you can. I'll just be a minute.'

'Hey dude! How you doing?' Vinnie asked as he came in, high-fived Archie and patted Becks on the head.

'To tell the truth, Vinnie, I think Mum is a bit nervous about tonight.'

'Oh, is that right? There's nothing for her to be nervous about, you know.' Vinnie had a suspicion that Archie was using his mum as an excuse and that it was him who was the nervous one. 'My sister and her family are some of my most favourite people in the world and now you and your mum are on that list too and I think you are all going to get along just brilliantly. The kids are going to love you, you are going to love them too and they are so looking forward to meeting you. They are really rather excited, so my sister tells me.'

'Really? OK, cool,' Archie replied. 'I have to just go to the loo. Dad kept giving me Coke all afternoon and I can't stop weeing. Sorry if that's TMI by the way. Dad kept telling me not to be nervous but I think it's made me worse.'

Vinnie smiled. So Mark had been trying to wind him up. Nice touch, Mark!

Grace bounded down the stairs. She'd worried about what to wear all day, but after hearing Monica's voice in her head as she rummaged through her wardrobe, she'd finally settled on a purple-and-pink wrap dress and neutral-coloured wedges. She grabbed her black faux-fur jacket from the coat rack and popped it round her shoulders as she grabbed a warm coat and a Minions rucksack containing Archie's pyjamas. 'Let's go! See you, Becks.'

They arrived at Ruth's fifteen minutes later. Before they'd even had the chance to ring the front door bell, the door was flung open and Ruth appeared with a pinny on over the top of a lovely flowery vintage tea dress. Grace had only ever seen her in her coffee-shop uniform so it was lovely to see her look so feminine.

'Uncle Vinnie!' yelled three voices, and a hoard of children suddenly appeared at the door, fighting to see who could hug their uncle first.

'Darlings, come out of the way and let these wonderful people through the door and meet Grace and Archie. You've probably already gathered that this is my brood,' she said as she introduced her children one by one. You could tell by the look in her eye that they were her pride and joy.

Archie stood close to Grace, seemingly too shy to say anything, until Harry said, 'Hey, Archie, would you like to come into the den and play FIFA with me? Uncle Vinnie says you are amazing at it and know lots of tricks and I wondered whether you'd teach me.' Archie looked up at Grace for approval, and she bent down to his level, as she always tried to when speaking to him about something important.

'Are you going to go and play, sweetie? I'll be right here if you need me.'

'OK, Mummy,' he said as he turned and smiled at Harry, and before they'd reached the den, Grace could hear laughter.

'Phew! That went well,' said Ruth. 'You look fabulous, darling! Those colours really suit you. Now, what can I get you? We have red, white or rosé wine, or do you fancy a G&T or a Pimms?'

'Oh, a G&T would be perfect please, and I love your dress too,' Grace replied as Ruth led the way to a large kitchen-diner where a very handsome, grey-haired, tall man was stirring something on the cooker.

'Well, I'm in my uniform all day, and when I

come home I normally change straight into my jim-jams. Mike told me I should dress up more often. Didn't you, darling? You can stop stirring now, by the way.' Ruth went over and put her arms around his waist and hugged him tight. Grace could see the deep love that these two people had for each other shining through. They looked adoringly at each other and she hoped that one day, she'd still feel like that about a special someone after they'd been together for years, and she hoped that special someone wasn't too far away.

'And this, Grace, is my gorgeous current husband, Mike.'

Grace went to shake his hand but instead he enveloped her in a bear hug.

'Ha! My wife likes to keep me on my toes! Now, from everything that Ruth has been telling me about you, you are exactly how I imagined you. It's so lovely to meet you, Grace. I've heard so much about you that I wasn't sure if my wife had a girl crush. Oh, and by the way, I love the fact that we finally get Vinnie out of our hair now he's met someone lovely to spend some time with. He's here all the time and we just can't get rid of him.' He grinned.

'Oi, I am here, you know,' Vinnie said as he went forward and gave his brother-in-law a hearty hug.

'You know you're part of the fixtures and fittings here, mate! You're always welcome in our house.'

Grace could instantly see the special bond the men had.

'Right, let's get the bar open! G&Ts all round?'

'Not for me, mate, I'm in the driving seat tonight and I have two very important passengers that I'm taking care of.'

Grace smiled at him across the room as Ruth tucked her arm inside hers and led her through to a lounge which was large, beautifully decorated and impeccably tidy with candles glowing on the mantelpiece and fairy lights shimmering above a huge mirror.

'Crikey, I wish my lounge was this stunning and tidy!' Grace said, envying the gorgeous room.

'I'd like to take the credit for that, but I can't. The cleaner came in yesterday and I've not allowed anyone in this room since, apart from to light the fire and the candles.' She laughed. 'The poor children are banned from here as it's the only grown-up room in the house and we like to keep it that way. I love my children, but I also love the fact that we have a huge family room that we spend most of our time in so that we can have somewhere that we can keep clean and tidy for visitors.'

'Wow, you have a cleaner, how fabulous.'

'We both work hard and the last thing I want us to do on our days off is to spend it cleaning. Life is for living and making memories with your family. It's too short to spend doing dull things like cleaning, and worse than that, arguing about the cleaning and who's going to do what. We made a decision a long time ago that this was our treat to our family and it is an important cog that helps the family to be in harmony. We don't go out that much, don't drink too much, and don't smoke, so our cleaner is our little bit of luxury while we can afford it. You should do it, it'll change your life.'

'What a great idea,' Grace said, silently adding finding a cleaner to her list of things to do in her head. She spent a lot of time at the weekends cleaning and Ruth was right, life was too short to spend doing such mundane boring stuff. And with a dog and a child to clean up after, she felt like she was on a constant treadmill vacuuming up dog hair and sweeping mud that came off Archie's football boots.

They chatted comfortably, then Mike came through to the lounge after about ten minutes, announcing that he'd fed the kids and that the grownups' dinner was ready and invited them through to the dining room. He placed an enormous plate on the table, which consisted of chicken and fish goujons, raw vegetables, hummus, and a selection of amazing breads and dips.

Grace was sat facing Vinnie, who grinned at her constantly. Ruth and Mike were at the opposite ends of the table.

'So Grace, tell me about yourself,' Mike joked, 'and I'll tell you if you've got the job.'

They all laughed and Grace started by saying that she was mum to Archie and Becks and she talked about her job, which she said she enjoyed. He asked about her family and Grace talked about losing her beautiful mother to cancer after a ten-year fight and how her father had gone rapidly downhill after losing his life partner, but that he'd found a new lease of life since he'd moved into the retirement village. She talked about her sister and how much she missed Hannah who was now happily creating a life in the US.

After she finished eating, she said, 'That was divine.'

'All home-made too, even the hummus. Isn't he the best?' Ruth explained how Mike was a closet chef and his hobby was cooking. 'What a stroke of luck,' said Grace, 'as my hobby is eating!'

'Give us a hand, mate.' Mike asked Vinnie to help

clear the table and she could hear their low voices in the kitchen while she and Ruth chatted amiably. She thought she heard Mike say, 'Have you told her yet?' and Vinnie say, 'Just drop it mate, please.'

As they came back into the dining room, Mike was frowning but was soon smiling again. He came through holding a huge casserole dish full of the most gorgeously aromatic chicken she'd ever smelt. Vinnie followed, carrying a dish of garlic roast potatoes, and a huge bowl full of fresh vegetables, which Ruth explained had been picked from their allotment by Mike and the children that afternoon.

After that, Grace didn't think she could possibly eat another thing, until Ruth brought out a deliciously light lemon mouse and a huge Eton Mess which she declared the easiest pudding to make, and insisted that Grace had a bit of each.

They were all fit to burst, Grace exclaiming, 'Mike, you should apply for *Masterchef*!' Mike cleared the table. As they moved into the lounge, Ruth asked Grace how she'd coped with not having her mum around. Grace mentioned that she'd been to see a medium a few months after her mum died and had been many times since and how much it had helped her.

Grace saw Ruth glance at both Mike and Vinnie

and a very strange expression came across their faces. 'Oh no, I'm so sorry. Have I said something to upset you all?' she asked.

'No, darling, it's just that we have a standing argument in this family about going to see a medium. I would love to go but am petrified, Vinnie would love to go and hasn't done anything about it because he's a big wuss and Mike is totally against us going. I know that Vinnie has told you about our darling Meredith, but we'd love to see if she comes through to us. It's a bit of a sticking point, to be honest. Would you mind telling us about your experiences and perhaps it'll help us to decide whether we need to take it further?'

* * *

It was nearly the middle of December, the year they'd lost their darling mum, and the whole family were unsure how they were supposed to get through a Christmas without her. How would they sit around a Christmas dinner table without someone that had always been there, an empty chair where she should be sitting? Just thinking about it had made Grace want to cancel the whole day.

While out shopping one day for Archie's

presents, Grace had walked past a shop that she'd walked past many times, which was advertising a spiritual event in a church with a number of local mediums. The need to find out more completely overwhelmed her and she went into the shop and asked the lady behind the counter if she knew anything personally about the event.

It turned out that the lady who owned the shop was a medium and did private readings and Grace's heart soared as she considered the possibility of an appointment, but it soon came crashing back down to earth when she was told that the woman was booked up for months ahead. Grace had said that she'd pop back in again after Christmas and turned to walk out of the shop. Unbeknown to the shop owner, tears started to fall from Grace's eyes but quickly stopped when she was called back by the medium. Gently, the medium asked her to come back the following Tuesday night as she felt an overwhelming urge to help her. As Grace walked out of the shop, wondering what on earth she'd done, her mobile rang and it was Hannah.

'Hey babes, just phoning to say hi. How are you doing today? I'm struggling a bit to be honest. Hope you don't mind me calling. I just felt the need to pick up the phone to you. I didn't want to talk to anyone else. Just my little sis.'

'Of course not, love, in fact you'll never guess what I've just done! I've only gone and booked a session with a medium. I was just going to message you to tell you.'

'You haven't! How could you do that without me? I want to come too.' She laughed.

'Shall I see if you can come with me? I can pop back in and ask.'

'Oh, I don't know now. I want to but I don't want to. Oh, bugger it, yes please. Will you ask?'

Grace went in and asked if she could take someone along and the medium smiled and said of course. She dropped Hannah a text to tell her it was all sorted.

The following Tuesday, just before they went into the shop where they were due to see the medium, Grace felt the strangest sensation in her legs – it felt as if there was no circulation in them at all from the knees down. Hannah laughed at Grace as she rubbed her legs to warm them up, but Grace brushed it off, putting it down to the fact that it was a very cold December night.

The room smelled of incense and candles and was warm and cosy. 'So, my name is Michelle, as you know. Please sit and try to relax. The way this works is that if any spirits come through to me, I will give you evidence so that you know who they are. Is that OK?'

Hannah and Grace nodded, nervous and full of anticipation, clutching at each other's hands.

'There is a lady here trying to make contact with you but she's struggling because she's so upset. She's someone who has very recently passed to the spirit world after battling with cancer and is devastated to leave her family. Do you know who that could be?'

Michelle became very emotional at this point and said that she needed to hold her chakra stick to ground herself because the spirit's sadness was flowing through her and was making her feel a little overwhelmed. Tears started to stream down both Hannah's and Grace's cheeks as they hoped and prayed that this was their mum trying to get through to them.

'Your mum wants to thank you girls for all you did during her illness. She knows how you both sat for hours on end at her bedside and she wants you to know that even though she couldn't communicate for the last few days, she could hear everything that was going on. She says that she is glad that you are wearing her rings, Grace, and that she loved the freesias that you put in her coffin.'

The next thing she said stunned them all as Michelle explained that their mum was new to the spirit world and had to find her own way of communicating with her girls. She would do this by letting them feel a cold sensation in parts of their bodies. Grace and Hannah were astounded and both smiled through their tears at the fact that their mum could make contact in this way.

'Your mum says that she will always be around her girls and will never leave your side. Just as she tried to be the best mum she could be in life, she will continue to do this in death; the only real difference is that you can't see her any more. She wants you to carry on talking to her; she hears everything you say and she wants you to try to see through your sadness by knowing that she's really not far away and will still always be there to wipe away your tears.'

At the end of the reading, the sisters, who were still a bit dazed by the events of the evening, as well as extremely emotional, went back to Grace and Mark's house. Seeing their distress, he asked them what had happened but then sneered when Hannah told him, saying that they were both ridiculous for believing in someone who was clearly a charlatan and taking advantage of two people who were going through immense grief.

Despite his attempts to belittle everything they felt, Grace and Hannah felt a huge sense of peace and calm, something they hadn't felt since their mum had passed away.

* * *

After Grace relayed the story, she looked up to see tears streaming down Ruth's cheeks. She went over to sit by her and put her arm around her. 'Ruth, I'm so sorry for making you cry. I've spoilt your evening.'

'But darling, you couldn't be further from the truth. It's beautiful, the fact that you connected to your mum that way. I'd love to have that experience with Meredith, wouldn't you, Vinnie? Mike, darling, surely you would want that for me. I don't know how else I can find peace since she was taken away.'

Grace turned to Vinnie and his cheeks were tear-stained too. Mike was still sceptical and asked, 'But how do you know that the things she said weren't just general and that you latched onto them because you were so deep in your grief? I'd hate to think that someone was capable of doing that to people who were so vulnerable.'

Grace explained further. 'There were things she couldn't possibly have known. Like the rings – how could she have known that I was the one wearing them and not Hannah? And she didn't say thanks for the flowers, she said thanks for the *freesias*. Who would know that? I went back to see Michelle a few days later and took her some flowers, and she told me that she was thinking of giving up because she hated the fact that she had to take money from grieving people, but that she needed to earn a living. I was devastated because I felt like I'd found a way to communicate with mum and that she was taking it away again, but it also showed me that she wasn't a charlatan out to exploit anyone. Michelle did explain that the bond between my mum and us was so strong that she didn't feel like it mattered who made that connection; that my mum would always find a way to tell us that she was around.

'She must have seen the sadness on my face though, so she offered to book a date in. The day before I went to see her again, I'd found out I was pregnant. When I walked through Michelle's door at that appointment, she sat me down immediately and said, "Your mum has been bothering me all morning and couldn't wait for you to arrive. She says that she wanted to give you something very special and decided that the best gift she could give you is the gift of a child. She wants to know whether you will keep her present.'"

Tears were once more streaming down Grace's cheeks at this point and Vinnie got up and moved to sit next to Grace and held her hand, stroking it gently as she continued her story.

'There was no way that I was doing anything but keeping this gift from my mum, and Michelle went on to give me all sorts of proof that these messages were from my mum. She told me Mum knew that Mark wasn't happy about the pregnancy and that it didn't matter and that she'd help me through it and that I'd never be alone. She told me that Mum was delighted that she could send me this very special present and would always be around me and my baby. That's probably why I mollycoddle Archie so much, because I see him as a very special gift from heaven from my mum.

'I've been back another seven times or so and was constantly told that Mum thought that Mark wasn't right for me and that I needed to sort my life out. Michelle even gave me a crystal once, charged with Mum's energy, and told me to wear it on a chain around my neck so that whenever I needed to feel close to her, I could just touch it. When I did, the crystal throbbed in my hand. It was bizarre! She even told me at one point that Mark was carrying on behind my back, but I chose to ignore that part – more fool me. The last time I saw her was just after Dad had moved to the retirement village; she told me that Mum was really happy that he had lifted himself up and was living his life again. And since Archie's dad and I have split up, I don't feel the constant need that I did before. It's strange but I feel that I know everything I need to know and I feel her around me all the time.'

Ruth hugged Grace tightly. 'I know I'm crying but what you've told me is just so beautiful and I would love to have that peace and calm when I think of Meredith. I worry about her all the time and wonder if there was something more that I could have done to save her or worry that I should have spent more time with her. If only I'd known that we only had a short time together. That's why I'm so hell-bent on creating memories for my children. Life is a gift and can be snatched away at any time. Life is for living and enjoying.'

'Do you know, Grace, I was really against this when Ruth mentioned it before,' said Mike. 'But now I hear your story and see how it's helped you through the years without your mum. I'd love you to pass on this lady's number if possible and I'll arrange for Ruth to go. You too, Vinnie, if you fancy it.'

'Not sure, mate, it's a lot to take in. I'll think about it,' Vinnie replied. He seemed really quiet for the rest of the evening, but as usual was very attentive to Grace.

Archie came through from the den. Grace smiled at him and he beamed back at her. 'Hello, gorgeous, how are you? I'd forgotten you were here.'

'Hey, Mum, I've had the best time ever. But I'm getting a bit tired now.' He climbed up on to her lap. *It doesn't matter how big he's getting, he always nestles into me when he is tired and he still fits into my body perfectly*, she thought as she snuggled him tight.

'Shall we get you home soon, tiger?' Vinnie asked.

'Yes please.' Archie yawned and his eyes looked heavy.

'Fancy a piggy-back out to the car?'

Archie's face lit up. 'You bet I do!'

Ruth hugged Grace long and hard and thanked her for sharing her story. Grace conveyed what a fabulous evening she'd had and once again apologised for the emotional outpouring, but Ruth brushed it away, saying how much it had helped her to reach a decision. Mike dropped a kiss on his wife's head as he stood with his arms around her shoulders at the door as they waved Vinnie, Grace and Archie off into the night, with promises of being in touch very soon.

Within seconds of being in the car, Archie was fast asleep.

'You're quiet, Vinnie, everything OK?' she asked him.

'Yep, fine, thanks. Just pondering on everything you said earlier. Do you really think that Michelle is the real deal? For the first time in a few years, I've seen Ruth really get excited about trying to make contact with Meredith. I couldn't stand for her to build up her hopes and have them come crashing down around her and set her back again. I'm just worried, that's all.'

'I can only talk from my own experiences, Vinnie. And I know how I felt each time after going to see her. The last few times it felt like I was going to meet mum and have a coffee and a catch-up with her and I would give anything to be able to do that with her again.'

'I'm sure you would, I just worry about Ruth, that's all. I know she's a big girl, but I only have one sister now and I want to make damn sure that she's happy and content in her life. I can't let her go through something that would devastate her all over again. I feel really confused.'

They pulled up outside her house and Vinnie dipped his head. Grace turned to him. 'I'm sorry. Should I not have said anything, Vinnie?' she asked.

'No, you weren't to know, babe. I've just never seen Ruth look so determined to do something. I just hope it gives her what she needs. Come on, let's get this little fella indoors.' He reached across and kissed her tenderly on the lips.

'Do you know, Vinnie, it could be just what Ruth needs to help her move forward.'

'You're right, Grace, I know that, it just feels a bit strange. The thought that we might be able to make contact with Meredith is both exciting yet terrifying at the same time. It'll sort itself out, I'm sure.'

As Vinnie lifted Archie out of the back of the car, the boy stirred and moaned a little but was in a deep sleep. Vinnie carried him straight upstairs and placed him gently on his bed. Grace took off his shoes and his jacket without waking him, kissed his forehead and whispered, 'Good night, my little angel.' Archie snuggled down under his duvet, rolled over and farted.

When they stopped giggling like a pair of teenagers, Grace put the kettle on and while they waited for it to boil, Vinnie put his arms around her and held her tight. She felt safe in his arms. Safe and loved. It was a feeling she hadn't had for a long time. Half of her was filled with joy and the other half was petrified. Could she really pour her heart and soul into someone all over again, with the possibility that it could one day be taken away from her again? And now, there wasn't just her to consider. She had Archie to worry about too. Could she let him get close to someone when there was a possibility it could all go wrong? She really felt like Vinnie was someone very special but there was just a nagging doubt in the back of her mind that he might just be too good to be true. Or was Mark right? Should she get her family back together so that her son could be with both parents? Her heart was saying one thing and her head was saying another. And she remembered that insecure feeling in the pit of her stomach when she'd seen that text message. Half of her wanted to ask Vinnie about it and the other half just wanted to ignore it and hope it went away.

Vinnie put his hands under her chin and tilted her head and looked her in the eye. 'You know I'd never hurt you and Archie, don't you, Grace?' It was as if he was reading her mind. 'I'm too old and sensible to play games. Watching you tonight with the people I love most made me realise how much I want that and how I'd love you to be a part of our family. Ruth adores you and I think I'm falling just a little bit in love with you. When I'm not with you I'm thinking about you. I can't concentrate on my work. I want to talk to you all the time. I think I've got a huge crush!'

Grace felt her heart swell with joy.

'I think I'd better go before I whisk you upstairs and ravish you,' Vinnie said, grinning. While she wanted nothing more than for him to stay over, his words calmed Grace's nerves. The thought of sleeping with somebody new after all those years still terrified her. She said that she'd speak to him tomorrow and waved him off at the doorstep. She went to bed thinking of what a fabulous evening she'd had and how much she'd felt like she fitted in with their wonderful family.

* * *

Oh darling, you have started something wonderful. Meredith has been desperate to get Ruth to see a medium and make contact with her. We've spent a while up here chatting and she knows that Ruth feels like she should have done more to help, or to spend more time with her. But none of it matters. Meredith just wants to show Ruth that she's around her all the time and watching out for her and, more than that, she wants Ruth to stop worrying about her and move on. She wants that for Vinnie too. What better legacy to leave than to help your siblings live their lives to the full and enjoy every minute? That's all I want for you too, darling. Don't worry if this thing between you and Vinnie doesn't work out. Sometimes you can ruin something by thinking the worst all the time and you'll make it go wrong. You just have to let go and trust in something higher than you. Meredith and I are here and we're always watching over you all. I'm your mum and I've never told you to do something that wouldn't be right for you. Just open your heart and let love in! Trust me, darling. I love you, Mum xxx

20

Grace had invited Vinnie for an early dinner on the Sunday afternoon. At eight o'clock that morning, her phone pinged and she saw that she'd got a text from Ruth.

Hey gorgeous girl, how are you today? Such a lovely evening even if we did have a few tears between us. Can't stop thinking about what you said last night. Can you pop me Michelle's number over when you have a sec please? X

Grace replied:

> Of course, here you go. And thank you again for a wonderful evening. Hope there's lots more of those to come x

The reply that came back was:

> Thanks sweetie. And I know there'll be years ahead of evenings like that. You know we all love you and the kids adore Archie. They said they'd had the best night ever. X

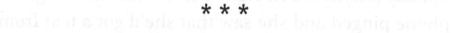

* * *

Grace had put a beef casserole in the slow cooker on a timer, which had started cooking overnight, and the aromas emanating from the kitchen were divine and were making her mouth water. She thought she'd better do a bit of maintenance in the lady department and made the effort to shave her legs and her lady garden just in case. For the first time in what seemed like ages, she was wearing matching underwear under her jeans and shirt – *orange* underwear. She hoped Monica appreciated her taking notice of what she said. Grace was feeling good and, although nothing would probably happen, she wanted to be prepared. Nothing like getting a bit of bedroom action with your skanky old pants on and a manky old grey bra!

Grace and Archie had had a tiring and emotional morning which all started with a battle over homework. Archie never wanted to do it when he came home from school at night, so it was always a weekend job. Grace wanted to get into the habit of doing it before he went to football late on a Sunday morning but it was a constant struggle. Archie was good with his English but really struggled with his maths and got easily frustrated. That morning it had ended with him throwing his pen across the room and stomping off to his bedroom. She'd let him off before she took him to his football match where his team had lost 3–0. Reeling from the result, he answered her questions with curt responses all the way home, until Grace finally lost her cool when they were sitting on the drive.

'You cannot keep speaking to me this way, Archie. I'll not stand it.'

'Well, perhaps if you had more time to play football with me in the garden, I'd be a better player and we'd be a better team. But you're always too busy to play with me these days, Mum, or too tired. But you always seem to find time for Vinnie. It's not fair!' He opened the car door and stomped off through the back gate into the garden.

Just something else to feel guilty about, Grace thought. When did the parental guilt ever end? Perhaps she needed to look at the time she was spending with Archie and spend it more wisely, as he clearly wasn't happy. It didn't seem to matter what she did, she never seemed to get it quite right even though she was trying so hard to please everyone. She left him out in the garden to cool off for a while and he eventually came in.

'I'm sorry, Mummy! I'm an awful son.'

'Darling, you are not an awful son at all. You are a wonderful son. But sometimes you have to be a little more patient. I know you've had me to yourself for years, and that was because I didn't have a job before, but now I have a job and a house and a dog to look after. And I can't do everything all of the time. I'm sorry, darling, I wish I could.'

They both sat on the kitchen floor, crying. Archie was getting older, and with that came a difficulty in coping with his emotions. Grace made a mental note to mention to Mark that it was happening more and more and they needed a plan to deal with it. She wanted to do the best by Archie but knew it was important for him to have male role models around.

Vinnie arrived around three o'clock. Grace was sorting out the final dinner preparations while Archie sat in the lounge watching the football with Vinnie, when there was a knock at the door. She wasn't expecting anyone till six when Archie was due to go to his dad's for the evening so was mighty surprised when she opened the door and there was Mark.

'Hope you don't mind,' he said. 'Just wanted to come early and see my boy!'

'Oh,' she replied. 'It's not really convenient to be honest, I have a friend here.'

'So you are refusing to let me see him, are you, Grace?' he asked shirtily.

Grace sighed to herself. Sometimes Mark's combative nature really deflated her, although she tried not to let it. 'I'm not refusing, Mark, I'm just saying that you can't just turn up here as and when you feel like it. We have plans, we're only ten minutes away from having dinner.'

Archie must have heard the raised voices and came into the hall.

'Dad!' he yelled and flung himself at him.

'Steady on, son,' Mark replied, laughing. Becks

jumped up at Mark, taking him by surprise, and Mark lost his balance and toppled backwards as Becks jumped up and stuck his paw right in his privates. Mark bent double on the floor dramatically and Grace had to work really hard to stop herself from laughing.

Bless Becks. Whenever Mark came into the house these days, he always jumped up at him and practically pushed him over. It was funnier because although he jumped up at Grace and others as well, he never tried to knock anyone else over. She knew that it really annoyed Mark and although she tried not to laugh, a little bit of her found that really funny. She was quite convinced that Becks did it on purpose; they did say dogs were a good judge of character, after all!

'Dad, come and meet mine and Mum's friend, Vinnie, he's really cool.' Grace put her head in her hands as Archie helped Mark up off the floor and led him into the lounge.

Vinnie had obviously been keeping his head down while all the excitement was taking place in the hallway but stood up as Mark walked into the room. Vinnie held out his hand to him. Grace could see that Mark wasn't going to shake his hand, and Archie said, 'Isn't it nice and grown-up when everyone shakes hands?' At that point, Mark would have made himself look incredibly stupid if he hadn't, so he leant forward and briefly shook Vinnie's hand, wincing as he did so at the fact that his son had shamed him.

'Can Dad stay for dinner, Mum, please, please? You said you'd done enough to feed an army.'

Grace cringed inwardly. 'I'm sure Daddy has lots to do and will need to get back to Lorraine.'

'No I haven't, not today. She's gone out with some friends for the afternoon, which is why I thought I'd call over early. I was at a bit of a loose end. I'd love to stay for dinner, thanks.'

Grace went into the kitchen, silently fuming. She hadn't even invited him. This was *so* Mark. She couldn't work out if he was extremely dense or extremely clever and whether he was playing another of his little games. She called Vinnie through to the kitchen on the pretence of asking him to lay an extra place at the dinner table.

'Oh my bloody God!' she whispered. 'What a cheeky bastard he is! Vinnie, I'm so sorry, I just didn't know what to say or do.'

Once again, Vinnie always seemed to know the right thing to say.

'Grace, we're adults, we can get through this.

Don't worry. There was nothing you could do without upsetting Archie. Let's just get through the next hour or so, for Archie's sake, then we can get rid of him and relax.'

'You are a star, do you know that?' she said, kissing him gently as he went through into the dining room to lay an extra place. She opened a bottle of Pinot and poured a small amount into a glass. She took a sip and tried to steady her nerves. Then she knocked the lot back and filled up her glass again.

'Shall I serve up, like old times?' asked Mark when she placed the casserole dish on the table. He smirked annoyingly. It was clear that Vinnie's presence had brought out his territorial instincts.

'No, it's fine thanks, I've already asked Vinnie to do it,' she replied, handing a serving spoon to Vinnie, smiling sweetly at him. He winked back at her and she calmed a little.

It was a really painful hour, with everyone except Mark trying to be as normal as possible to keep the pretence up for Archie. Archie didn't even notice as he talked animatedly about football and Mark promised him that he would get him a new kit for his birthday.

'Vinnie's going to take me to a Villa match one of

these days, aren't you, Vinnie?' Grace's and Vinnie's eyes met across the table.

'Oh, you don't want to go there, mate, they're rubbish!'

'No, they're not, Dad, don't say that!'

'Only joking, buddy!' Mark laughed it off.

Mark had spent the meal bringing up situations from the past, situations that he and Grace clearly had very different views on. He reminisced over an apparently fabulous holiday in Spain, waxing lyrical about the incredible food at the hotel and the attentive staff at the resort. Grace had a very different view, and actually remembered the week away as being a catalyst for the end of their relationship because one night he took off on his own for a few hours, returned back worse for wear then started an argument with Grace while Archie was sleeping.

As soon as they'd finished eating, Grace cleared the plates and said to Mark, 'As you're here early, you may as well take Archie now and then you can spend a couple of extra hours with him.'

'Oh, OK then.' Mark was surprised. 'I was just going to go and sit and watch the rugby in the lounge.'

'Not in my bloody lounge you don't,' she muttered. 'Go and get your stuff together then, Archie.'

While Grace hated the fact that she was losing a couple of hours with Archie, the trade-off was that she didn't have to put up with Mark lording it up in her house.

Grace's stomach was in knots, knowing that the time had come that she had to leave Vinnie and Mark alone. In all honesty, she was dreading it. She ran up the stairs to Archie's bedroom. She had never packed his bag so quickly before. They came down the stairs and, before going back into the room where Mark and Vinnie were making awkward small talk, Archie turned round to her and said, 'Mum, can I have a great big hug please?'

'Of course you can, darling. Are you OK?'

'I don't like it when Dad says things are rubbish that I like and I don't like it when he's being horrible to you, either. I love you so much, Mummy, I wish I didn't have to go to Dad's today.'

'I love you so much too, my angel. But Dad likes to spend time with you too. And I'm sure he's only joking.'

'But jokes are supposed to be funny, not cruel. At least you have Vinnie to keep you company now,' he said. 'I like him, Mum. I like him a lot.'

'Yes, darling, so do I. Come on, let's get you and Dad sorted out.'

Mark and Vinnie went quiet as they walked into the dining room and Grace wondered how they'd got on. Vinnie smiled at her and gave her a wink and she felt a flutter in her heart. She knew that he wasn't mad at her, and that he didn't hold her responsible for having to share their meal time.

She practically shoved Mark and Archie out of the door and then, when it was shut, leaned up against it, closed her eyes and let out an enormous sigh. Vinnie appeared and put his arms around her. 'Shit, that was awkward! Hope I didn't say anything wrong to make anything worse.'

She laughed, realising that there was probably so much more that Vinnie wanted to say about Mark but was much too polite. 'You were amazing. Believe it or not, Mark was really lovely when we were first together. But he has changed over the years, and now he's somewhat of a Jekyll and Hyde. Still, he's gone now, so let's not give him any more air space because that's what he would want. Why don't you go and sit down in the lounge and relax and I'll be through in a minute?'

She went to the downstairs bathroom, took ten deep breaths, pulled herself together and came back into the living room. In her hands, she had a bottle of brandy and two glasses.

'Are you trying to get me drunk and have your wicked way with me, young lady?' Vinnie smiled at her and she thought he'd never looked more sexy than he did right then.

'Do you know, I just might be,' she replied, taking a huge gulp of brandy.

'Thank God for that!'

Her heart was beating so fast. Was she ready for this? It had been so long since she'd had sex with anyone but Mark. Could she go through with it?

A voice in her head said, *Just do it, Grace. Don't think, just do.*

Vinnie took the glass from her hands and kissed Grace like she'd never been kissed before. She melted into it and cast aside her hang-ups and anxiety of being naked and sleeping with someone new. She was just desperate to be closer to this man than she'd ever been with anyone before and she needed to feel him inside her.

She put her hands under his shirt and felt bare skin and his deep muscly stomach. She wanted to feel his skin on hers.

'Are you sure about this, Grace?' Vinnie looked deep into her eyes and she felt like she was forever lost in them.

'I've never been more sure of anything in my life,'

she replied. She took him by the hand and led him up the stairs and into her bedroom where she propelled him towards the bed, kicking the door shut behind her. With all her inhibitions flung out of the window, she took a deep breath and showed Vinnie just how sure she was.

* * *

Afterwards, she lay in his arms while they snoozed. Eventually, she needed to go to the bathroom so she eased herself gently from underneath his arm. He groaned and turned to face her.

'Where do you think you're sloping off to, young lady?' he asked.

'I'll be back in two secs,' she replied as she went into the bathroom. She looked at herself in the mirror. *Well, girl!* She said to herself. *That was an extremely fabulous way to spend a Sunday afternoon!* She felt like a new woman. She wondered if she looked different. Her eyes were definitely sparkling. It had been so long since she'd had enjoyable sex, she couldn't actually remember when it was. And she hoped that she'd never forget again.

She remembered that Monica had bought her a silky kimono for her last birthday, which was normally hidden under her purple fleecy dressing gown, so in an effort not to kill off the romance as soon as it had started, she grabbed it off the back of the bathroom door and decided to go barefoot. She went downstairs and returned with two steaming mugs of tea and the biscuit tin.

When she returned, Vinnie said, 'You really are the girl of my dreams, you know. I didn't think I'd be hungry after that mammoth Sunday dinner you cooked, but I seem to have lost some of my energy! This is just what I need to get it back again.'

They sat side by side in her bed and chatted comfortably as if it were the most normal thing in the world and they'd been doing it for years. She couldn't quite believe it. She'd been worrying about that moment for weeks. When was the right time to have sex with a new partner? How many dates should she go on first? When would they be alone? When would it happen? Would they enjoy it? What if she did it wrong? Would she know what he enjoyed? Would he like her body? Should she ask him to stop over, or leave? It was a minefield. But everything with Vinnie was just so easy. Grace realised that she was more relaxed and calm than she had been for years. Sod meditating, what she'd needed for inner peace was a damn good shag, clearly!

Vinnie finished his mug of tea and took hers from her and put it on the bedside table. He pulled her towards him again and when she felt his hardness against her, she realised that he seemed to have got his energy back after all. She grinned and kissed him and he rolled her over so he was above her and eased her legs apart gently with his knees. He looked deep into her eyes as he pushed inside her and groaned with pleasure. 'You are amazing. What are you doing to me?' he asked, as this time their love-making was slower and even more intense. Just perfect.

* * *

The sun shone brightly through the gap in the curtains and filled the room with light. Grace opened her eyes to find Vinnie leaning on his elbow, watching her. He smiled and tucked a stray strand of hair behind her ear.

'Morning, sleepyhead.'

'Morning, you! It wasn't all a dream then?'

'Not at all, it's real, alright. No regrets I hope?' he asked.

'None whatsoever.'

'I am so glad to hear that. You snore, by the way!'

'I do not!' Grace squealed, blushing.

'I'm afraid you do, but you are forgiven because they're sexy little snores. I let you sleep, but to be honest they were making me feel extremely horny and I just wanted to wake you up and show you just how much I liked them.'

'Good job you didn't. To be honest, even if David Beckham woke me up saying he wanted to roger me senseless in the middle of the night, I'd slap him and say, *David, don't bloody wake me up. Now get over your own side of the bed and go back to sleep.* I really hate being disturbed in my sleep.'

Vinnie laughed. 'It's not really etiquette to mention another man wanting to have his wicked way with you when I've only just had mine, you know. However, as it is the mighty Golden Balls Beckham, I will, on this one occasion, ignore it.

'Right then, lady. Much as I'd like to stay right here and show you how much better in bed I am than that Beckham stud-muffin, I think we should get our lazy butts out of bed on this Bank Holiday Monday and make the most of this sunshine. There's a dog downstairs who I'm sure would love to go out for a walk in the forest and I know I'd like to get some fresh air. How do you fancy a nice long walk, then I'll buy you a slap-up breakfast?'

'Oh, Vinnie, you sure know how to treat a lady! I bet David never says that to Victoria first thing in the morning. I'll have to back by three as Archie is back then, is that OK?'

'Of course. And I've had a text from Ruth this morning asking what your plans are for next Saturday night. She wondered if you fancied going over for a karaoke and games night. They do tend to get a little raucous but if you think you can cope with that, then I'm game!'

'That sounds fun, but I don't do karaoke! I'll join in from afar but there is no chance that you will get me in front of a microphone. I am tone deaf. The only singing out loud I do is when I'm in my car. But what I lack in tone, I make up for in enthusiasm!'

'We'll see!' He winked at her. Every time he did that, her heart fluttered a tiny bit. She wondered if that was something she'd ever get used to.

While she jumped in the shower, Vinnie threw on his boxers and jeans and went down to the kitchen to make them some coffee. Since Grace had been going to Ruth's café, she always picked up some of her special blend of coffee that he loved so much, and it was now her favourite too.

When Grace came down from her shower, she saw Vinnie engrossed, looking at her noticeboard which hung on the kitchen door. There were the usual doctor and dentist appointment cards and school reminders, but also pictures that had been cut out of magazines pinned on there. There was an image of a stunning summerhouse, all decked out with cushions, lanterns and fairy lights. It looked like a magical place. There was also a fabulous rattan garden set and a tidy, clean, perfect garden with beautiful buddhas and cascading water features and a big statue of a stunning angel.

Sipping her coffee, Grace said, 'Oh, you've spotted my dream board then! It's a bit far from reality, isn't it?' She laughed as she pointed out of her dining-room window at her shabby garden shed.

'What are the drawings for?' he asked.

'Oh, nothing really. It's my dream garden, all zen and buddha-like. Somewhere I could go to escape the world and sit in peace and tranquillity. I do have a buddha, but sadly Becks pees up it. I'm sure that's probably bad luck in ancient Japan.

'I bought some garden furniture last year, which is in the garage and I can't assemble it myself, so it's still there. The plans are exactly what I want to do. I don't have the resources to implement it right now, but it's on my dream board because you never know! One day, if I dream it enough, it might happen.'

'Well, perhaps one of these days we can sort your furniture out. I'd love to help you, Grace.'

'Thanks, Vinnie, you really are a sweetheart, you know. And I might just take you up on that offer. Now, let's get this furry beast out for a walk.'

She smiled and thought about what a long way she'd come from the day Monica had started her make-over. At one point, she'd never thought she'd find someone she'd want to be with romantically. She just couldn't be bothered and was just happy to wait around for Archie to come back from his dad's, but she thought that she might just be falling for Vinnie. He made her feels things that she'd never thought she'd feel again. Perhaps it was worth it, after all.

21

Vinnie asked if they could swing by his house on the way out, so he could pick up his hoody. The weather was definitely warming up, but it was cool in the shady parts of the forest. As they pulled into the cul-de-sac he lived in, she noticed a car parked outside his house, but when the driver spotted Vinnie's car, they quickly pulled away. It was a pretty young woman in a blue Fiat 500. Grace's heart began to beat faster and she went silent, not knowing whether she should mention it and prick the little bubble of happiness that had descended on her since last night with Vinnie. Was she just imagining things – seeing things that weren't even there? When she was with Mark, he said she did that all the time. Her thoughts

were racing; she needed to calm down and pull herself together.

They pulled up in the car park at the forest and
Becks jumped out of the back of the car and waited
patiently for Vinnie and Grace to put on their hood-
ies. Vinnie kissed her gently then took her hand as
they headed down towards the lakes. Grace couldn't
stop wondering again if everything was too good to
be true. Once you'd been severely hurt, half of you
always wanted to protect your heart, however much
the other half of you wanted to just let things flow.
And it wasn't just her that she had to think about;
Archie was also attached now. She knew that Vinnie
was someone very special and she desperately
wanted to trust him with her heart – but could she?
They had a lot of getting to know each other to do.
What happened when the honeymoon period was
over and they both stopped being on their best behaviour? She knew she had to stop comparing him to
Mark, but they'd been together for such a long time
that she found it difficult. Perhaps whoever was inside the car she'd seen was visiting his neighbour
and just happened to have parked outside his house?

A voice that seemed to whisper through the trees
and sounded just like her mum came into her head.
Darling, you have to love like you've never been hurt or

you'll turn love away. You deserve love, you have love right here and you have to grasp it with both hands, eyes wide open and an open heart. Trust me, even if you trust no one else! Things aren't always what they seem.

Vinnie shouted, 'Race you to the bench!' and took off, Becks charging at his heels.

'Totally unfair! You knew you were going to do that, so you were always going to win.' She panted as she reached the bench where Vinnie was sitting. He pulled her down onto his lap and kissed her passionately.

'Grace, Grace, Grace, what are you doing to me?' he murmured. 'I thought that feeling like this was something you read about in books. I didn't realise that you could feel so wonderful with someone so quickly. When I'm with you, there's nowhere else in the world I'd rather be.'

One of the many things she loved about Vinnie was how honest and open he was. There was no playing games, he just said what he was feeling. OMG! She just realised she'd thought the word 'loved'! Did she love him? Already? In such a short space of time? She hadn't thought it possible that she would ever love anyone apart from Archie ever again. But yes, she was definitely well on the way to falling head over heels with this man.

Grace had been guarding her heart and protecting herself from possible further hurt, never even considering meeting anyone else. But she realised now that she'd been missing out. Perhaps that expression 'love like you've never been hurt' was right after all, rather than 'don't bother loving, because you're going to get hurt'. She realised that she'd gone from being a glass-half-empty to a glass-half-full person and she felt happier because of it.

A grey-haired couple who were probably in their late seventies were walking past hand in hand and they stopped and smiled at them. 'Good morning,' said the gentleman. 'So lovely to see couples in love! And what a beautiful morning too.'

'It is indeed,' said Vinnie. 'We're making the most of a beautiful sunny day.'

'Glad to hear it, son. When you get to our age, every day you wake up is a bonus. We have our aches and pains but I'm delighted to say that my Vera and I have been married for fifty years today and I just want to share it with the world.'

Vinnie jumped up and shook the man's hand. 'Congratulations to you both. How wonderful to hear that. Are you doing anything special to celebrate?'

'We're flying out to Australia tomorrow morning to see our son. He's been out there for five years now and he's paid for us to visit him and his family as our golden wedding anniversary present. We're just off to grab a coffee now and a late breakfast and then home to finish the packing. We're thinking of staying in the country around three to six months, depending upon when they get fed up with us, so we've had to think very carefully about what to take. Vee obviously wants to take everything she owns.' He smiled as he winked at his wife.

'I'm very excited,' she said. 'I get to hug my son again. We Skype each other every week since he bought me an iPad last Christmas, but to feel him in my arms again will be such a special moment. I cannot wait. I thought this day would never come.'

'I'm Vinnie, by the way, and this is Grace. How wonderful for you. I know we've only just met you but would you do me the honour of allowing me to buy breakfast for you both to say Happy Anniversary?' Grace thought that this was quite possibly the nicest thing she'd ever known anyone to do for a stranger. Vinnie really did have a kind heart.

'Oh, Vinnie. What a lovely young man you are. You do remind me of my boy.'

'Hardly a boy any more, Vee! He's forty next week.'

'He'll always be my boy, Reg, you know that,' Vera retorted, nudging her husband with a grin.

'It would be lovely to have breakfast with you,' Grace said. 'We'd love to hear all about your plans for your trip. What do you think?'

Vera and Reg looked at each other and smiled. 'We'd love to.'

Reg and Vinnie walked ahead with Becks trotting along at Vinnie's side. The dog really had taken to Vinnie in a way that Grace hadn't expected. Becks always seemed calm in Vinnie's presence, which reflected her own feelings when she was around him.

Vera walked along beside her and when they came to a particularly rocky part of the path, Grace offered her arm and Vera happily tucked hers in. When they got over the rocks, Vera didn't remove her arm and Grace realised how nice it felt. It reminded her of the days when she used to walk with her mum for hours arm in arm. She smiled as she realised that this was another happy memory instead of a sad one even though it tugged at her heart.

They meandered along, chatting like they'd known each other for years. Vera talked about her son who she was still quite clearly besotted with. He was an IT consultant who had moved out to Melbourne for a six-month period, but while he was there, had met Amy, the love of his life. They'd married quickly and recently discovered that they had a baby on the way. The baby would be born while Vera and Reg were visiting, another reason they were so excited about the trip. When Vera talked about her son, her whole face lit up.

She asked Grace if she and Vinnie had children. Grace explained that they'd only recently got together and that she had a son who spent time with his father as well as her. Vera slowed down, turned to face Grace and took her hands in hers.

'I know we've only just met, but I'd like to say something. If I can teach you one thing in life, it's that you can't just be a mother. Don't get me wrong, being a mother for me was the best job I ever had. And for years I felt that it was all I ever needed. But one day, your children flee the nest and you become lonely. When your child leaves home, you feel like your heart has been ripped out. It's almost like you have a limb missing. That's when you realise that the man you chose to spend your life with is the one who you will grow old with. I can see how much you love your son by the way you talk about him and I know we don't know each other, but I bet you are an amazing mother. But you need a love of your own. One day your son will meet the love of his life, and if you are lucky, like I am, you will not lose a son, but gain a daughter.

'I know that your son leaving home is a long way off, but trust me on this. I think you've found yourself someone there who's a little bit special!' She nodded towards Vinnie. 'He's a good man. I can feel it in my bones. I feel that you are guarding your heart, but I also feel that you need to let go. Trust in love and trust in each other and you'll be just fine – I hope maybe one day you will be celebrating a milestone anniversary! Life is short and when you get to our age, you know that you have to live it to the full.'

Vera reached up to Grace and wiped away a tear, which she hadn't realised was trickling down her cheek. 'Special love comes around just once in a life-time. I found mine and I think you've found yours. Now you just have to grasp it and enjoy it. Don't push it away before you've given it a chance to bloom and flourish. Now come along, let's go eat. I'm ravenous!'

Vera reminded Grace of her mum. She had grey hair and looked sophisticated in her bright russet-coloured raincoat over a pair of brown jeans and walking boots. She had very subtle make-up set off by a bright orange lipstick. Grace smiled, thinking how much her mum would have liked this lady.

They sat outside in the sunshine and Becks settled nicely under the table. Breakfast was ordered and the two couples chatted companionably. It didn't take long for them all to demolish their full English breakfasts and a huge pot of tea and then, reluctantly, Reg reminded Vera that they had to go and pack. Grace said that she would love to know how their Australian adventure was going and Vera reached inside her handbag and found a notepad and pen. She asked Grace to write down her email address and promised to let her know when they arrived in Australia.

The two women hugged when they parted as if they'd known each other all their lives. Reg pumped Vinnie's hand and said what a pleasure it had been to meet them, thanking them for their breakfast. As Reg and Vera walked towards the car park, Vinnie slung his arm around her shoulders and planted a kiss on her head. 'Well, that was a surprise meeting if ever I've known one. What a fabulous couple.'

They heard the roar of a deep throaty engine and they turned around to see a bright-red convertible Ferrari pull out of a parking space. There was the loud beep of a horn and Reg and Vera waved as they wheel-spun out of the car park, leaving a cloud of dust behind them.

Vinnie and Grace laughed as she said, 'I guess that's what Vera meant by living life to the full!'

They arrived back at Grace's house just after one o'clock and as she was expecting Archie back later in the afternoon, Vinnie said that he would go home as he had some planning to do for the week ahead and would leave them to have some quality time together.

'I've had a wonderful long weekend, Grace.' He kissed Grace tenderly after she got Becks out of the boot and he walked towards his car. She did wonder what the neighbours would be thinking, having her bedroom curtains shut in the middle of the afternoon and then a car at hers overnight. She'd be getting a text from Belinda soon, she was sure of that.

She waved as he drove off. As she shut the door behind her, Grace realised that she was missing him already.

22

On Tuesday at lunchtime, while Grace was making herself a sandwich before going out to another house viewing, her mobile rang and she saw Ruth's number displayed.

'Hey, Ruth, how are you?' she asked. 'How did it go?' There was a very strange noise coming from the other end of the phone. 'Ruth? Ruth?'

'Oh, Grace,' she sobbed. She sounded so upset.

'Where are you? I'm coming to you. Just tell me where you are.'

'I'm at the shop. I can't face going home right now.' It was difficult to decipher what Ruth was saying, and her tone of voice was strangely muted.

'I'm on my way,' Grace said, feeling concerned.

When she arrived at the café, it was in darkness, but there was a light coming from the staff room at the back. The door was locked so Grace hammered on it. Ruth appeared, her face blotchy, looking like she'd been crying for a week.

When she opened the door, Grace slammed it behind her and turned the lock again. She led Ruth back into the staff room.

'What happened, darling?' she asked.

'Oh, Grace,' she sobbed. 'I spoke to Meredith through Michelle. It was incredible.'

Grace's body tingled from her toes to the top of her head as Ruth recalled her session.

'When I arrived at Michelle's house, she was eager to get me in and settled and said that she had a young lady who desperately wanted to speak to me. Michelle described the woman and I knew straight away that it was Meredith. Michelle said that she was getting the feeling that this young lady had been taken way ahead of her time and that the young lady was telling her that it was OK; that she was fine and well, and that while she knew that her family were so very sad, it was just her time to go.'

Grace passed Ruth a tissue as she noticed a tear fall slowly down her cheek.

'She said that she knew that her family wouldn't

ever forget her, but that it was time we started to build a new life without her and that there was no better legacy for her to leave behind than to watch her family live their lives to the full. She said that we needed to know that life is so very precious and short, and that it is about the people you meet and the memories you make with them along the way. She said she wanted us to make amazing memories with the people that are around us; to remember and cherish the past, but that we should take and make opportunities to have an amazing future. To live life like every day counted. She made me promise to do this, Grace.'

Grace held Ruth's hand as she could see how emotional her friend was getting and she just wanted to comfort her.

'She talked about the leukaemia and said that there was nothing anybody could have done to save her. She said that she was around me and my beautiful family all the time and that she walks with us when we go on our family walks. Apparently she's never far from her brother or her sister and she wants us to continue to talk to her as she hears everything we say, but she gets frustrated because she couldn't answer us before now.'

Ruth explained that during the session she was

trying to write things down so that she wouldn't forget what was said, while listening as hard as she could so she didn't miss a thing. Grace was trying really hard to hold it together as Ruth continued her story; she felt so emotional, and she was taken right back to that very first contact she'd had with her mum.

'Finally Meredith talked about Vinnie and how he's met someone new who he feels is his soul mate and that she hopes they will go on to have a fabulous life together. She said that she wanted to thank Mike for being a wonderful husband and so supportive to me and that he really is a sincere person who genuinely adores his family and his wife.'

Ruth seemed to have calmed down slightly at this point and Grace wiped her own tears away and asked her how she felt about her visit to Michelle after sharing the experience.

'Oh, Grace, I am so pleased I went. I know I'm upset now but it's because it's all so raw. I've had this amazing connection with my kid sister that I never thought for one minute I would ever have again and that is such an incredible feeling. I didn't realise how much I'd pushed all these thoughts aside, and it's brought all my emotions back to the surface... but in a really good way. I know I'm totally drained now, but that aside, the one thing that I'm sensing more than anything is peace. I feel at peace with what has happened. I really needed this.'

'Ruth, I am so delighted for you. I know that going to see Michelle was a massive help to me. In fact, I don't know how I would have coped without her in my life at a time when I needed so many answers. I can't tell you how pleased I am that you have done what you needed to do. Perhaps now your heart might start to heal.' She turned to Ruth, tears shining in her eyes, and embraced her friend, knowing exactly the emotions that Ruth was experiencing.

The shrill ringtone of a mobile phone interrupted the moment. 'Oh my!' Ruth exclaimed, as she spotted Vinnie's name on the caller display. She clutched her hand to her chest. 'I need to tell Vinnie and Mike. I told you first.' She smiled through her tears. 'I knew you'd understand and I instinctively just needed you to be the first to know. I know neither of them will mind. Will you speak to Vinnie for me and ask him to come round to mine and Mike's house now please?'

Grace answered Ruth's phone and Vinnie laughed. 'I knew she'd ring you first. I just knew it.'

'I'm so sorry, Vinnie,' Grace replied. 'I know she

probably should have told you and Mike but she called me instead, probably because I understand better than most what she's just been through. She asked me to get you to meet her at their house as soon as you can.'

'I don't mind, Grace, why would I? She loves you nearly as much as I do. And that's a huge amount. See you there in ten minutes.'

Grace smiled as she handed the phone back to Ruth, her heart beating ten to the dozen and set on fire by Vinnie's words. Had he really just said that he loved her? She wanted to jump up and down on the spot in excitement, but on reflection decided that probably wouldn't be particularly cool.

'Can I ask a massive favour, Grace?' Ruth asked.

'Of course. Anything you like,' Grace replied.

'Can I have a hug? I just need a great big sisterly hug right now.'

Grace and Ruth stood and hugged like they were never going to see each other again. Tears poured from both of them, but they both knew they were good, cathartic tears. They knew there was a bond between them that no one could ever break; that whatever happened, they would be friends for the rest of their lives.

'I'll leave you to it then,' Grace said.

'You will not, you daft bat, you're coming with me. You're a part of our family now, Grace, whether you like it or not, and you are included in everything we do.'

The women shared an understanding smile as they got into their respective cars and drove the short distance to Ruth's house. Grace was still officially on her lunchbreak, although it was a rather extended one today. Once there, Grace made a pot of coffee and took it into the lounge where Mike sat on the arm of the sofa, arms round Ruth's shoulders, while she sat next to Vinnie, holding his hand tightly, telling her brother and husband everything that had been said at Michelle's.

There wasn't a dry eye in the house. Mike went into the kitchen and returned with a bottle of Veuve Clicquot and four flutes. The anticipation and then the delightful noise of the cork popping made them smile and, through their tears, they raised their glasses and made a toast. 'To Meredith!'

* * *

Yay! I told Meredith she could do it. I knew that between us all we could get her to speak to Ruth. How amazing is that! I know she's made up. Being up here in heaven is so difficult. I am so chuffed that Meredith got through to her sister. I'm so proud of her and of you for helping it to happen. And Michelle needs a medal. She is so amazing and I'm so glad that we found this way of contact. It's miraculous, isn't it, this universe that we live in? Well done, my darling, thank you for sharing your experience with others. I know some don't believe, but we do. I always told you I'd find a way to let you know I was still here. Always was and always will be. Love you, Mum xxx

23

Ruth called round on Saturday morning unexpectedly and said that she was taking Grace for a surprise day out because they had some planning to do to organise fat club – although they agreed they really must stop calling it that. If nothing else came from their day, it would be a new name for the group. Grace was stunned and totally unprepared. She told Ruth that she couldn't go out for the whole day because of Becks and Archie. It had been a long time since Grace had been able to be spontaneous; she was always fully aware of the responsibilities she had at home.

With a twinkle in her eye, Ruth said that she had already sorted that out. 'Vinnie is going to arrive here any moment to look after Archie for the day – between them, they will make sure that Becks is looked after, too.'

She added that it would be good for Vinnie and Archie to spend some 'bonding' time together and that Grace needed to grab a swimming costume. Grace groaned internally. There were few things she hated more than showing off her wobbly bits in beachwear. However, she did what she was told, touched by the fact that someone had actually taken the time to make some decisions for her, as she seemed to spend her whole life making decisions for everyone else.

Grace had tried to get out of Ruth where they were going, but she was giving nothing away. They chatted on the journey about how they were going to run the slimming club. They were both delighted that they had the same ideas and shared the same beliefs and values. They were so in tune with each other and it was a wonderful feeling for Grace.

When she saw the sign for the spa, Grace gave a little squeal. And then thought she'd better not get too excited, just in case that was not their destination. She was beyond ecstatic when they pulled up in the car park.

'Little bro's treat to his lady and his sister!'

'Really?' Grace asked. 'Your brother is a proper Prince Charming. I really do love him to bits.'

Ruth smiled at her and Grace didn't notice that she'd admitted to loving him.

They were greeted with a fruit cocktail and the strong fragrance of essential oils which, along with the sound of ambient music, gave an immediate feeling of peace and tranquillity. Grace thought she'd died and gone to heaven. She'd dreamed of having a spa day for so long, but because so many other things came first in her life, she had never thought it would happen. In fact, not only had Vinnie arranged a spa day, but he had booked the very spa she had always wanted to go to. There was an image of it on her dream board. He was amazing. He was doing everything he could to make her happy and she loved the feeling that someone wanted to make her dreams come true. She felt loved and valuable.

After a morning of relaxing, they ambled along a corridor, following signs to the restaurant where they were seated at a table by a window which overlooked a beautifully serene lake. Swans gracefully glided on the surface and the women watched them, sharing a comfortable silence. Even speaking seemed to be a bit of an effort; they were so blissfully relaxed.

They devoured the most exquisite meal and,

stuffed to the brim, spent a bit of time after lunch brainstorming names for the club. They laughed till they cried as they tested out names on each other.

'Skinny Minnies!'

'Cakes Be Gone!'

'Cakes No More!'

'Get Stuffed!'

'Hippy Hippy Shakes!'

'Spare Tyres United!'

'Lard Arses No More!'

Ruth shouted out, 'Fat Fuckers Anonymous!' and an elderly lady who was reading got up, threw her book down on her lounger and stormed past them in disgust, which, though Grace tried to blurt out an apology, made them roar with laughter until neither of them could breathe.

Calming down but realising how good it was to laugh, they decided to head over to the relaxation lounge where they grabbed a chaise longue each. They pulled cashmere blankets over themselves and snuggled down for a rest while watching the dancing flames of the huge log burner, which hypnotised them to sleep. A minute later, Grace heard a strange noise and realised that it was herself, snoring. Maybe Vinnie was right and she did snore, after all! She was mortified but as she looked around, it seemed that no one else had heard her and it looked like Ruth was equally sparked out. She looked at the clock and to her surprise, she saw that an hour had passed.

She grabbed a passing waitress who returned with two steaming coffees in gorgeous blue-and-white polka-dot Emma Bridgwater mugs accompanied by a selection of pastries on matching plates. 'Oooh, I couldn't possibly eat anything else,' Ruth groaned as she woke and immediately reached for a cinnamon swirl. 'OMG, these are exquisite!'

Grace laughed and took one herself. She didn't know how they could possibly eat any more after the three-course lunch they'd not long devoured, but it seemed that it was possible after all.

Grace pointed out two fifty-something ladies who were sitting drinking out of champagne flutes around the hot tub area. 'Bet the glamorous one on the left is a rich widow and she's brought her friend along on a spa day for a bit of company. I hope those glasses are plastic. Health and safety, you know!' Ruth laughed at her, which encouraged her to gossip some more. 'And what about that couple over there? They can't keep their hands off each other and she keeps sticking her tongue down his throat in full view of everyone.'

'Clearly having an affair,' Ruth giggled. 'Ew!

You'd never do that with your husband now, would you? What about her behind the desk? What's her story do you reckon?'

'Oooh, we're proper busybodies, aren't we?' Grace laughed. They both stopped dead still and looked at each other.

'Busybodies! *Busy Bodies*. That's it!' The name they'd been looking for. It was perfect.

They high-fived each other and toasted Busy Bodies with their mugs.

They were quiet in the car on the way back, not because they had run out of things to say, but because they were so relaxed and there was no need to fill the time with anything. It had been such a perfect day. Adult company had been missing from her life for a while, but no longer.

24

As they drove down the street towards Grace's house, she realised that the outside lights were on. Vinnie, Archie and Becks were all standing on the doorstep waiting for her. Archie seemed to be jumping up and down with excitement about something. She gave him a great big hug, ruffled the fur on Becks' head and then gave Vinnie a kiss full on the lips and told him what a wonderful day they'd had. She whispered in his ear that she'd show him later how much she had appreciated his wonderful gesture.

'Mum, Mum! You have to put this blindfold on because me and Vinnie have something to show you!' Ruth smiled at her, nudging her to do what he said. Grace bent down to let Archie put the blindfold on. She recognised it from an old beauty kit of hers – it had a dog's face on it. Knowing just how ridiculous she must have looked, she went with it anyway; Archie's enthusiasm was infectious.

Vinnie took one hand and Archie the other, and they led her through the wrought-iron side gate and down the path along the house.

'OK, Mummy, you can take it off now!' Archie squeaked with excitement.

What Grace saw when she took the blindfold off took her breath away. A huge lump formed in her throat and she couldn't speak. Her whole garden had been transformed into her dream. In one corner stood an angel statue which had been stored in the garage. It was something that she'd spotted in a salvage yard just before they'd moved into the house, and the reason she'd bought it was because she wanted to think of an angel watching over her and Archie and protecting them in their home. In another area, her rattan furniture had been assembled and arranged with loads of cushions on the chairs, and on the table in an ice bucket was a bottle of Bollinger and lots of glasses. In the far corner was what used to be her old ramshackle creosoted shed. Now it took pride of place, painted in a beautiful rich cream and duck-egg blue, with bunting and fairy lights round the doorway and Moroccan glass lanterns hanging outside each window. She still couldn't find any words. She wandered over to it and inside it there was bunting and more decorative lanterns. In one corner was a desk and an office chair and in the other, a sofa covered in technicoloured throws. Bookshelves lined the other walls.

She turned around and flung herself at Vinnie, clinging on for dear life. 'You did all this? For me?'

'Not just me, I had a great deal of help from my wing man.' He swept his arm round to Archie who had the biggest, proudest smile on his face that Grace had ever seen. 'And Mike and the kids, too. I'm not Superman, you know!'

'You guys are amazing! I just don't know what to say! And you!' She turned to Ruth, who was chuckling naughtily. 'You knew, didn't you? That's why we've been out all day, isn't it?'

Ruth smiled at her. 'Grace, if my little brother wanted to give you your dream garden, how could I refuse? Especially when he offered me a spa day as a bribe to get you away. As mum to three kids, I'm very easily bought, you know.'

Archie insisted that they all have a group hug, and how could they refuse? Apart from the day that

Archie was born, Grace had never felt so blessed in her life.

She felt totally overwhelmed. These people, who she'd only known for a short time, had turned her world around. They were kind, they were generous; they were beautiful souls. Just a few months ago, she had never felt more alone and sad, not knowing what the future held. And then one day, Vinnie had knocked on her door and it seemed that her luck had changed. And she'd never been happier.

* * *

Mike appeared from the conservatory with the karaoke machine in one hand and an extension lead in the other.

'We decided that we'd have the party at your house instead of ours. Hope that's OK?' he added apologetically.

'That's a fantastic idea,' Grace replied. 'I'm never leaving this garden again, anyway. Hope the neighbours don't mind the noise!'

As if by magic, they heard laughter coming from the side passage and Belinda appeared with a bottle of wine with Bill following behind, staggering under the weight of a huge pot filled with chilli con carne.

'The first rule of being neighbourly is to always invite the neighbours to the party,' Bill laughed. 'Surely you know that, Grace. Although I'm not sure how we got conned into cooking most of the food too!' He winked at her and once he'd plonked the pot down on the table, stooped and gave her a kiss on the cheek.

Monica then appeared from the kitchen carrying a huge bowl full of jacket potatoes, a tub of butter and a big dish of grated cheese. 'Hello, darling, hope you liked your surprise.' She grinned.

'Dinner is ready!' Vinnie announced. 'But before we start the food and the evening's entertainment, I want to make a toast to Grace. A few months ago, I'd never even met this amazing lady. And now, I feel like she's always been in my life. She's made me happier than I thought possible. I hope you love your new garden, Grace. I just wanted to do something nice for *you* for a change as you seem to spend your time making everyone else's lives better. So, ladies and gents, please join me in raising your glasses to Grace.'

'To Grace,' they chorused, and the kids cheered. Then from the karaoke machine, Pink started singing 'Get the Party Started.'

Grace was insistent that she wasn't going to sing,

saying that she had never done karaoke before in her life and did not intend to start at the ripe old age of thirty-seven.

Vinnie thrust a flute of Bollinger into her hand as the kids decided to kick off the singing and were dancing along to the music. Becks had plonked himself under the food table, just in case anything dropped onto the floor and he was required to hoover it up with his mouth.

Belinda came over and slung her arm around Grace's shoulders. 'Grace, I've never seen you look so happy. I had a feeling that day when Vinnie turned up that he was going to be someone significant in your life and I couldn't be more delighted for you. I used to worry about you so much, in the house on your own; I always wished that someone special would come along and show you that there was more to life than sitting around and waiting for your son to come home. I'm so pleased for you, my love.' Tears sprang to Grace's eyes as she hugged this beautiful lady that she was so lucky to have living next door.

Grace looked around at her friends and took in the scene. She thought that she had never seen Archie look as happy as he did right now. She'd always wished she'd had more children. She and Archie adored her sister's kids and missed them dreadfully now they were in the US. He was certainly in his element with his new friends, who felt like family already.

Ruth had had a couple of huge G&Ts by this point and decided that she would sing 'Firework' by Katy Perry. It was certainly a very different version from the original and she really didn't care. Mike looked like he couldn't have been prouder when she hit the high note at the end, even if she didn't quite get there.

None of them tried in any way to get Grace to have a turn. They knew and appreciated how she felt and didn't try to do that 'oh go on' annoying thing with her. Because of this and how much fun they were all having, and how easily those G&Ts were going down, Grace asked whether there were any songs by The Carpenters on the machine.

Nobody commented, they just looked for the track she wanted. When Ruth asked her who was going to sing it, Grace said, 'You, Monica and me, Ruthie! That's who!'

There was a big cheer and when 'Top of the World' started playing, the three ladies sang at each other rather than looked at the screen. They all knew the words off by heart and sang a fairly acceptable rendition. When they finished, Vinnie flung his arms around her, and gave her a great big hug. 'I'm so bloody proud of you, Grace,' he said. 'I thought you didn't do karaoke.'

'I don't and I never have and I never thought I would. But right here and now, I don't think I've ever felt more comfortable. I don't think I've ever felt more myself. And you're the reason for that, Vinnie. You're the one who makes me feel like I can do anything I want to. Like nothing is out of my reach. You're amazing, Vinnie, do you know that? I... er... love... the way that you make me feel.' She had come dangerously close to telling him that she loved him but she didn't want to scare him off. She thought it was too early for that, but she knew deep down that it was only a matter of time before those words came out of her mouth.

They spent the rest of the evening pretending to be The Sugababes, Little Mix and One Direction and they had a complete whale of a time. She couldn't remember when she had enjoyed herself so much. It was soon midnight and she realised that Archie was starting to get really tired. It was a good job it was school hols so he could have an easy week and some lie-ins to make up for it. A late night once in a while was OK; and tonight had been a special occasion.

* * *

Darling girl, I hid tonight behind that angel in your garden. I don't know why because I know that you can't see me. I am apparently allowed, once and only once, to be seen by you. I am saving that moment for a time when you really need me because it really will be the last time that you ever see me. Tonight though, my love, I was so proud of you. So proud that you have turned your life around. So proud that you have made such wonderful friends. People that you deserve in your life and who deserve you. And I'm so pleased that you have someone like Vinnie, who I really do think will treat you exactly how you are meant to be treated. Someone who will do everything in his power to make you happy, which is what love should be all about. I'm so happy for you, my darling.

Please think carefully about what Mark has suggested, about bringing together your family for Archie's sake. And make the right decision. I'm right here beside you all the way, whatever you decide. I love you, Mum xxx

25

A week later, the time had arrived for the first meeting of Busy Bodies. There had been a little response to the Facebook posts and a few people had put their name down on the list that Ruth was keeping on a clipboard at the café. To support Grace in her new venture, Belinda had very kindly offered for Archie to go to hers for tea, which he was really excited about, so Ruth and Grace had been at the café since five that evening setting up everything, and Ruth had spent the day making low-calorie snacks in the hope that people might like to order some. The start time on the poster was seven thirty and at seven fifteen the doorbell tinkled and two ladies popped their head round the door asking if they were in the right place. They introduced themselves as Gill and Maureen.

Grace took down their details while Ruth got the scales ready. She asked Gill to pop on first while Maureen went to the ladies', and when she'd finished it was Maureen's turn. Maureen was about to get on the scales when she shrieked '*Wait!*' and proceeded to take off her earrings, her necklace, her glasses and her jumper. They all laughed when she said how she'd definitely weigh less without them. Gill muttered, 'Perhaps if you hadn't just shoved a jam doughnut in your face when I came to pick you up, that might have helped too.' Ruth and Grace grinned at each other.

Their weights were written on their record cards, which were then stored in a lockable box. By this time, Beryl and Alma, two ladies who looked to be in their early seventies, had trickled through the door and joined the queue. They all said how delighted they were at how quickly they were weighed and their details taken. A young man, who introduced himself as Ben, was the next to sheepishly come through the door, asking if he was in the right place for the slimming club, followed by a married couple, Dawn and Dave. The last lady who entered the café had a figure to die for and Grace couldn't understand for the life of her why she was even there.

Everyone seemed really friendly and after the weighing, Ruth went round the group, offering the healthy snacks. There were murmurs of 'delicious' and 'this can't possibly be slimming' and 'oh my God, I need the recipe for this'.

Ruth tapped on the side of her glass with a spoon to get everyone's attention.

'We just wanted to say thank you for coming along tonight to our little club. Grace came up with the idea, I had a venue and we both wanted to lose some weight so it was the perfect combination. Our promise to you is that it won't be painful; you won't have to queue for ages while other people get weighed, because we don't have the room for massive numbers. You can come and be weighed and leave straight away if you want, or you can stay for a group chat about anything we've tried that might help others. You won't get told off if you've eaten something you shouldn't have.' She looked at Maureen at this point and raised her eyebrows. '*You* know you've done it, so you don't need someone else to tell you.' Everyone in the room laughed and visibly relaxed.

Grace spoke next. 'This is a club that we want you

to enjoy coming to, not dread. So if there's something you think would be a great addition, do let us know.'

The slim lady coughed and raised her hand. 'How about those of us who want to maybe go for a group walk? I'd love to go out for a walk in the evenings but feel daft and not particularly safe on my own. I'm Bev, by the way.' She had one of those faces that completely transformed when she smiled.

'What a great idea. We'd definitely be up for that, wouldn't we, Dawn?' Dave asked his wife, and she nodded.

'Definitely, I'd love that. What if we all shared recipes for something we've cooked that we think would be worth sharing with the other people here too?'

'Another fabulous idea,' agreed Ruth. 'And if you wanted to, I could even cook us something for tea on the night of the club which you could either eat here or take home for just a small charge.'

Again, there were oohs and aahs all round and lots of nodding heads.

'And what if you set up a Facebook private page that we could all be in, so that we can all support and motivate each other and share recipes and ideas?' Ben suggested. There was a unanimous nod of heads.

'I always feel awful at this type of group,' explained Bev. 'Because I'm reasonably slim, people wonder why I'd like to lose weight – but it's not about how you look, it's about how you feel inside. Perhaps this group would benefit from doing some things to help us raise our self-esteem and confidence? Maybe we could ask some guest speakers to come along to help us.'

Once again, there were yesses all round and Ruth and Grace looked at each other and grinned. Monica would be the perfect choice for a guest speaker. They had hoped that their idea of a small local slimming support group would be a good one, but now they knew it was going to be a resounding success.

Beryl came over and thanked Ruth and Grace for a great evening.

'Ladies, can I just say that I have thoroughly enjoyed myself tonight. Since my Keith died, I've not gone out much. Everyone I know is in a couple and I feel like a spare part, and I'd much rather stay in and read a good book anyway. I feel like I've already made some lovely new friends and I'm really looking forward to the next one. Thank you so much for giving me a new lease of life.' She held one of Grace's hands and kissed both her and Ruth's cheeks. She practically skipped out of the door. Grace felt her heart swell at the thought that they'd been able to create something that was quite life-changing for someone else.

Maureen and Gill waved as they left and Grace laughed as she heard Gill say, 'Shall we just get a cone of chips on the way home then, instead of a full portion, Maur?' She knew that these two were going to be a lot of hard work but a lot of fun, even if they didn't lose any weight!

As the last member of the first group shut the door on their way out, Ruth high-fived Grace as she said, 'God, I think I love you, Grace! Don't we make an awesome team? Roll on next week!'

Ruth and Grace cleared away all the plates and put the chairs up on the tables. It was a habit of Ruth's that she'd got from her days of being a teaching assistant years ago and she insisted that it made it easier for the floor to be cleaned the next morning. It was time for home; they were both exhausted but still buzzing from such a brilliant evening.

'You're pretty awesome, Gracie, do you know that?' Ruth flung her arm round Grace's shoulder as they walked towards their cars.

'You're not so bad yourself, gorgeous!' Grace

replied as she kissed her on the cheek and waved goodnight.

* * *

The next day the shrill ringing of the telephone interrupted Grace and Archie from making low-fat flapjacks as a tester for Busy Bodies. It was her father.

'Grace, I have something very important to tell you and I really hope you are sitting down.'

Lord above, she thought, her heart starting to race in her chest. 'What on earth has happened?'

'I'm going on a cruise with Gladys. I really hope you don't mind, but we will be sharing a cabin. I would never want or be able to replace your mother,' he blurted out, 'but I have realised that it is nice to have company in my twilight years and that I think your mother would want me to not waste a moment longer being miserable and wishing she were here.'

Grace stifled a giggle of relief. 'Oh! That sounds good. Tell me all about it.'

With the relief evident in his voice, he told her all about the cruise. A few of the residents from the retirement village were going and some of the staff were going along too, to be on hand should they be needed. Grace thought it sounded a wonderful idea and realised that it must have taken a lot for her dad to have plucked up the courage to make this call.

'I am happy for you, Dad,' she said. 'And for what it's worth, I'm sure you're right and that if Mum were here she'd be gallivanting around the world with a sugar daddy so I reckon you should go for it!' They said goodbye and hung up.

Despite her words of encouragement to her dad, Grace felt a pang of sadness when she put down the phone. She knew that no one would ever replace her mum. How could they? While Gladys was a lovely lady, she was very different to the vibrant, beautiful, vivacious lady that her mum was when she was taken way before her time. While these days she had wonderful memories when she thought of her mum, she was always going to be sad for the future they'd never have together; sad for Archie that he wouldn't know how it felt to have a proper nanna who adored him.

Grief is such a strange thing, she reflected. *One minute you feel perfectly fine, then the smallest trigger can devastate you all over again. A song, some words, a place you drive past, a memory, a voice, or the sight of someone who reminds you so vividly of the person you've lost, and all of a sudden you are back in a moment when you realise they are no longer here.*

This was all on her mind when the doorbell rang, but her thoughts paused when she saw Mark standing there. Quietly, he asked whether he could come in and have a word. Archie appeared behind Grace, delighted to see his dad unexpectedly on his doorstep.

'Hi, Dad!' he said, grabbing him in for a hug.

Grace smiled at the love Archie had for his father, and after Archie had greeted Mark, she told him to go upstairs and get ready for bed.

She took Mark through into the kitchen and she stood as he made himself comfortable sitting at the breakfast bar. Realising that he didn't look like he had any intention of going for a while, she sat down opposite him. He started talking about what a lovely sunny day it had been and he didn't seem to want to get to the point of why he had come.

'Well, what did you want to talk about, Mark?' she asked. 'I presume you haven't come to talk about the weather.' She was starting to feel braver when speaking to him.

'I've been thinking about us, Gracie. I have a serious proposition for you.'

Grace raised an eyebrow and thought, *This is going to be interesting*.

'Lorraine is going away soon for a week with her

friends on a hen party. I've decided that you and I should use that time to see if we can put the past behind us to build our family again. We, as Archie's parents, have a duty to our son to be family, and I know that you, as his mother, would want to do what's right for him. It's only ever been you, Grace. I wouldn't be with Lorraine now if you hadn't kicked me out.

'It makes sense to do it while Lorraine's away, then she won't know about it and if it doesn't work out, we can go back to how things are now and she need never know.'

Grace laughed out loud. A short, sharp laugh. She couldn't believe what she was hearing.

'So, let me get this right. You want us to get back together for a fortnight while your girlfriend is away to see if we can make it work out? If it does, you'll leave Lorraine, if it doesn't, you won't tell her that it even happened. Is that what you are saying?'

'Yes, that's right,' Mark said blithely. 'You, me and Archie back together, trying to do stuff as a family. This is the best thing for all of us. Just think, you'd have Archie with you every night and every day. Isn't that what you've always wanted? I know I've been a bit of an arse in the past, Grace, but I've changed, I truly have. I can be the man that you want me to be. I can help you more. Let's be a family again.

'I know you've been seeing that Vinnie bloke, but really, Grace! He's not Archie's dad, I am, and you know our son wants nothing more than to see his mum and dad back in the same house.'

Grace wasn't sure, but her mind went back to the occasions that Archie had got his parents to join in group hugs, and how his little face had lit up on the rare times they had both made it to sports day.

'And anyway, I saw that Vannie, or whatever his name is, in the petrol station earlier. I said hello and told him what a wonderful evening we'd had at your awards do. He seemed surprised. Didn't know a thing about it, but I filled him in on what a fantastic night we'd had,' he smirked.

Grace was lost for words. It would be just her luck if Mark managed to turn their very innocent night out into something more sordid in Vinnie's eyes. She tried to pretend that she wasn't affected by what Mark had done, knowing that she had to tread carefully.

'You know that deep down you, me and Archie all back together again is what you really want. It'll be great, just like old times. So what do you say?'

Grace was still reeling, unable to comprehend

what damage Mark might have done to her relationship with Vinnie. Mark, for some strange reason, took her silence as acquiescence and, without warning, strode over to her, taking her by complete surprise, and kissed her. Somehow, he got his sleeve caught in her necklace and as he pulled away, the crystal broke into two pieces and dropped on the floor. Distraught, she dropped to her knees to pick them up. He winked at her and walked to the front door, saying over his shoulder, 'Don't worry, Grace, I'll buy you a much nicer one. If you play your cards right, it might even be a diamond!' As quickly as he had walked into the house, he walked out again, leaving Grace feeling completely dazed.

Despite his apparent desire to get back together and his protestations that he had changed, it was clear he was the same old Mark. But there was just a tiny part of her that wondered whether there was truth in his words. *Was* she being unfair to Archie by not being with his dad? Archie was the centre of her life and she'd always put him first. She couldn't bear it if she caused him any unhappiness.

* * *

She phoned Vinnie the minute that Mark left but he didn't pick up, so she left a message on his voicemail.

'Hey, Vinnie, it's me. Er, Grace, that is. Can you give me a call when you're free please? Thanks. Bye.'

He didn't call back.

She tried to stop the tears forming in her eyes. All this time she'd been worried that he might have something to hide, and now Vinnie would be the one who thought she was lying to him.

That night when Archie had gone to bed, Grace phoned Hannah. They talked about their father's revelations earlier that day. Hannah was also really pleased that he was starting to enjoy life again.

Grace told her sister about Mark's proposition. Hannah ranted down the phone: 'If you are even considering this one tiny bit, you do realise that I'm going to have to jump on a plane to the UK and come and batter you senseless, don't you? You know that he's only doing this because you've found someone new.

'Grace, my darling, don't you dare allow him to mess up what you have with Vinnie. He sounds really special. Even from this far away, I can tell that you really like him. Your voice is different and I can hear that you are smiling when you speak about him. I've never heard you speak about Mark like that.

Mark is an asshole. He's just poisoning you because you've found someone new and he doesn't like it.'

Grace smiled to hear some Americanisms creep into her sister's vocabulary.

'I know what you are saying but this way, H, I'd get my boy back. I'd get to be with him all the time. You know how much I hate it when he's not here. I feel like part of me, my heart and my soul, is missing. Perhaps I could put up with Mark and his ways. We loved each other once, very much. We could try to get that back. Perhaps I just need to accept that family is more important than what I really want?'

'Darling, I understand, but you have to live for yourself. You cannot live your life for Archie. It won't be long before he's going off with his mates. He'll be going to high school soon and he won't even want you to walk to school with him. I know that you can't see that now but I can. I've been through it and I know how it feels. Don't throw away what you have with Vinnie now and certainly not for Mark! I know it's early days but I have a real good feeling about you and Vinnie. Don't you *dare* throw it away for that good-for-nothing jerk!'

'I haven't decided anything yet, sis, but I have to consider all the options and think about what is right for Archie. As his mum, that's my job. And anyway, I know that on the surface Vinnie does seem perfect, but there's something niggling away at me.'

'What?'

'When I saw him on my night out with Monica, his friend said something about Ellie not liking the fact that he was talking to a woman. And then, when I was at his house, I saw a text message from a woman, telling him to ring her. And then when we went to his house, there was a young girl driving away from his house.'

'So have you asked him about it?'

'Erm, well, no.'

'For goodness' sake, Grace, you have to ask him. There could be a perfectly reasonable explanation. Do you not think you are reading too much into it?'

'Yep, I know that. But I could also find out something that I don't want to and the whole Vinnie situation could come crashing down around me. And I can't do that to Archie.'

'Babe, I know you love Arch and hate it when he's away, but I beg you to remember how unhappy you were when you were with Mark. You seem to have forgotten all of that. He treated you badly and I can't believe you would even consider having him back. He'll never change, you know. Remember all those times when you used to sit at my kitchen table and cry because he'd upset you again?

'You're a different person now. Look how far you've come in the last few months. You're back to the old Grace. My little sister, who I adore, who is full of life and just wants everyone around her to be happy. Think about Archie – he must love to have his mum being cheerful around him all the time, instead of how sad you used to be. And think about your future. You would be turning down the opportunity of a new life with Vinnie. He's a man who loves you for who you are and not who he wants you to be. He accepts you and loves you and you are better for having him in your life. I can see that for myself and I'm all the way over here.

'Just please think very carefully and talk to me before you make your mind up. You have to promise me that! And maybe you should just ask Vinnie about the other things that are winding you up?'

Grace felt so sad when she put down the phone after speaking with her sister. She was so far away. There was a whole ocean between them. She knew that her sister had chosen a life in the States for her family and she had to respect that, but she also felt that her sister had chosen that life over being close to her. *You really just have yourself to rely on*, Grace told herself. *People have to do whatever it takes to be happy.*

Without her mum around to chat to, Grace had never felt so alone. She had a huge decision to make. Perhaps it would be easier all round for everyone if she just gave it another go with Mark.

Mark texted her that evening, to see whether she'd considered his proposal. He was probably texting her while Lorraine was cooking dinner or something. The thought of having Archie with her all the time was like a carrot dangling over her head. He knew it and he was playing her. Grace couldn't help feeling that she was being manipulated by him all over again and she ignored the message.

If and when Vinnie called her back, she didn't really know what to say to him. She shouldn't have kept the fact that Mark had attended the awards ceremony with her secret from him, but the only reason she hadn't told him was because it wasn't important to her. However, it had been too long now since it happened to bring it up with Vinnie without it sounding like a bigger deal than it was. She didn't know what to do. She also needed to ask him about the text she had seen and other things, because it was really playing on her mind.

She tried to call him once more before bed but

again it went to answerphone. Perhaps she'd bug-gered everything up already.

'Vin, it's me again. I wanted to explain everything to you. I know that you bumped into Mark and that he's trying to cause trouble between us. Please, call me so we can talk. Please, Vinnie. I miss you.'

That night, Grace didn't sleep a wink. Her mind was all over the place. She'd met someone wonderful and she hadn't thought that was possible, so he de-served to know what she was thinking. But the trouble was, she didn't really know what she was thinking herself. How could she explain anything to someone else when she didn't understand herself? She thought perhaps that if she ignored the problem, it might just go away. Knowing that she had a busy couple of days coming up at work, she vowed just to get stuck in and try to forget all about it for a while.

* * *

But that was easier said than done and when she still hadn't heard from Vinnie by the next morning, she was starting to panic. She couldn't believe that Mark had managed to ruin what she and Vinnie had built together, but she also couldn't believe that Vinnie wouldn't even talk to her and let her explain.

She rang Ruth.

'Oh, Gracie, what on earth has happened? Vincent has told me that he's taken an emergency job in Hull and is going to be away for the week. I said that I knew he'd miss you and he said that you weren't everything that you appeared to be. He sounded really cross. Has something happened?'

Grace explained it all to Ruth; that Mark had spun their night out into some sort of romantic date and Ruth sympathised, but told her she was a total idiot for not mentioning it to Vinnie at the time. Grace tried to explain that she hadn't even wanted Mark to accompany her, and hadn't really even had an option as he'd decided *for* her, so she'd just blocked it out. That was the only reason she hadn't told Vinnie. She had nothing to hide.

'I just hope he finds it in his heart to listen and to forgive you, Grace, I really do. I could bash your blooming heads together. You are so perfect for each other but this has come between you. I'll try to talk to him, but sometimes he's so pig-headed that he won't even listen to me. I can only try. I also know that Vinnie has something that he needs to share with you. I wish I could go into it, but it's not my story to tell. He needs to tell you himself.'

Grace knew that she would miss him terribly

during his week away but it had at least come at the perfect time, giving her some head space so that she could try to make sense of her thoughts and feelings. She'd never been happier than she was with Vinnie, yet there was something about him that she clearly didn't know. She was torn – wanting to do the right thing for her son and her family.

Grace had always believed that a family should stick together, taking the cue from her own parents, who had been through hell and back but had always kept the family as a unit. She understood from certain things that her mum had said over the years that her father had never been an angel, and while she never knew exactly what he'd done, she knew that there was something in their life that had caused major turmoil. But her mum had insisted that they stay together for the sake of her family and it was that example that weighed heavy on her mind as she wrestled with what to do. Mark had always been good at manipulating her, making her believe that it was her duty to not think about her own feelings but put the feelings of others before herself. She was at a loss, held back by her sense of duty that she needed to put Archie first, even before her own happiness.

She knew that Vinnie was due back on Saturday night because before Mark's revelation, they'd made arrangements to go to Ruth's, so she decided to leave it at that for the time being and not bother him. She felt like her brain was going to explode if she kept trying to fathom out what she should do. She knew what she wanted to do in her heart, but her head kept pulling her another way.

* * *

On Tuesday afternoon, Grace went to visit her dad. When she arrived, Gladys was there and they all had a cuppa together. They were so excited about their cruise and showed Grace the brochure and went through the itinerary with her.

Her dad was also rather excited to show off his new mobility scooter, something else that was giving him a new lease of life.

'How's Mark?' he asked. 'I was so grateful for all his help with this scooter business. I could never have done it without him.'

Grace was shocked. Mark had visited her dad? He'd been helping him? Why had neither of them ever mentioned this before?

'You never said he came to see you, Dad. Why would you not tell me that?'

'To be honest, I thought you knew that he pops in

for a cup of tea every now and again. He did so much research on the best type of scooter for me to get and then took me along to pick up the one that we'd chosen. I really don't know why you can't sort everything out with him. He's a decent bloke and he's Archie's father. A boy needs his father around.'

Grace was stunned. It wasn't like Mark to put someone else before himself, but perhaps he really had changed after all, like he said he had. Was he now proving himself to her, knowing that it wouldn't be long before she found out from her dad that he'd done him a huge favour? She was more perplexed than ever.

Her dad went out to the toilet, shaking his head, and Gladys asked her if she was OK, saying she looked down-hearted.

'Not really, Gladys. I'm so confused.'

'I know I'm an old fuddy-duddy, darling, but if I can help in any way, do let me know. I'm a great listener.'

'Thank you, Gladys, I really do appreciate that. Mark and I were not happy when we were together and he wants us to be a family again, but now I've met someone else who I really like and have the chance of a new but unsure future. So how do I choose?'

'Is he only saying this now, because you have the chance of happiness with someone else though, Grace? I do know that in life, you have to do what makes your soul sing. And be with someone who always puts you first and loves you for what you are, and not for what they want you to be. And someone who makes you laugh. I met Mark the other day and he seemed to be charming, but his eyes are too close together for my liking. You should never trust a man whose eyes are too close together.' She laughed.

'Seriously though, you're a lovely woman and a wonderful mum. And you deserve to be with someone who treats you like a million dollars all of the time, not just when it suits. And you need to be sure that he's not just trying to spoil your happiness with your new man. That old chestnut, where he just doesn't want anyone else to have you. But then what do I know? I'm just a silly old woman. Just remember that the person you choose is the person you're going to grow old with. So decide wisely.'

Grace smiled and thanked her as her dad walked back into the room, and she realised that Gladys wasn't the only person to have said this to her. She'd made up her mind.

26

Grace sent a text to Mark and said that she'd like to see him on Thursday night, suggesting that he could take her out for a meal and to pick her up at seven fifteen, trying for once to take control. His cursory response agreed to the dinner, but said that she'd have to arrange a babysitter as he was far too busy and he would be there at seven thirty. Gritting her teeth, her next text was to Monica, asking if she'd help out by sitting with Archie for a couple of hours.

Thursday afternoon came round and she received a text from Mark to say that he'd had a hell of a day at work and that it would be nice if she could drive so he could have a drink. Once again, Grace tried out her new-found assertiveness, replying that she'd had quite a week too so it would be nice if he drove. He didn't respond until early evening, once again leaving her hanging till the last possible moment, when he reluctantly agreed.

When Monica came round and saw her friend, she wolf-whistled. Grace was dressed in a red crossover top, which showed off her magnificent cleavage, a snug-fitting black pencil skirt, and black knee-high suede boots. She knew Mark had always had a thing for boots, even if it was nearly the height of summer.

'Wow! You look *a-may-zing*! I hope Vinnie appreciates the effort that you've gone to.'

'It's not Vinnie I'm going out with, Monica, it's Mark.'

'You can't be serious, Grace. What are you even thinking?'

'Mon, you have to trust me on this, I've thought long and hard and I've made my decision. I'll be back within two hours.'

At seven forty-five, fifteen minutes later than they had arranged, Mark turned up. Monica answered the door, glared at him, shouted for Grace and then shut the door in his face, but it was re-opened by Archie, who ran to the door, eager to say hi to his dad, who hugged him. It was clear that Mark had come straight from work as he was wearing his work suit and tie.

Grace came to the door and they both said goodbye to Archie, Grace giving her son a huge cuddle.

'So, where have you booked?' she asked Mark.

'Booked? I haven't booked anywhere. I thought you were booking somewhere.'

A great start, Grace thought, but she kept calm.

Mark walked straight round to his side of the car and let her sort herself out getting in. His phone pinged to signify he'd got a message, which he checked, and as he always had done, tilted it away so that she couldn't see who it was from. He smirked as he read it, took a minute to respond, then realised that she was watching him and put it in the side pocket of the car.

'Why don't we head up to the Plough & Harrow,' she suggested, knowing that they could normally get a table there at short notice.

'I can't believe you wouldn't drive. I've had a really shitty week at work this week and I could have done with a drink, you know,' he said.

'Yep, my week's not been brilliant either, to be honest.'

'Yeah but a problem in your little job is nothing

compared to the scale of the problems I have. I have the future of the country to think about, educating the little shits I have at my school. And the parents, for that matter.'

It was obvious that Mark was already irritated and, as usual, it immediately put her on edge. But she was determined this evening that she would not let him rile her.

They arrived at the pub and were lucky to be seated straight away at a table in the conservatory area. While they sat and looked at the menu, a silence descended upon them; clearly they were both finding it difficult to even think of anything to talk about. She thought of Vinnie and the hours they had spent chatting about their lives, their hopes, their fears, and felt a wave of sadness knowing that Vinnie didn't even want to see her right now. The waitress came over and Mark ordered his food without even asking Grace what she wanted or even if she was ready. Sometimes she forgot quite how inconsiderate he was; and this was a time when he was trying to impress her and apparently woo her back!

She placed her order with the waitress and Mark said he was popping to the gents'. Uncharacteristically, he left his phone on the table, so after a quick look over her shoulder to make sure he couldn't see her, she picked it up. She knew it was wrong, but couldn't help herself. She flicked onto his messages and found the last one that had arrived when they were in the car.

> Have a good time at your conference, hope you learn loads. Sorry you couldn't join me on this holiday but look forward to having lots of sex when I get back!

His reply read:

> It'll be dead boring. I'd much rather be on holiday with you. I'll be thinking of you as I'm in our bed at night, imagining how hot your tan looks. You can imagine what I'll be doing while I'm thinking of you! Can't wait to see your white bits! Xxx

So, that's why he'd been smirking. Leopards really don't change their spots, do they? He was just keeping all his options open, wasn't he? What a bastard! Why she expected differently from him though, she couldn't imagine. She knew now that the decision she had come to was the absolute right thing to do. For her, for Archie and for Mark. She'd been thinking about it all week. He'd always made out that the split was her fault and she permanently felt guilty about taking Archie away from his dad. She'd spent the week wondering whether Mark could ever change and whether they really could have a happy family life together, reunited. But she knew now that he wouldn't change, and that for once she had to be strong.

She put his phone back in exactly the same place he'd left it and dropped Ruth a text to ask if she could do her a massive favour. Ruth responded in exactly the way she hoped she would. She also asked the waitress to hold their dinner order.

When he returned, she asked him what he was doing at the weekend, just to get the measure of what he had planned, considering that he was supposed to be trying to work hard to get her back. He said he was going to the pub to watch the rugby with his mates on Saturday afternoon then going out for a curry, and playing golf on Sunday. Grace noticed that he hadn't even asked her what her plans were. Clearly he'd already slipped back into his old habits of doing what *he* wanted to do, when *he* wanted to do it, without any consideration of her or Archie. They were just an afterthought in his life, as they always had been. And sadly, always would be. She'd been so focused on what she thought would be the right course of action, bringing her and Mark back together for Archie's sake, that she hadn't realised it until now.

The door to the pub opened and there stood Ruth. Grace acknowledged her with a nod, watching as she headed over to sit in a chair by the door.

'Mark. I've considered your proposal.' She looked up and saw he had a smug grin on his face. She had a feeling it might not be there for long. 'Thank you so much for thinking of Archie and me, and how we could once again be a family.'

His smile became even bigger, if that was possible. 'I'm glad you've come to your senses, Grace. You know it's the right thing to do.'

She held up her hand to stop him speaking, using one of his typical moves back on him. It felt good.

'Mark. I would appreciate it if you would just shut your mouth for one minute. It gives me such pleasure to tell you that I wouldn't want to be with you again if you were the last man on earth. You are arrogant, you are ignorant and you are inconsiderate. You think only of yourself, your own fulfilment and your own happiness.'

'Oh, and I suppose this is only because you've got yourself a new shag now?' he responded. 'Bloody fan-fucking-tastic Virtuous Vinnie waves his willy around and you think he's Mr Fucking Wonderful.'

'Do you know what, Mark? Yes, Vinnie has waved his willy around, and I have to say it's bigger and more beautiful than yours will ever be and he knows how to use it a whole lot better than you ever used yours! He's kind, he's considerate, he's gorgeous and he's bloody perfect for me. And he's nicer to our son than you've ever been. And you're his father! You have never put your family before yourself. *You* are the only person that matters in your life. You should be ashamed of yourself.'

Mark turned red with fury and went to speak.

'*Do not speak right now!*' she bellowed at him. Grace didn't know where this strength of purpose had come from but she did know that this was the very last time her ex was ever going to treat her this way.

'So, yes, Vinnie is a hundred times the man that you have ever been or ever will be. He treats me with kindness and respect, something that you don't appear to have for anyone, not even your own family. And I suggest that if you ever want people to like you, go look those words up in a dictionary. And for the record, I would rather be alone than be with you. Because being alone is better than being in a relationship where you are lonely and disrespected. Being alone is better than being lied to and cheated on. And you're still doing it now to Lorraine. I am worth far more than you, Mark. It's just taken me a very long time to work that out. But now I have, I have never been more serious about anything in my life. Now go and fuck yourself!'

And with that, she picked up her coat, strode over to Ruth who hugged her so tightly she thought she might have cracked a rib, and walked out the door, to the applause of the bar staff.

27

There had been no calls or texts from Mark since she'd left him in the pub the previous night. She knew he'd be furious but she was sure he was giving her the silent treatment on purpose in order to keep her on tenterhooks so that she'd be worrying about what he was planning. It seemed like none of the men in her life were speaking to her.

In a total state of daydreaming, she got Archie ready for school and took the short walk hand in hand with this adorable child. She knew that one day soon would be the last day that he would want to hold her hand and so took every opportunity to do so now. His chubby little hand fitted into hers perfectly, although she noticed how big it was getting. Soon, he'd be taller than her and she dreaded the day when he wouldn't fit on her lap any more. When they got to school, he did what he always did and squeezed her hand three times, one for 'I', one for 'love' and one for 'you'. This way he didn't have to say it out loud while his mates were around. She squeezed his back four times, the extra squeeze meaning 'I love you too.' As he walked off, she called him back. When he got back to her, she hugged him tight and kissed him. '*Mum!* You're embarrassing me!'

'Yeah, but I'm your mum and that's my job!' She laughed as he rolled his eyes at her, but he gave her a great big smile so she knew she was forgiven already.

As she wasn't working that day, she decided to throw a joint of beef in the slow cooker and go and blow away the cobwebs by taking Becks for a walk. It would give her some time to think, which, after the past week, she sorely needed. She drove to the forest and walked and walked. Becks was in his element but she couldn't help but remember the lovely walks she'd had here with Vinnie, holding hands and getting to know each other, and she realised how much she missed him.

Before she knew it, it was lunchtime and they'd been walking for over three hours, but it had been good for her to be in the countryside and have some space to think. She wondered whether she'd dreamt everything that had happened last night. Whether she really had stood up to Mark once and for all.

Whether she'd dreamt it or not, she felt stronger than she'd felt for as long as she could remember and she had hope in her heart. Hope and positivity that her future was going to be rosy and that everything was going to be OK. Normally she felt a constant worry that Archie was never going to grow up a well-adjusted child, and that felt like such a responsibility on her shoulders, but today she felt like even that was sorted. She felt calm and peaceful. She also felt loved. She wasn't sure what the situation was with Vinnie and while that made her feel sad, she knew it was something that she'd get over. It wouldn't destroy her.

She'd been at low points in her life; when she lost her mum, she knew that a huge part of her heart had been broken and that although it would never heal, she would eventually move forward and get used to the fact that, much as she wanted her to be, her mum wasn't around and she just had to suck that up and get on with her life. Another really low point was when she and Mark split up, but again, she knew at the time that she would get over it eventually, and she had. She'd got used to a new life without a partner and it wasn't so bad. Love came from lots of different sources, and she had love in abundance from her friends and family. Maybe she didn't need that romantic love to make her complete. She just needed to be comfortable in her own skin, so that she could be happy with her life. It was better to be happy and alone than to be in a relationship and be lonely. And it was better to have loved and lost than never to have loved at all.

The aroma of the beef cooking hit her as soon as she walked through the front door and made her feel hungry for the first time that day. She peeled some potatoes so that they could have hot buttery mash and got some veg ready to boil in the evening.

After making herself a ham and cucumber sandwich, she sat with her feet up and her iPad on her lap, thinking that whatever will be will be. She had a feeling that however much she stressed about things, it wasn't going to change the situation. She flicked through her Facebook updates and friends' posts and before she knew it, she was looking at Vinnie's profile pic. He wasn't one for using social media, even though he had profiles set up. She gazed into his eyes and hoped in her heart that they could at least be friends, if nothing else. She wasn't going to let Mark destroy the last few months totally.

Whiling away her afternoon on the internet meant that it was soon time to pick up Archie from school. While she was waiting in the playground and chatting to some of the other parents, Archie's class came out and his teacher looked at her a bit strangely. When all the class had been dispersed to their parents, there was still no sign of her son. She went over to his teacher and asked where Archie was.

'Have you forgotten that he was at the dentist?' she asked. 'His dad picked him up at two o'clock.'

Grace's heart sank to her boots. 'No – his dad never takes him to the dentist. His dad doesn't even know where his dentist is. And his dad is always at work.' She felt unease deep down in her stomach and knew that Mark had collected Archie to wind her up. He was taking revenge on her for humiliating him in the way that he knew would hit her hardest.

She'd left her phone at home so ran all the way back on trembling legs and grabbed it from the hall table. She purposely never took her phone to school, so that she and Archie could concentrate on chatting about his day while they walked home. These were their few special moments of the day. She rang Mark's number but it rang out and then went to voicemail. She left a message asking him to call her straight away. She rang Mark's school and asked to be put through to him, only to be told by the receptionist that he'd phoned in sick that morning. Despite her deep breaths, she was now starting to panic.

There was one other person that she needed by her side to help her right now. Vinnie's phone also went to voicemail. She left a message blurting out what had happened in short sharp phrases. 'Archie's gone. Rang Mark. No answer. I don't know where they are. I'm scared. Think I might need the police!'

Having said the words made it sound so real, and she started to fall apart. She really didn't know what to do. Her breathing became erratic and panic was really starting to set in. When the phone rang, she grabbed it, seeing Vinnie's name flash up on the display.

'I'm on my way back from Hull. I came back early and I'm nearly home. I can be there in less than fifteen minutes,' he replied. 'Stay by the phone in case he rings. Don't ring the police yet as they won't be far away. He's just trying to frighten you. I'm coming, Grace!'

Two minutes later, the house phone rang and she snatched it up. 'Mark?'

'No, darling, it's me,' said Ruth. 'Vinnie just rang and told me to keep you on the landline till he got there.'

'Oh, Ruth,' Grace said as she fell to her knees, breaking down in floods of tears. 'He's just taken him to get back at me. I can't believe he could do this to me.'

Ruth tried to keep her as calm as possible and got her to think about all the places that they could have gone.

'I have to go, Ruth, Vinnie's arrived.' She flung the phone down and ran out to the car and he quickly swept her up in his arms, where she clung on for dear life. He stroked her hair and wiped the tears from her eyes as she wailed, 'How can he do this to me? How could he do this to his son?'

'Come on, let's go inside and get a drink and we'll think about our plan of action. Mark might be an arse, but he is Archie's father and surely Archie will be safe with him. They can't be too far away as they've not been gone long. We just need to find them.' Her hands shook as she spooned coffee into a mug, spilling most of it on the work surface, and poured the hot water. She realised that Vinnie wanted to keep her busy to try to calm her down a little, but she was utterly distraught, although seeing Vinnie being so calm and supportive, she felt her heart swell with gratitude, and she couldn't bear the gap between them any more.

'Vinnie, I owe you an explanation about the event I went to with Mark.'

His face clouded over. 'Not now, Grace. There's a lot of stuff that we probably should have talked about and didn't. But right now, we have something way more important to do.'

He suggested she get a piece of paper and write down a list of all the places she thought that Mark may have taken Archie. She couldn't even write the words, her hands were shaking too much, so he took the pen and pad from her.

'I know it's hard, but it would really help if you could have a good think about it, honey,' he said gently.

'They don't really have a place that they go. They don't go anywhere in particular. Mark never takes him anywhere. I can't even focus my mind. Think, Grace, think!' She hit her forehead with the ball of her hand. 'Can't we just phone the police? They'll find him, surely. They'll know what to do.'

'Involving the police might just wind him up more though, Grace. You need to be really sure. Once they're on board, there'll be no turning back. And you know he could lose his job because of this if they're involved.'

'OK, let's just wait a bit longer. I'll try his phone

again.' Once more, it rang out and went to voicemail. She left a message, trying to be as calm as possible. 'Mark, please ring me. I know that Archie is with you and that you'd never harm him but I need to know where you are and why you've taken him. Please, call me.' Her voice broke on the last three words.

She remembered then that a while ago Mark's phone had broken, and he had borrowed Lorraine's. She had put Lorraine's number in her phone at the time, so as a last resort, she phoned it now. It had the international dial tone but went to answerphone. She left a message asking Lorraine to call her urgently.

Snatching up her car keys from the dish on the hall table, she said that she was going to drive round to Mark's flat, but Vinnie told her firmly that she was driving nowhere in that state and grabbed his keys. After diverting the house phone to her mobile, they went round to Mark's and rang every intercom on the door until someone let her into the block. Grace ran up the stairs, heart racing, and banged on Mark's front door, Vinnie following close behind. Mrs Brown, the old lady from the flat over the landing, appeared when she heard the commotion.

'You won't find him in. He's gone away for a few days, dear, he told me this morning. Why are you here?' she said. 'He said he was taking his son away on a little holiday. I did think it was a bit strange to be honest, as the children are still in school, aren't they?'

'Oh my God! No!' Grace fell to the floor in a crumpled heap, her head pounding and a dizzy feeling overwhelming her.

'My darling, whatever is the matter?' Mrs Brown asked as she bent down to Grace and put her arm around her shoulders. Vinnie was starting to look anxious, although Grace could tell he was attempting to calm himself.

'He's taken my son out of school and they've disappeared,' she exclaimed. 'Did he mention where he was going at all?'

'Let me think now. Yes. Yes, he did. He said he was taking his son to his friend's house in the Lakes. Do you know where that would be?'

'Mrs Brown, thank you, thank you, thank you.' She scrambled up from the floor and kissed the dear old lady on the cheek. 'You've been a massive help. I owe you everything. Come on, Vinnie,' she yelled behind her as she ran down the stairs two at a time. 'I know where they are.'

Grace looked at her watch as they jumped in the car. It was three hours since she'd gone to pick up

Archie from school and that had been an hour and a half after Mark had picked up Archie. They would have already arrived in the Lake District if they'd driven straight there. She told Vinnie to just get on the M6 and drive north.

Grace's phone rang and she saw an unknown mobile number flash up. Normally she wouldn't answer unknown numbers, but she had a feeling deep down in the pit of her stomach that she needed to answer this one.

'H-Hello?' she stuttered.

'Good afternoon. Is this Grace Carnegie?' a woman's voice asked.

'It is.' Her heart was in her mouth.

'This is Police Constable Sarah James here from Cumbria Police. Please don't worry, but I have a young man here who says he's your son. He's quite distressed but had your number in his coat pocket and asked me to ring you. I'm going to pass you over to him.'

Her heart skipped a beat or two.

'Mummy!' Archie cried down the phone. 'Mummy, is that you?' She could tell that he was trying to be really brave but could hear tears in his voice.

'Archie! Where are you?' she asked him, trying to stay as calm as she possibly could.

'We're at a service station on the motorway. Dad picked me up from school saying I had to go to the dentist, but I knew that there was something wrong because you always take me there. When we got in the car, he said that we weren't going to the dentist but that he was taking me away to the Lake District for the weekend. I knew that if I was meant to be going somewhere with Dad, that you would have known about it and would have told me.'

He was now crying hard but trying to talk between his sobs. 'I told Dad that we had to speak to you. We kept seeing that you were trying to call but Daddy kept laughing and saying that it served you right. What did he mean, Mummy?'

'Oh, darling, I'm so sorry that this happened. You're my wonderful brave boy. Where is Dad now?'

'I don't know, Mummy, he went to the toilet ages ago. He sat me down with a McDonalds and told me to stay still till he came back but this nice police lady came over and asked me why I was alone. I started to cry and she asked me what had happened so I told her. I had your number in my pocket. You always told me to keep it somewhere safe in case of emergency. I think this was an emergency, wasn't it, Mummy?

Have I done the right thing? Will Dad be mad with me?'

'It was absolutely the right thing to do, darling, yes. You are a very clever boy. But please don't worry any more, I'm on my way to you. I'll be there as soon as I can. And I'm going to give you the biggest squeeze ever. Now, do everything that the nice police lady asks you to, OK? And remember that your mummy loves you so very much and I'll be there really, really soon. OK, sweetheart?'

'Yes, Mummy, I love you too.'

Grace's heart melted once more now she knew that her son was safe and that within hours she could hold him in her arms again.

'Can you pass me back to the nice police lady please, sweetie?'

The policewoman explained that she'd seen a young boy sitting on his own in his school uniform when she and her colleague were grabbing a coffee at Knutsford Services on the M6. They thought it was strange so just kept an eye on the situation. When they saw that he'd been there for quite a while and no one appeared to be with him, she spoke to Archie, who said that his dad had gone to the toilet a while ago, and that he'd been told not to move. Her colleague had then gone into the toilets and located

Mark. He was locked in one of the cubicles, crying, and the police officer had had to climb over the top to open the door and get to him. Mark had admitted that he'd taken his son out of school without the consent of his mother and that he knew it was the wrong thing to do but didn't know what to do next. He said he'd messed things up big time, but he'd thought he wanted to get back at his ex-wife. They had taken him and Archie to the offices in the service station and put them in separate rooms while they rang her.

Listening to the whole sorry story in the policewoman's soft northern tones calmed Grace's fears a little, but she couldn't feel totally relieved just yet. Not until she had her boy back in her arms once more. But at least she knew now that he would be safe till she got to him.

Vinnie put his foot down, driving far faster than he should, while Grace explained what PC James had told her, until she was interrupted by the shrill ring of her phone. It was Lorraine.

'Grace. What's happened?' Lorraine sounded bemused to be hearing from her partner's ex-wife and Grace couldn't blame her.

'He's taken Archie, Lorraine. Why would he do that? Why would he do that to me?'

'Oh, Grace, we had a huge row last night on the

phone. He was in a foul mood when he called me. I'd had far too much to drink and so had he. I told him that I was sick of him and sick of playing second fiddle to his ex-wife. Sorry, Grace. I told him I wanted him gone. I tried to call him this morning but he hasn't returned my calls. I think you've borne the brunt of it.'

'Well, I think I'm probably the one who put him in the bad mood he was in, Lorraine. But right now, I know where they are so I'm going to fetch my son. Good luck with everything.'

'You too, Grace. I'm sorry. I never meant for you to get hurt in all of that.'

'Well, perhaps you should have thought about that before you started shagging my husband behind my back.'

Grace ended the call. The only thing that mattered now was seeing Archie safe and sound.

* * *

Vinnie's car screeched to a halt at the entrance doors to the service station just under an hour later, and Grace hardly waited for the wheels to come to a stop before she opened the door, jumped out and ran in. There, sitting at a table near the door, was Archie with a policewoman. Her heart was pounding as she stopped, took a breath and slowly walked towards her son, trying not to panic him.

'*Mummy!*' he yelled when he saw her. 'It's my mum,' he explained to the police officer, who smiled at Grace. Archie threw himself into Grace's arms and burst into tears again. Grace did the same. They hugged each other like they never wanted to let go.

'Miss Carnegie, we need a word with you in private when you're ready. Take your time, though. I think this little man is very pleased to see you.'

Grace nodded and turned round to see Vinnie, who had now parked the car and was standing behind her.

'Grace, why don't I take Archie into the shop to get some sweets and by then I'm sure you'll be right back. Archie, Mummy just needs to go and have a chat with your daddy and this nice lady.'

Archie smiled up at Vinnie and put his hand in his and Vinnie ruffled his hair. Grace's heart soared with love for them both and then sank with sadness as she realised what she'd thrown away.

They walked past a room where, through a tinted window, Grace could see Mark sitting with his head in his hands. She took a deep breath and walked into the room. Seeing her, he stood up and walked over to her. He was just inches away from her and she wanted to throttle him but held herself back.

She stayed silent for a moment, not knowing what on earth to say to him, then all her emotions came rushing to the fore.

'Mark! What the hell were you thinking?'

'I don't think I was thinking, Grace, I just needed to get away. After you left the restaurant, I spoke to Lorraine and she told me that she didn't want to be with me any more either. I can't be on my own, you know that. I just flipped and decided that I needed to get away and wanted to be with my son. If you hadn't pissed me off last night, none of this would have happened.'

He didn't even mention the word 'sorry' in his explanation and Grace was now seething. Before she knew it, she'd slapped his face. She'd never in her life laid hands on anyone before, but the rage inside her was just too much. The police officer, who was also in the room, looked away.

'You bloody bitch! I could do you for assault.'

'Do it then, Mark. Go on, do it! And I'll do you for kidnapping. See how the education authority reacts to that, shall we? See if you'd ever be able to work again with children, let alone be a head teacher.'

Mark's expression changed as he realised how

much trouble he could be in. He clearly hadn't thought about the repercussions when he planned his little escape. As reality kicked in, he hung his head in shame. Not because of what he had done to Grace and Archie, but at what it could have cost him.

'I'm sorry, Grace!'

'Are you, Mark? Are you really? Do you know I could quite happily kill you right now with my bare hands? You need to realise now that *this is it*. We are *over*. I've tried so hard to be reasonable with you. You come to my house as and when you feel like it, demanding to see Archie when it suits you, and I'm even good enough to invite you for dinner, all because I want the best for our son. Then when I stand up to you and do something for myself, that's the right decision for both of us, this is how you repay me. I will never, and I mean *never*, forgive you for this, Mark. What sort of a father would do this to his own son? He'd be better off without you in his life, but I wouldn't do that to him. This ends now, Mark. *Do you understand?'*

Mark said nothing. His face looked ashen. He clearly saw the truth in her words.

Grace moved closer to Mark until she was mere millimetres from him and could feel his breath on her skin. 'I said, *do you understand*?' she yelled right into his face.

'Yes,' he murmured and held his head low.

And with that, Grace turned round, took a deep breath, lifted her head up high and left the room. PC James asked Grace if she'd like to press charges, to which Grace replied that she didn't, but the constable told her that she should go away and seriously think about it and get in touch if she changed her mind. She passed her business card to Grace and stroked her arm comfortingly.

'If anyone had done that to me and my son, I'd have done far worse than slap him. Although I didn't see a thing, of course.' She grinned and Grace returned the smile. They walked out to where Vinnie and Archie sat in the coffee shop.

Grace stood in front of them and reached out both of her hands, which were still shaking. She took Vinnie by one hand and Archie by the other and said, 'Come on, my two favourite boys in the whole world. Let's go home.'

28

Vinnie made sure that Archie and Grace got into the house safely. He told Grace that he knew they needed to talk, but that tonight she should be with her son, so he kissed Grace on the forehead and said he would call her tomorrow. She was totally exhausted.

Grace took Archie straight up to his room, then hesitated and thought that just for tonight, he could stay in her bed with her. She needed to feel him close to her, to know that he was under her protection.

After letting Becks out in the garden, she went upstairs, kicked off her shoes and, fully clothed, tucked herself into bed next to her beautiful boy. Within seconds, she was sleeping like a baby.

* * *

Grace often dreamt about her mum, but this time she knew it was different. It didn't feel like a dream at all.

She woke with a start in the middle of the night and as her eyes adjusted to the moonlight streaming through the curtains, she felt the bed dip and saw her mum sitting on the bed beside her.

She looked radiant and healthier than she had looked for years, dressed in a beautiful pair of white trousers and a white loose shirt. She looked stunning.

Grace couldn't believe her eyes. She stared at her mum's face as her mum moved closer and took her hands.

Darling girl, you need to listen to me and listen carefully. Do not interrupt, just listen.

I am, and always will be, your mother whether I am on earth, or in heaven. We have a bond between us that even death will never break. I will always love you and lead the way for you.

I have left you to your own devices over the last few

years. However, where your love life is concerned, you've made such an appalling mess of things that I'm taking matters into my own hands now and taking over. It is now time for you to enjoy your true love and this is the second gift which I give to you. The gift of love.

The first gift I gave you is that gorgeous little boy that I am so very proud to call my grandson. My only regret is that I never knew him while it was my time on earth. I wish I'd physically been there to hold your hand through the early stages of motherhood and to give you support when you needed it most.

But I want you to know that I watched him come into the world. I watched you hold him up to the sky to show him to me. I love that you never closed the curtains in your hospital room because you wanted me to see everything. I saw it all, my love, and I'm still seeing it all. I've never missed a thing!

I've watched you and I'm so very proud of how you throw yourself into being his mum. I've wiped away your tears and I know how sad you are that I'm not there by your side, but I promise you faithfully, my darling, I am around you all the time in spirit. I'm just a breath and a heartbeat away.

I know that Archie sees me, and we talk. And I catch every one of those kisses he blows me each night. I will always watch over him for you and will ensure that he is always safe and loved. And no matter what happens in his life, he will always love you more than anyone and I will never let Mark take him away from you. I make that solemn promise to you.

The third gift I give to you is that of abundance. In all things. Finances, so you never have to worry about money and are able to do what you love in life. Health, so that you will always be physically able to do the things you want to do. Happiness, in your job that you love so it won't feel like work. And finally, love, that you will be loved and cherished by a man who truly deserves you and who you will love back.

And now, let's get back to gift number two. That of love. I'm really rather proud of myself for finding someone who is so utterly perfect for you. I have watched him now for a long time and feel strongly that he is the one that you should spend the rest of your life with. He is kind, generous, loving and understanding – all the things you should ask for in a partner. I am very happy to leave you in his capable hands. My darling, Vinnie is your soul mate, your partner for life. Grab that love with both hands and never let him go.

I've met someone while I'm here in heaven. A very special lady. Her name is Meredith. She's been looking to find someone that she knows is worthy of her big brother. And she'd been watching you. I was trying to work out *why this beautiful young lady was watching my daughter and I couldn't fathom it, so I just asked her. You know subtlety has never been my strong point. She told me that she had a big brother and she just wanted to see him happy in his life. She felt that the lady she was watching was very special and was perfect for him. We talked for ages and we decided that you would both complete each other. We congratulated ourselves on creating a match made in heaven. No pun intended!*

I hope that you now take notice of what I am saying, and yes, I know that this will be a first!

I will always love you and watch over you. Never stop talking to me; I hear you all the time! I will continue to visit you in your dreams but you have to start to let me go. Go and be happy with Vinnie. You no longer need me in the forefront of your life but I will always be around you and I promise that I will never, ever leave your side.

'Mum, is it really you? Am I dreaming? Are you real? Don't go. Don't leave me again! I need you!' Grace sobbed so hard, gasping for breath.

Grace's mum wiped the tears away from her daughter's eyes for the last time. She placed her hand upon Grace's stomach and she felt a warm glow radiate through her body.

I do have to go now, darling, I'm sorry, but you really don't need me any more. Go and be happy with Vinnie

and Archie. I love you, my darling, my angel, my world!
But now it's time for me to go. Goodnight, sweetheart! I
love you with all my heart.

With that, she held her daughter's head in her
hands, kissed her lingeringly on the forehead, then
faded slowly into the distance.

And Grace felt a sense of peace wash over her
and radiate within her that she'd never felt before.
She laid her head back on the pillow and drifted
back to sleep.

EPILOGUE

The sun was shining. It was a beautiful afternoon in late August and she could hear the string quartet playing the 'Flower Duet', which was one of her favourite pieces of music.

'Ready?'

'Yes, darling, I am. Are you?'

'I am, let's do this.'

She looked down at this handsome young man she was so very proud to be a mother to as he put his hand in hers and squeezed it three times. She squeezed it back with an extra one as he walked her through the manor-house courtyard towards the out-door-seating area, decked out in white organza, flowers and fairy lights.

Halfway down the pathway, her father stood up from where he'd been sitting next to Gladys, who was already dabbing at her eyes with a tissue. He was looking particularly dapper in a grey suit and crisp white shirt with a grey floral tie, and he had his trademark twinkle back in his eye as he beamed at his daughter. He took her other arm and between him and Archie, they walked her towards a wooden gazebo where the registrar and the man she was due to marry were waiting for her.

She glanced over to the left-hand side of the audience and saw Vera and Reg, who had flown all the way from Australia for this special day, sitting behind Hannah and her family, next to Belinda and Bill, all of them grinning from ear to ear. Monica and Carlos sat with tears streaming down their cheeks – and that was before the service had even started. 'You look stunning!' Monica mouthed across to her friend, blowing her a kiss with both hands.

Grace glanced to the other side of the walkway, where a number of Vinnie's mates were sitting. And in the row behind them were the crowd from Busy Bodies. Every single person in the group still came to meetings once a week, but not only that, they'd become a wonderful group of forever friends, not just meeting up at the slimming club but also at other social events too. Grace could never have wished to meet such a nice group of people.

'Thinking Out Loud' by Ed Sheeran started to play.

Vinnie turned and it appeared that the sight of his bride literally took his breath away.

She was stunning, in an exquisite floor-length ivory gown, with a fitted silk bodice sparkling with hand-sewn crystals and a flowing chiffon skirt that sashayed as she walked towards him. A simple chignon hairstyle, with gypsophila braded through tousled curls, complemented her dress beautifully. She had never looked more beautiful. The love shone from within him, as he sighed, grinned and kissed her cheek.

Archie shook Vinnie's hand and his voice warbled slightly as he said, 'Look after my mum please, Vinnie!'

'I promise I will, buddy. I'm going to spend the rest of my life making your mum the happiest lady alive,' Vinnie replied.

Archie beamed back at him, took his mum's hand and kissed it.

A loud gurgle came from the front row. Grace, Vinnie and Archie turned round to see little Meredith giggling and being tickled under the chin by her Aunty Hannah. Now six months old, Meredith was a chubby little bundle of joy and Hannah was loving spending time with her niece. She was looking forward to taking Archie and Meredith out to Florida where they would be joined three days later by Grace and Vinnie who were having a long weekend away, the destination of which Vinnie was keeping under wraps, although Grace had heard him and Ruth talking about Italy one day before shutting up when she approached. She hoped it would be that wonderful hotel that he'd talked about.

The sisters had shared a very special moment that morning when they were getting ready in their hotel room. Hannah came out of the bathroom to see Grace gazing into space out of the window, in a world of her own, a sad expression on her face and with tears in her eyes.

'You know she'll be here today in spirit, don't you? She's around us all the time, babe. You don't think she'd miss a day like this, do you?'

'I know, but she's missed out on so many important days in my life. The day I had Archie, the day I had Meredith and now the day I get married. Although some of that might not have been in the order that she would have approved of!'

The sun came out from behind a cloud and as Hannah looked across at her sister, the sun framing her in the window, she looked like she had a huge pair of wings behind her. She thought at that moment that her sister had never looked more beautiful and knew for sure that their mum was with them in the room.

'But more than anything, I just wish that she was here to give me some help with the babysitting!' Grace said, laughing. Hannah knew how much her little sister missed her mum. They both did, but today was a big day for them, Hannah knowing that her sister was not alone any more and was truly loved by Vinnie, both about to start a new chapter in their lives.

Grace adored her baby girl and Archie doted on his baby sister. From the minute his mum and Vinnie told him that they were having a baby, Archie was over the moon. When she was born, he kissed Meredith and said, 'Hello, beautiful. I'm your big brother and it's my job to love and protect you forever.'

Her two pregnancies couldn't have been more different. Vinnie was the perfect partner, practically wrapping her in cotton wool. He wouldn't let her lift a finger, and single-handedly decorated the nursery to her exact wishes, in stark comparison to her first pregnancy, where she'd felt very alone, devastated that her mum wasn't around to share this precious time with her. Grace had loved being pregnant with Archie, completely amazed by this little miracle growing inside of her, but she had also carried around a terrible sadness that Mark wasn't more interested in the baby.

There was no doubt whatsoever that Mark loved Archie, in his own way, but he was such a selfish man that his own happiness had and would always come first. After the episode where he took Archie from school, he and Lorraine had patched up their differences and moved to Spain.

Without having to worry about joint custody and being near to Mark, Vinnie and Grace bought their dream holiday home on the Cornish coast. The stone cottage mixed traditional and modern styles and boasted a first-floor living room, which opened through tri-fold doors onto a spectacular decking area with panoramic beach views. Through a gate at the bottom of the garden they just had to saunter through the sand dunes and they were on the beach. Never in her wildest dreams had she thought she'd ever be lucky enough to have a place like this, but Ruth and Vinnie had inherited some money from a distant relative and the couple ploughed money and hard work into their place by the sea.

Grace would never tire of this stunning view from their second home and walks on the gorgeous sandy beach with Becks frolicking in the sea. Vinnie dipping Meredith's toes in the cold water and her squealing with laughter as Archie jumped over the waves made Grace's heart swell with joy.

It was their special place of peace, tranquillity and happiness, and she and Vinnie hoped one day to retire there and grow old together.

After they'd both come clean about the reasons that they'd been keeping secrets from each other, things had never been better. The day after Mark had taken Archie, Vinnie had gone round to Grace's and she'd asked about the text and asked who Ellie was.

Vinnie explained that Ellie was a horticultural student who he was mentoring via the local agricultural college. She was also a friend of Meredith's, and she had developed a huge crush on Vinnie. Because she was quite vulnerable, and she'd always looked up to Vinnie, he didn't want to do anything to upset her, so didn't really discourage her either.

Since she had found out that he'd been seeing Grace, Ellie had transferred her affections to a young man on the same course who totally idolised her and for the first time in ages, she was really happy.

When Vinnie had asked about why Grace hadn't told him about taking Mark to the awards evening, Grace explained that it just wasn't important to her, and that she had also been trying to block it out. She knew in her heart that the only real reason that she'd ever considered getting back with Mark was because of Archie and she realised that within months, they'd have been back to the way they were before they split up.

Grace and Vinnie laughed through their tears and vowed that if they had any chance of a future together, there would be no secrets at all, however big or small, and that they would discuss everything.

However, there was one more secret that both Archie and Vinnie had been keeping and that was the incredible pre-wedding present that Vinnie had bought for her.

Her mind drifted back to that very special evening when Vinnie and Archie had very clearly been up to something. They loved their surprises and were as thick as thieves.

'Mummy, we have a surprise for you, so you have to do as we say, OK?'

She nodded at Archie.

'OK, so you have to walk with us into town,' he continued, 'and just keep doing as we say. Would you take these keys, please.'

Puzzled, Grace didn't really think she had a choice in the matter. She took the keys that Archie handed to her, and his face broke into a grin as they drew towards the high street.

They walked down the street, past Elizabeth's bar, before they suddenly stopped. Grace wondered what on earth was going on. At this point, Vinnie took over giving out the instructions.

'Put the key in the lock, Grace.' She looked up and saw that they were standing outside the empty shop on the main street, the one she'd always dreamed of owning.

'Don't be silly, Vinnie!' she laughed. 'It's hardly going to fit, is it?'

'Put the key in the lock, Grace,' he repeated calmly.

She looked at the big black heavy door with the brass handles and searched for the lock. She slotted in the big iron key and looked up at Vinnie, puzzled as it clicked into place.

'Now turn the handle,' Vinnie told her.

She looked at him, totally bewildered, her heart

pounding with apprehension and confusion. She had no idea what the hell was going on.

As she turned the handle, Vinnie placed his hand on her back and gently guided her into the shop. There on the floor making a path to a huge wooden fireplace in the centre of the first room were what seemed like a million tea lights twinkling away in glass jars.

She glanced around at the vastness of the room. It felt like she'd known this place for years. It felt like home. Again, she looked towards Vinnie, bewildered.

'But I don't understand. What are we doing here?'

'It's yours, my darling! You told me your dreams and I just want to make them all come true. This is your chance, Grace. This can be the bookshop you want it to be. You just have to follow your dreams. You always find a way, and I admire that quality in you so much. If you think something is right, you'll do everything in your power to make it work. And now this is something you can make work.

'I've done the easy part. I've signed the lease on the building, now you need to tell me how we can move to the next step and make it the bookshop that you've always wanted.'

'Vinnie, what have you done?' Grace put her

hands to her mouth. 'I just cannot believe my eyes and ears right now. Thank you, thank you, thank you.'

She turned and hugged him so tight he could hardly breathe.

'Vinnie, before Archie came into my life, I just existed. When he was born, he completed my life but I was only truly happy when it was just him and me. And when Mark and I split up, I thought that my life was just going to stay the way it was. But then I worked out that even though I was alone, it was actually OK and I found that I didn't need anyone to complete me. That I was enough. That it was up to me to make myself happy, no one else.

'Since the day I opened up my front door and found you standing there, my life has changed so much. You make me so very happy. I love you so much. It's almost like a guardian angel has been watching over me and sent you to me!'

She glanced skywards and smiled. Once she'd started to trust in her own judgement, trust in herself and realise that she had a right to be happy as well as making others happy, she'd found true love. She'd had to love herself before she could truly and fully love someone new.

'Mum, that's not all! You have to follow the lights.' Archie was jumping about excitedly.

She stepped through the room, her heels tapping on the wooden floorboards, and followed the two lines of candle jars, which led to the fireplace, where on the wooden mantelpiece lay an old, worn book.

'Open the book, Mum!' he instructed her. He went to stand next to Vinnie and put his little hand into his. Her heart skipped a beat when she saw Archie look up into Vinnie's eyes, his eyes shining with love.

Grace looked down and her hands were shaking as she opened the cover of the book. Hidden inside it was a delicately wrapped black velvet box and she gasped as she opened the box with trembling fingers. Inside was the most exquisite white gold ring, its centrepiece a beautiful aqua aura crystal, in a stunning setting of what looked like a million sparkling diamonds.

Look up, darling! she heard her mum's voice say. She lifted her gaze from the ring and glanced up at the mirror above the fireplace.

MARRY ME! it said in bright-red lipstick.

Another gasp escaped her mouth as she turned to look at Vinnie. Archie and he looked first at each other, nerves getting the better of both of them, then looked back at her. It felt as if time had stood still.

Vinnie stepped towards her and took both of her hands in his.

'Well, how about it?' he asked nervously after what seemed like minutes but was only a second or two.

'How about what?' she replied, laughing as he grimaced then grinned as he got down on one knee.

'Grace, I've adored you since the minute you opened your front door to me. I want to be with you every morning when I wake up, and every evening I want you to be the last person I see. Please, Grace, will you do me the honour of being my wife?'

Grace flung herself at him and dropped to the floor, wrapping her arms tightly around him. 'Yes, yes, of course I will!'

She looked over at Archie who was beaming from ear to ear, then opened her arms and was nearly knocked over as he flung himself at them both.

That was the moment that she not only became a fiancée, but also the proud owner of the Amazing Grace Bookshop.

* * *

Breaking out of the memory, Grace turned to the registrar as he said, 'Ladies and gentlemen, friends and family, we are gathered here today to celebrate the joining together in matrimony of Grace Christine Carnegie and Vincent Walter O'Loughlin...'

* * *

Grace's heart caught in her mouth as she stood outside the bookshop that had lived inside her imagination for so long. She took a deep breath, made her wish and pushed open the heavy glass door. A Tibetan windchime bell tinkled quietly as she gently closed the door behind her and entered the room. It was everything she had dreamed and hoped it would be and more.

Brown leather winged-back armchairs were strategically positioned around the warmly lit room, the smell of cinnamon and spice-scented candles making it so inviting and cosy.

Grace smiled as she noticed him sitting on a squashy, fawn-coloured leather bean bag near the fireplace, a book open on his lap, reading. His glasses were perched on the end of his nose, and he was totally mesmerised by the book and oblivious to everything else going on around him. For a few moments, she just stood and stared at him while her heart melted a little bit more.

A bookworm, just like his mum, she thought as she tiptoed across the distressed wooden floor and bent down to kiss Archie. He looked up at her and his broad grin lit up his face.

'Oh, hi, Mum. I was just reading this awesome book.' He got up and hugged Grace and gave her that special smile, the one he saved just for her.

'I just wanted to see what it looked like from outside,' she said.

'Again though, Mum? That must be the tenth time today. And what did you think this time?' he asked, far more grown up than the twelve years he'd been on earth.

'I just love it! I think it's pretty much perfect!' she replied.

'It is pretty cool,' he said with a big grin. 'I can't wait till it opens tomorrow morning.'

'Me too,' said Grace. 'Come on, dude, time to get you home. Big day tomorrow.' She ruffled his hair and looked around her at the shop one last time before tomorrow's grand opening.

The bookshop was the talk of the town. The three-bedroomed flat above the shop had been featured in a national paper the week before, which described the luxury accommodation as 'the perfect backdrop for those looking to explore their creative side' and since then the phone had been ringing non-stop with potential writers and authors, interested in booking it as a writer's retreat. The French doors from the flat's lounge opened up onto a huge terrace above the shop, which was decorated with rattan sunbeds, chairs and tables with a breathtaking view of the rolling green countryside. 'Authors,' said the piece, 'could not fail to be inspired to write in such a stunning location.'

She couldn't believe that her childhood dream of owning a bookshop had finally come true after all this time, and that the following day would be the start of a whole new adventure for the O'Loughlin family.

* * *

My darling big, brave girl. You have travelled such a journey, and I am so incredibly proud of you.

You learned through heartache and tears that you had to believe in yourself and love yourself and all your flaws enough to stand up for yourself and let go of those who don't treat you right. Loving yourself is not selfish;

it's essential to growing, achieving your dreams and to developing wonderful relationships with others.

Yes, you are a mother, but that is not the be-all and the end-all of your life. You deserve happiness and to have dreams and goals of your own too.

When you realised all that, you let love into your life and I can see how much you and Vinnie adore each other. And you have a beautiful family. When your children go off into the big wide world, and have their own adventures, that's when your next adventure can start too.

I love you, Grace. You are amazing.

Until we meet again.

Mum

Xxx

ACKNOWLEDGMENTS

The list of people who have offered help and encouragement on my writing journey so far is endless. My heartfelt gratitude goes out to each and every one of you, whose involvement, in whatever way, has been invaluable and appreciated more than I can ever put into words.

The biggest thanks of all go to my son, Oliver. The love of my life. Thanks for putting up with me writing and talking about my book. I hope I've made you proud and shown you that if you want to do something, you have to make it happen. You are my world, son. I love you to the moon and back and back again!

Thanks to my sister, Lisa, who has become my surrogate mum. Thank you for your love, your support and your delicious Sunday dinners! Love you guys!

Big love to my buddies, Lisa Baker and Sara Moseley; two of the most inspirational and amazing people that inspire me every time I speak to them and make me realise that anything is possible, you've just got to go and work out how to make it happen.

I have so many blogger and author friends who have supported me along my journey, and who have become amazing friends, and who have taken the time to read and review my debut novel. Unfortunately there isn't enough room on the page to thank everyone individually but thank you for being so fabulous and being wonderful champions of *Amazing Grace*. Huge thanks to my colleagues at Bookouture HQ. I am inspired by you guys on a daily basis. Your talent knows no bounds and your support has been incredible.

And to the Bookouture authors – you are again a wonderful group who have cheered me on offering advice and encouragement every step of the way. Big love and thanks go to Angela Marsons, Carol Wyer and Patricia Gibney, who if they haven't heard from me for a few days check in with me to see if I'm OK because I'm so quiet! LOL!

To Sue Watson and Emma Robinson, my soul sisters, and to Susie Lynes for making me roar with laughter when a hilarious message pops up on my screen!

To Olly Rhodes, thank you for taking a chance on

someone you never even knew a few years ago, and allowing me to become part of your company and part of the publishing world that I never dreamed I could be part of. You are a force of nature and I admire everything you have done. Thank you for your patience, your faith and your trust in me with your middle child. To my book club friends, Bookworms United! God, I love you lot! You've all become such good friends and we've had some fabulous times since our book club started. What amazing memories we've made and wonderful friendships formed. I cannot thank you enough for your love and support. Long may our book club continue and long may we continue to ask 'who was the author' and 'what's it called' for years to come.

To Miranda Dickinson. You and your #WriteFoxy workshops have been such an inspiration to me. Thank you for being part of my journey.

Thank you to Keshini and Lindsey at Hera Books for giving me the opportunity and for making my dreams of becoming a published author come true. Also huge thanks to Emily Yau and Boldwood Books for re-launching them into the book world.

ABOUT THE AUTHOR

Kim Nash is the author of uplifting, romantic fiction and an energetic blogger alongside her day job as Digital Publicity Director at Bookouture.

Sign up to Kim Nash's mailing list for news, competitions and updates on future books.

Visit Kim's website: https://www.kimthebookworm. co.uk/

Follow Kim on social media here:

facebook.com/KimTheBookWorm

x.com/KimTheBookworm

instagram.com/kim_the_bookworm

bookbub.com/authors/kim-nash

ALSO BY KIM NASH

The Cornish Cove Series

Hopeful Hearts at the Cornish Cove

Finding Family at the Cornish Cove

Making Memories at the Cornish Cove

Standalone

Amazing Grace

Escape to the Country

LOVE NOTES

LOVE IN EVERY CHAPTER

WHERE ALL YOUR ROMANCE
DREAMS COME TRUE!

THE HOME OF BESTSELLING
ROMANCE AND WOMEN'S
FICTION

 WARNING:
MAY CONTAIN SPICE

SIGN UP TO OUR
NEWSLETTER

https://bit.ly/Lovenotesnews

Boldwood

Boldwood Books is an award-winning fiction publishing company seeking out the best stories from around the world.

Find out more at www.boldwoodbooks.com

Join our reader community for brilliant books, competitions and offers!

Follow us
@BoldwoodBooks
@TheBoldBookClub

Sign up to our weekly deals newsletter

https://bit.ly/BoldwoodBNewsletter